"Why Do You Wear Your Hair Up Like That?"

he asked softly. "It looks so beautiful down about your shoulders." He reached out and loosened one of the pins that held it. The flaxen mass cascaded over his hand. "Ah," he murmured. "That's better. Aislinn, with the amber hair. You should always leave it just like that."

Linn caught his hand and held it to her cheek.

"I'm dirty," he protested, making no move to pull away.

"I don't care," she whispered.

"Aislinn, why do you encourage me?" he muttered harshly. "I'm the man you said no to on the mountain. Why did you refuse me?" He whirled away from her, incensed again at the memory. "Do you wish so much to hurt me?"

DOREEN OWENS MALEK

always wanted to write. For years lesson plans and legal briefs kept turning into love stories, until she stopped fighting the muse and published her first novel. She lives in eastern Pennsylvania with her husband, who doesn't mind sharing her with her seductive heroes.

Dear Reader:

There is an electricity between two people in love that makes everything they do magic, larger than life. This is what we bring you in SILHOUETTE INTIMATE MOMENTS.

SILHOUETTE INTIMATE MOMENTS are longer, more sensuous romance novels filled with adventure, suspense, glamor or melodrama. These books have an element no one else has tapped: excitement.

We are proud to present the very best romance has to offer from the very best romance writers. In the coming months look for some of your favorite authors such as Elizabeth Lowell, Nora Roberts, Erin St. Claire and Brooke Hastings.

SILHOUETTE INTIMATE MOMENTS are for the woman who wants more than she has ever had before. These books are for you.

Karen Solem
Editor-in-Chief
Silhouette Books

The Eden Tree

Doreen Owens Malek

Silhouette Intimate Moments

Published by Silhouette Books New York

America's Publisher of Contemporary Romance

Silhouette Books by Doreen Owens Malek

Native Season (DES #86)
A Ruling Passion (SE #154)
The Eden Tree (IM #88)

SILHOUETTE BOOKS
300 E. 42nd St., New York, N.Y. 10017

Copyright © 1985 by Doreen Owens Malek

Distributed by Pocket Books

ISBN: 0-373-07088-8

First Silhouette Books printing March, 1985

10 9 8 7 6 5 4 3 2 1

America's Publisher of Contemporary Romance

Printed in the U.S.A.

For my editor, Patricia Reynolds Smith,
who understood the spirit of this story
with the kindred soul of a fellow Celt.

Say, are you she that came to me last night
Brought by enchantment in a vision?
My spirit ravished by the wondrous sight
Knows naught aright for deep distraction. . . .

For tho' last night I saw her beauty plain,
Another such I never shall discern
In dream or vision till she come again,
And all the wonder of that time return.

From *The Second Vision*
by Tadhg Dall O'Huiginn (1550–1593)
translated from the Gaelic by the
Earl of Longford

Chapter 1

"No!"

Aislinn Pierce sat up in bed, trembling from head to foot, her heart pounding. It was the same dream: her father, surrounded by flames, calling for the help which never came.

Linn glanced around wildly, trying to see in the enclosing dark. What was this place? Whose bed was this? She tried to put her feet to the floor, and discovered that her blanket was wrapped around her like a winding sheet. She yanked it aside and got out of bed; the stone floor was a cold shock to her bare soles. Linn leaned against the side of the feather mattress and steadied herself with the aid of the brass bedstead. She was still shaking with the effects of the nightmare.

After a few seconds she passed a hand over her clammy forehead. She remembered now where she was. This was her grandfather's house in Ballykinnon, Ireland. He was dead. Her father was dead. And except for the violent, terrifying visions that disturbed her sleep and caused this emotional reaction, she felt dead herself.

Linn's grandfather, whom she'd never met, had died a month before, and her father had flown to Dublin to settle the old man's affairs. The two had been on bad terms and, to Linn's knowledge, had not communicated in thirty years. But her father had been the estate's sole heir, and when the news came, he had journeyed to his boyhood home to take charge of "Ildathach," or "Colorful Land," which he had called the "home place."

But he was never to reach it. The plane he'd chartered at Shannon Airport for the short hop to Ballykinnon had crashed. He and the pilot had been trapped inside, and both had been burned alive in the wreckage.

Since Linn had learned of her father's fate, she hadn't had a single night of uninterrupted sleep. During the day she felt numb and inert, lifeless, but at night her constantly active mind called up specters of her father's torment that gave her no peace.

Linn took a deep, ragged breath. She padded silently across the hard floor to the leaded casement window, which opened outward to the courtyard below. She was the owner of all this now, the flower beds and the impossibly green lawns, the outbuildings and the fertile acres which stretched away as far as she could see. How strange life was. She'd hardly realized this place existed until Dermot Pierce had died, setting into motion the chain of events that had taken her father, Kevin, too. And here she was, the recipient of a bequest whose name she hardly could pronounce. Ildathach. Her tongue tripped over the word.

She heard a sound deep within the house, and the hairs on the back of her neck stood on end. She listened, and it came again, followed by the crash of something breaking. Oh, God. The terror of the dream returned, compounded by the sense that she was not alone in the unfamiliar, shadowed house. Irrational in her fear, Linn bolted from the guest room, darting down the passage, across the entry hall with its woven carpet, and out into the yard.

The cobblestones bruised her bare feet, but she ran on, over the gravel path and onto the grass, dewy and clinging. There was a crisp, cool breeze, redolent of midsummer, and it lifted her hair and flattened her gossamer gown against her as she moved. Linn raced into the stand of trees at the edge of the road, going into the woods, as if by running from the house she could run from the stark terror of the dream. But it was no use. She heard again the shrieking voices, saw and smelled the fire. Tears streamed down her face, and the nightdress billowed behind her as she ran, heedless of the stones and pebbles that abraded her bare feet. The moon was full, illuminating her path, and the night was chill. A fine mist pearled the leaves on the trees and hung in the air like a curtain of gauze. Magical whitethorn bushes scraped her legs, and the throaty song of night birds contributed to the otherworldly atmosphere. But Linn was unaware of the scene around her, pummeling along, stumbling on the rough terrain, choking and gasping until she came to a clearing where the trees stopped. She halted, astonished. There was a man in the field before her, stripped to the waist, stacking wood against the side of a small stone cottage.

And such a man. His body was beautiful, perfectly formed, like a classical statue. He had broad shoulders and muscular arms and a strong, slender waist. The tendons in his back and arms flexed as he bent and straightened, bent and straightened, shifting the cords from the base of the chopping block to the pile at the wall of the house.

Linn watched, transfixed, unable to speak or to move. He was partially turned away from her, but she could still see strong features and a square, no-nonsense jaw. His hair was dark and curling, not black but a deep, vivid brown, falling loosely over his forehead and down to the nape of his bare neck. His tanned skin gleamed wetly with perspiration, which stained the waistband of his corduroy jeans. They clung to his narrow hips and long, racehorse legs as if molded to his body. A line of dark hair twisted downward from his belly and vanished beneath his pants.

Suddenly he moved in her direction, and she gasped involuntarily. He whirled on her, and their eyes met.

Even at a distance of fifteen feet his gaze compelled her, direct, intense and very blue. Startled, he dropped the slab of wood he held and took a step toward her. Linn backed away.

He held up a hand. "No fear," he said in a soft, deep voice tinged with a lilting brogue. "No fear."

Linn stopped, hypnotized.

And who might this be? the man thought. Not one of the locals, surely. He knew them all, kept track of such things. A beauty she was too, with pale hair streaming over her shoulders, and the curves of her slender body clearly outlined against the piece of nothing she wore, backlit by the moon. He could see her nipples, taut from the night chill or from fear, pressing the thin material, and the outline of her lovely legs below the line of her waist and hips. He swallowed, his mouth dry. He felt the tightening in his gut that signified arousal. He had no idea who she was, but he wanted her. Instantly.

He came closer, and Linn could see a frosting of gray at his temples and in the wings of dark hair above his ears. But it was premature; he was young, in his early thirties, with strong, bold features.

They stood face-to-face, and he reached out gently and touched the wetness on her cheek.

"Crying, is it?" he whispered. "Why, lass, what's amiss?"

The tenderness in his voice undid her. Linn broke down completely, putting the back of her hand against her mouth to stifle her sobs. His brow knit in concern, and he gripped her shoulders. In the next instant she was in his arms.

He murmured words of comfort, this stranger she was clinging to as if he might save her life. Linn recognized Gaelic phrases from her childhood, half-remembered terms of endearment. They reminded her of her father, who had used them, and she could not stop the tears.

"Pastheen finn," he muttered, smoothing her damp hair back from her brow. "Fair little child." And *"mavourneen"* (precious one), and *"orlaith"* (golden lady). He crooned and rocked her as she clung to him, not caring how this miracle had happened, aware only of the comfort and strength of his splendid body, the mesmerizing sound of his husky voice. Her sleepwear was slight barrier between them; she could feel the moisture on his skin penetrating the silk chiffon, fusing them together. He smelled musky, masculine, and she closed her eyes, pressing her face against his naked shoulder, tasting the salt of him on her lips. At the touch of her mouth, she felt every muscle in his body contract.

She didn't know when he began to kiss her; she felt his mouth moving in her hair, and then the heat of his lips on her face, her neck. He spread his legs, straddling her, and she moaned when she felt him hard against her. He bent his head hungrily to seek her mouth with his, and in a pale shaft of moonlight he saw that she was that rarity of rarities, a brown-eyed blonde. The amber lashes fanned her cheeks as their lips met.

Nothing this powerful, this elemental, had ever happened to Linn in her life. She didn't question it, couldn't question it. She only knew that since she'd heard of her father's horrible death, *she'd* felt dead, and this man was bringing her alive. Her tears forgotten, she opened her mouth under his, and she heard his sound of satisfaction as his tongue found hers. Linn's head fell back in abandonment, and he clasped her waist on either side, lifting her and setting her against a tree. With this support he fell against her, enveloping her with his body. Her hands fluttered down his back as he strained her closer, ever closer. She dug her fingers into his firm, muscular body helplessly, awash in a sea of sensation.

The man had no other thought but that he had to have her, right then, right there. He tore his mouth from hers and ducked his head to her breasts, nipping and teasing her through the cloth that covered her until, in frustration, he finally pulled the gown off her shoulders and shoved it to her waist to clear his path. He took one rigid peak between his lips and covered the other with a large, caressing hand. She was small, and his palm engulfed her. She wrapped her arms around his shoulders and held his head against her, sliding her fingers into the wealth of hair at the back of his neck, then moving one hand to touch his as it massaged her sensitive flesh. The sensation was delicious; when he moved away from her, she whimpered her loss.

Watching her face, the heavy-lidded eyes and full, parted lips, he slid his palms along her sides and pushed her gown above her knees. Linn clutched him, her head dropping to his shoulder in submission. He ran his hand up the inside of her thigh, pausing until she sighed and shifted her weight to accommodate him. Then, his control fleeing, he touched her and found her ready for him. She moaned as he stroked her, moving in a rhythm that was almost involuntary.

Was it really possible, he thought dazedly as she responded to his slightest movement, was it possible that this exquisite, unknown creature would let him make love to her? She wanted him; she was almost crazy with wanting him; he could feel it. Her lips pressed his skin lightly, dazedly, as he reached for the clasp of his belt, and he was beyond thought in an instant. With an inarticulate groan, he lifted her into his arms and looked around desperately for a suitable patch of grass. Her hands moved over him restlessly as he strode to a small hillock and set her down gently, kneeling with her, feeling her trembling ardor, which met and matched his like a leaping flame.

"Now?" he asked hoarsely. "Here?"

"Yes, yes," she answered pleadingly. "Make love to me. Make me feel alive again."

These were the first words she'd uttered, and they betrayed her.

He released her so quickly that she fell back onto her elbows. He stood, breathing harshly, running unsteady hands through his hair, trying to calm down. He was trembling, forcibly stemming the physical and emotional tidal wave that had almost carried them headlong to shore. It was a few seconds before he looked her in the eye and faced her.

"American, are you?" he asked abruptly.

Linn gazed back at him, bemused by passion, uncomprehending.

He bent and shook her arm. "From the main hall?" he demanded, jerking his head in the direction of her grandfather's house. This time she nodded dumbly. His demeanor had changed completely; he was withdrawn, almost hostile.

"So," he said slowly, drawing out the vowel as only an Irishman could, "you must have been in a killing hurry."

"Wh . . . what?" Linn stammered. What had happened? What was he talking about?

The indigo eyes assessed her with a coldness that bewildered her. "To take possession," he said. The words were close to a sneer.

"I don't know what you mean," Linn said helplessly. He wasn't being very clear, and she had just crashed from the heights of sexual exhilaration to the mundane earth with a resounding thud. She was befuddled in her attempt to recover equilibrium.

"I stop at the gatehouse, there," he said contemptuously, indicating the cottage at the right. "I didn't expect you for a fortnight, but it seems Kevin's daughter was in as big a rush to get here as her father was to leave."

"Stop," in the vernacular, meant "stay." That much

she knew. He lived in the gatehouse. She was beginning to see the light.

"Mr. Fitzgibbon, the lawyer in town, said there was a caretaker out here, somebody named Clay," Linn said questioningly.

"Aye," he said, inclining his head. "I'm Clay."

Linn blinked in surprise. When the lawyer had mentioned the groundskeeper, she had pictured some elderly family retainer in tweeds and a cloth cap, hardly this virile dynamo who had taken her, in a few turbulent minutes, to the brink of fulfillment. Rick, her ex-husband, had not managed to do as much in two years.

"I came early; I didn't even tell Mr. Fitzgibbon. Ildathach is all I have left of my father. I was very anxious to see it."

Clay walked away from her and picked up his shirt from the ground, where he had evidently discarded it while chopping the wood. He shrugged into it. "Oh, I'm sure you were," he answered bitterly. "You've a perfect right to it, after all."

"Wait a minute," Linn began, but he interrupted her.

"You'd best dress yourself as well," he said calmly, nodding at her disarranged nightgown. "You're not accustomed to the climate here, and you can catch your death in one of these mists."

Linn glanced down at herself and flushed to the roots of her hair. She'd been having this conversation half-naked, her nightdress pooled in folds at her waist and halfway up her thighs. She got up hastily, drawing the flimsy material about her as best she could. It didn't help much. Whether from his statement or from adrenaline reaction to their passionate encounter, she began to shiver. She wrapped her arms about herself and stood still, trying not to tremble.

He was not fooled. "Come over a bit chilly?" he asked mildly. "It's no surprise, with you in that tissue thing." He took off his shirt, which he hadn't buttoned. "Here, have this," he said, walking back to her and extending the garment.

Linn shook her head. This was a bad idea for two reasons: the thought of his clothing next to her skin called up images that unnerved her, and also he was now uncovered again. She tore her gaze away from his body.

"Don't be a fool, girl," he said abruptly. "Take it. You'll shake yourself to cinders before you get back to the house." He held it up to help her into it, and she had no choice but to comply. She slipped her arms into the sleeves, which dropped over her wrists. The tails hung almost to her knees.

"You look grand," he said dryly.

"Yeah," Linn muttered. "I can imagine."

Clay met her eyes. There was a slight smile in his. Her awareness of the picture she made had touched him. Linn was hopeful. Perhaps they could be friends after all. They'd come close to being lovers.

She was relieved to see him bend and retrieve a sort of sweatshirt from the grass. He'd obviously been wearing both before he'd stripped for the work. He pulled it over his head and waited for her while she buttoned his shirt and rolled the sleeves up her forearms.

"Why were you running so?" he asked curiously, when she looked up to find his penetrating gaze on her.

"I . . . had a bad dream."

"You were sleeping in the house?"

"Yes. I arrived late today, and Mr. Fitzgibbon drove me out here and let me in with his key. I was so tired from the trip that I went right to bed." She looked down. "There was the nightmare, and then I heard a noise in the house. A crash. I'm afraid I ran right out and just kept running."

He looked disturbed at the possibility of an intruder. "What kind of a crash?" he asked.

"Like something falling, breaking. I thought somebody was there."

His brow cleared. "I doubt it. The cat, more likely. He jumps through the ground-floor window in the parlor. Bridie leaves it open for him. It wouldn't be the first time he tipped something onto the floor. It's stone, you know. The vases don't bounce." He eyed her quizzically. "Did Bridie not tell you about the cat?"

"I don't know anybody named Bridie."

"She's the housekeeper," Clay explained. "Comes in daily; walks up from town. You must have arrived after she left for the day. You'll meet her tomorrow."

Linn couldn't believe they were chatting this way, in the middle of the night, after that explosive meeting. She shifted position to take advantage of the flooding moonlight and see him as well as she could. His coloring was high, vivid, and complemented his blunt, almost harsh features. He wasn't conventionally handsome, but arresting in a way no merely handsome man could be. She knew instinctively that in any gathering her eyes would bypass the pretty boys and be drawn to him. It was hard to say why, exactly; she just recognized that it was so.

"I'm sorry that I startled you like that," she said falteringly. "I behaved stupidly, I suppose, charging out into the dark. I didn't think I would see anyone." She glanced around uncertainly. "I don't know where I am."

"Never trouble yourself," he said shortly. "I'll walk you back to the house."

"You're sure you don't mind?" she asked anxiously.

He shrugged slightly. "I sleep badly myself," he said, without explanation. "I'm often about the place at night."

Linn remembered his first remarks. "Correct me if I'm wrong, Mr. Clay, but I get the impression you resent my presence here. Why is that?"

Clay stared at her. How could she ask that question? Didn't she know what her father had done? Had she no idea why the man had left Ireland? She gazed back at him innocently, waiting for an answer. Apparently not.

When he didn't reply, she said, "I will not inconvenience you, Mr. Clay. I want you to go on as usual. I didn't realize that the cottage was your home. I misunderstood Mr. Fitzgibbon. When he said there was a caretaker, I thought he meant someone who lived elsewhere and came in by day, as you say Bridie does."

He looked at her a long moment, as if to see if she was sincere, and then said, "Do as you please. I'm the man by the wall in this anyway." He walked ahead of her, onto a dirt path.

The man by the wall? What did that mean? Linn hesitated to reply, and he glanced back at her. "Shall you come along, then?" he said impatiently. "You'll not find your way alone."

Linn followed him slowly, keeping to the depression in the earth worn bare of grass by the passage of many feet. It threaded through the trees. She could not remember if she had come along this way or not. Everything looked the same. Clay walked steadily in front of her, not glancing around, pushing overhanging branches out of the way, snapping off twigs and tossing them aside, making it easier for her as she came behind him. Linn studied the back of his head, thinking that his hair was attractive, the color of bittersweet chocolate, curling in soft profusion down to his collar. It had felt very silky, smelled very clean. Her glance moved downward over his strong torso, now concealed by the shirt. There was a fluidity to his movements, an economy of effort, that made her feel secure approaching the house from which she had fled. If anything or anybody was inside it, Linn was certain he could handle the situation.

Clay deviated from the path and took her arm. It was the first time he'd really touched her since he found out who she was, and she started at the contact. He looked down at her, and his eyes were twin blue coals smoldering in his still face. She realized she'd been deceived by his deliberately casual manner when he offered to take her back. He was as constantly aware of what had passed between them as she was.

"Walk with me," he said. "This is shorter than the way you came, but the ground is covered with rocks and fallen branches. You might trip. Stay close and hang on."

Linn did as he said, clinging to his arm and stepping only where he did. After a few minutes of picking their way through the beeches and maples, they came within sight of the house. As soon as they were out of the trees, he released her.

"Here you are, my lady," he said. There was an undertone of irony in his voice, which did not escape her.

"Why do you call me that?" she asked sharply.

"You're the mistress of the manor," he answered simply.

And for some reason you're convinced I don't deserve to be, Linn thought. Aloud she said, "Hardly that."

"I'll have a look 'round," he said. "Just in case." He made a circle around the outside of the house, and then followed her inside through the front door, which she had left ajar in her flight. The interior looked ghostly with most of the furniture draped in protective sheets. He went ahead of her into the parlor and returned carrying a large striped tabby. It purred loudly as he stroked its fur.

"This is your intruder," Clay announced. "Fearful-looking demon, isn't he? A scourge to every mouse in the parish. Meet Ned."

Linn felt ridiculous, as he had intended. "How was I supposed to know it was a cat?" she asked defensively.

He let the cat drop to the floor, where it rubbed against his legs affectionately and then stalked back into the living room, its tail held haughtily in the air. "You weren't," he said kindly. "The night is full of terrors in a strange place."

Linn melted at the gentleness in his voice. He was a contradiction, comforting one moment, ablaze with passion at another, aloof and resentful the next. The elements were certainly mixed in him, Linn reflected. She wanted to put the light on in the hall to see him, but as she reached for it, he said, "I'll leave you now."

"Let me return your shirt," Linn said, taking it off. He came to stand behind her, and when she turned to give it to him, he was closer than she'd thought. His hands sought her immediately, and the shirt slipped to the floor.

Clay embraced her with one arm, tangling the fingers of his other hand in her hair. He bent and brushed his lips lightly across her throat. Linn went limp and closed her eyes, arching to meet him.

"You see how it is with us," Clay said warningly. "I can take you anytime I want. And I do want. So have a care." He let her go and walked soundlessly to the door. "Good night," he said softly, and went out. She heard his footsteps in the cobbled yard, fading, then gone.

Linn sagged against the wall of the entry hall, her heart pounding. So that was passion, she thought. She'd heard about it all her life but had never experienced it until this night. And with a volatile Irishman she didn't even know. Would it be more appropriate to laugh or cry? She had no idea.

When she felt recovered enough, she made her way slowly to the guest room. She didn't realize that he'd left his shirt behind until she stepped on it. She picked it up and put her face against the cambric linen. It smelled like him. Then she shook herself and tossed the shirt on the entry hall table. She was not going to behave like a puppy with its master's blanket. She marched straight into the bedroom and climbed under the covers.

She was worn out and fell asleep almost immediately. Her last thought before drowsiness overcame her was, I wonder what his first name is?

In the morning, with the brilliant sunshine streaming in all the windows of the old house, she half imagined that she had dreamed the whole thing. But when she bathed in the old-fashioned claw-foot bathtub, she saw the faint purpled stain of bruises where his fingers had gripped her forearms. And when she pinned up her hair in front of the gilt-bordered mirror hanging on the plaster wall, she saw the reddened marks his mouth had left on the side of her throat. She gripped the wooden chest below the mirror, swaying slightly, feeling again his lips, his hands. It had been real. No phantom could have made such an impression.

Linn was still reeling from the shock of the experience, which had opened up a new world for her. After the years of frustration with Rick, she had almost believed that there was something wrong with her, that Rick had been unresponsive because she wasn't woman enough to generate a response. But one moonlit interlude with the caretaker had convinced her otherwise.

She heard the sound of a key in the lock, and then the hallooing of a feminine voice. Linn smiled. This must be the fabled Bridie. She picked up her robe from the bed and went out to meet her.

Unlike Linn, Connor Clay had spent a sleepless night. He'd gone back to the gatehouse and paced around, then went outside and paced around some more. She was the last woman on earth he would have chosen to need this way, but there simply was no choice involved.

So that was Kevin Pierce's daughter. Faith, she was lovely, with that cascading yellow hair, silver in the moonlight, and that sweet, slender body. She would have yielded to him, too, if he hadn't realized who she was and stopped.

He should have known from the look of her. He'd seen enough glossy American ladies during his year in the States to recognize the type. That style, that subtle sheen and glowing healthiness of skin and eyes and hair, was a uniquely American trait. It came of vitamins and expensive cosmetics and treatments. The little number she was wearing, silk if he wasn't mistaken, had probably cost enough to feed six starving kids from the Falls Road for a month. Connor slouched against the gatehouse door and watched the sun come up. God, how he'd wanted her. Still did, truth to tell. His hands itched to feel her satiny skin again, his mouth to devour hers, his whole body to merge with that slighter, softer one. He reared up in frustration and kicked a mound of hard-packed dirt. It broke and flew into particles, scattering clumps in a circle. This would never do. He hoped her visit would be a short one. Damn it, no he didn't. He hoped that she would stay.

Inside the cottage the phone started to ring. He cursed softly in Gaelic. He never should have gotten the thing installed; people were always calling him and interrupting his work. And who would be ringing at this hour? It was just past dawn. He sighed and went to answer it. Whoever it was would only call again.

The housekeeper proved to be a middle-aged woman in a print dress, a shawl tucked over her shoulders. Her graying hair was screwed tightly into a bun at the back of her head, and a pair of reading glasses dangled from a chain around her neck. She crushed Linn in a motherly embrace.

"Well, if it isn't Kevin's daughter come home to us, all the way from America." She stepped back, her hazel eyes dancing, and surveyed Linn smilingly. "Why, you're a pretty little thing, aren't you? You put me in mind of a cousin of mine from County Meath, so you do. That same fair hair. We don't see much of that hereabouts; we're all dark in the South, you know." She took Linn by the hand and led her into the kitchen. "Sit yourself down, lass, you've come a long way." She clapped her hand to her forehead. "Oh, I've lost my wits. I didn't say who I was. You must be thinking I'm mad. I'm Bridie Cleary, love; I look after the house for the old man." She quickly amended that. "For Mr. Pierce. At least I did. Terrible tragedy, both of them going so close.'' She removed her shawl and fingered the wisps of hair about her ears.

"I guessed who you were," Linn said when she could get a word in edgewise. "How do you do, Mrs. Cleary?"

"Oh, Bridie, love, Bridie. Mrs. Cleary is my mother-in-law, still with us at eighty-five. Would you like some breakfast? I don't know what we've got in; I'll have a look. Larry Fitzgibbon told me to keep on as I was, so I've been coming down every day like always, cleaning and keeping out the vermin, you might say." She went over to one of the cupboards and began removing some earthenware dishes.

"Just coffee would be fine."

Bridie made a mournful face. "Only tea, dear. We don't drink much coffee. Plus I'm told the brew we make tastes like dishwater anyway. What's your Christian name, love?"

"Aislinn."

"Lovely." The housekeeper beamed. "Lovely." She crossed to the black iron stove and got the kettle. Linn looked around the kitchen. Attempts had been made to modernize it, but by current standards it was still woefully out-of-date.

"You made reference before to my father," Linn said. "Did you know him?"

"Why, sure I did, lass, sure I did. When he was young himself, before he went to the States." The woman's mouth drew into a thin line. "That was his father's doing, and no mistake. He was a devil, that Dermot. Could cite Scripture for his purpose and get you to believe it." She crossed herself hurriedly. "I'll not speak ill of the dead," she added ominously.

Linn filed this exchange away for future reference. She might be able to get more out of Bridie at another time. Linn had always wondered about the source of the quarrel between her father and her grandfather, and this woman probably knew more than she was willing to reveal on first acquaintance.

Bridie filled the kettle and put the water on for tea. "I know I have eggs," she muttered. She turned to Linn. "Will you have an egg, and some biscuits? There might be stirabout too. Porridge, that is."

"An egg would be fine."

"I hope you'll stop with us for a while," the house-keeper said. "I'll have the cloths off the furniture this day, and you'll settle in. Larry Fitzgibbon, that old blather-skite, said you might be selling the place. That's never true, is it?"

"I'm not going to sell it," Linn said firmly. "Mr. Fitzgibbon thinks I should. He feels that it's too big for me to look after, too much responsibility. I know he means well, but I have no family left at all. My mother died when I was born, and now my father is gone too. My heritage is here, my roots." And Clay is here, Linn admitted silently. She knew he was part of it now as well.

So did Bridie Cleary. She shot Linn a sidelong glance. "Met the keeper, have you?" she asked slyly.

Linn could feel herself turning red. "The keeper?" she said, feigning ignorance.

"Him that lives in the cottage beyond, looks after the grounds. Good-looking young fella, strapping and won-derful tall, great mass of curly hair on his head."

"Oh, yes. I ran into him last night." That was almost the literal truth.

"I thought you might. He starts marching at sunset, like one of those vampires. Rattles 'round all night like Tim Doolin's ghost. It's a shame, I say."

"What is?"

Bridie shook her head sadly. "He can't sleep, poor man. His memories keep him awake."

"Why?"

Not surprisingly, Bridie was eager to talk about it. As a

matter of fact, since she'd arrived she'd done far more talking than cleaning. She was at the moment making some ineffectual swipes at the countertop with a disreputable-looking rag, and breaking eggs with her other hand. Linn smiled to herself. Bridie was a bit more garrulous than fastidious.

"Well," Bridie said, turning to Linn, "he was in the fighting up north. He was wounded, shot up terrible bad, almost killed entirely. Came south to recover and has been back these several months. All day he's inside writing books, and at night he walks. It's a sight more than a body can bear, I'll tell you that much. Fine young lad like that, it breaks my heart."

"Writing what books?" Linn asked, curious.

Bridie shrugged to indicate that it was all beyond her. "Some are translations from the old language, from what I've been told. I can't read it, more's the pity."

"He translates Gaelic?" This was unusual. It was a difficult tongue and had been banned in Ireland for so long that it had almost passed out of memory. There had been a succession of movements to revive it, but only a small group in the country were fluent in it. Linn had read an article about it coming over on the plane.

"Why did he come back here?" Linn asked.

"Did you not know? He was raised here, in that cottage. His parents worked for Dermot. His mother, Mary, was in service at the house; his father ran the Pierce mines. All sold now. Those days are gone forever. But Dermot gave the boy the gatehouse, rent free, for as long as he wished to stay. So when he was hurt, he came back home. And now he writes there and takes care of the place when it needs it. Not much to be done nowadays; most of it's gone back to woods." The woman removed the pan from the stove and put Linn's egg on a plate. "So you're a teacher, then? What do you teach?"

"I'm an associate professor of literature at a college in New Jersey," Linn responded automatically, her mind on what Bridie had said about Clay. It was fascinating information.

"A professor of literature," Bridie repeated, awed. "Grand, grand. There'll be some competition for himself about the place, I'm thinking. How long will you stop with us?"

"The summer. I go back to work in the fall." The phone rang in the hall, interrupting the conversation. Linn listened to the distinctive European ring—tinny, one-two, one-two. The sound echoed in the still house, making it seem louder than it actually was.

Bridie bustled to answer it, officious in this appointed chore. After a moment she returned, a sour look on her face. "It's Mr. Fitzgibbon, asking after you."

"I'll take it." As Linn walked past her, Bridie leaned in and whispered, "I wouldn't pay him much mind, dear. He's taken the pledge at least ten times, and it's never stopped him from having a jar in my presence."

Linn didn't even try to decode that message. They were all speaking English around here, but half the time she couldn't tell what they'd said.

"Hello, Mr. Fitzgibbon," she said into the phone.

"Dr. Pierce. How are you this morning?" His brogue was deeper and thicker than Clay's. He sounded like Barry Fitzgerald on the late movie.

"Fine, sir."

"Well, will you be coming in to go over those deeds, lass? If I'm to settle the estate legally, you have to sign the papers."

"Yes. I'll be in this morning, as I said."

"Grand. I've spoken to Con already and asked him to carry you along with him when he comes to town. It's a long walk, and I thought about you. He has a car and has to drop off a contract for me, so it will save you the hike."

"Con?" she said faintly. She knew who he meant.

"Connor Clay, girl; you met him last night. He said so when I called him."

"Oh, yes." Oh, God. She was not going to be able to recover. He would probably be on her doorstep at any minute.

"He'll call for you around ten," Fitzgibbon said, confirming her fears. "I'll say good-bye, then." The line went dead.

Linn replaced the receiver, wondering what else Clay might have said to the lawyer. Met her, indeed. He'd met her all right. She went back to the kitchen and told Bridie that she had to get dressed, she was going into Bally-kinnon with "Con."

"Just have your tea, then; it's all made," Bridie said, smiling knowingly. "Take a bite of that egg, too. You're all bones. You Americans are all starving yourselves to skeletons, I can't think why."

Linn downed the egg in two forkfuls and swallowed half a mug of tea. That should provide indigestion for the rest of the day. Then she sprinted for the guest room and tried to decide what to wear. She unfolded a skirt and blouse from her suitcase, then darted into the adjacent bathroom and dressed quickly. He would be on time; she knew it.

He was. She heard his voice moments later, talking to Bridie in the other room. The sound of it made her stomach knot. How could she possibly face him this morning after what had happened the previous night? Oh, well. There was no help for it.

Linn smoothed her skirt and grabbed her purse. She met him in the hall, where he was waiting. He looked up, and she saw him in daylight for the first time.

Her impression of his appearance was confirmed. He had heavily marked brows and a bold jawline, a high-bridged nose and thin, well-defined lips. He was very attractive in that special way that has more to do with coloring and expression than actual symmetry of features. He had the beautiful eyes for which the Irish were justly famous, expressive, thickly lashed. And his body, clad

today in the omnipresent blue jeans and a plaid shirt, was
as graceful as she remembered. He was perfectly propor-
tioned, as if sculpted from the earth he was named for by
some Gaelic Praxiteles.

He was watching her too, looking her over, comparing
memory with morning reality. And Bridie Cleary was
watching them watch each other.

"Hi," Linn said.

He nodded. "Hello, miss."

"Shall we go?" Linn asked. Bridie was taking too great
an interest in the proceedings.

"Will you be back for lunch?" Bridie asked.

"I don't know how long this will take," Linn answered.

"I'll leave a plate in the icebox," Bridie called after
her. Linn shuddered to think what that might mean. The
icebox was just that, an ancient relic that actually had to be
stocked with ice.

Clay held the door for her, pausing on the threshold to
look down into her face. Linn had forgotten how big he
was, or else his size had registered obliquely in the
confused passion of the previous night. His breathing was
visible in the slight stirring of his chest and shoulders as
he waited, motionless, for her to pass. Linn glanced up
and met his eyes, feeling the impact of his gaze like a
blow. The daylight was revealing, and they were very
close. His lashes were so long and thick that they tangled
at the corners of his lids, curling in on themselves. His
eyes, thus heavily and vividly adorned, had a startling
effect in his roughhewn face; the contrast seemed to
enhance his masculinity rather than diminish it. Linn was
riveted; while he looked at her out of those extraordinary
eyes, she could not look away. She was pinned, like a
butterfly to a mat.

Bridie stood quietly in the hall behind them, eyeing the
two young people silhouetted against the brilliance in the
doorway. Connor was frozen with his hand on the knob,

and the girl was standing with her face turned up to him as if he were the sun itself, shedding light and warmth. They were absorbed in each other, oblivious, for the moment, of their audience.

Bridie hummed a little ditty under her breath and then paused, coughing loudly. The two figures jumped guiltily. Con flung open the door and Linn hurried outside. The man favored Bridie with one long, level glance before he closed the door behind him.

Bridie resumed her tune, smiling slightly.

It was going to be one interesting summer.

Chapter 2

LINN GLANCED AT THE MAN BESIDE HER AS THEY DE-
scended the steps. I almost made love to him last night,
she thought, incredible as that seemed. He moved ahead
of her, and she watched the play of sunlight on his hair.
He wouldn't be modeling for *Esquire* anytime soon; he
was too primitive, too original for that. But Linn had the
feeling that once you met him, you never forgot him. He
was definitely memorable.

She stopped short at the foot of the stairs. A comfortable Bentley was parked in the yard.

"Is that my grandfather's car?" she asked.

He opened the door on her side and, once she was
seated, leaned in to reply. "It is not. Some things about
the place are actually mine." He slammed the door shut
and walked around to the driver's side.

Damn. She had said the wrong thing. She hadn't meant
to insult him.

He got in beside her and started the car, looking over at

her. She couldn't meet his gaze. She bent her head, and her hair fell away from her collar. She almost jumped out of her seat when he reached across suddenly to touch her neck.

"I didn't know I was so rough," he murmured. "I'm sorry."

He had seen the marks on her skin. She recoiled from his touch as if burned. If he did that again, she would make a fool of herself. But then, she had already accomplished that the previous night.

"It's all right," she said. She forced herself to meet his eyes. She would have to deal with this, and now was as good a time as any. Pretending that nothing had happened between them was ludicrous.

"You don't have to be sorry," she went on. "Last night was as much my responsibility as yours. You didn't force anything on me."

His blue eyes were fastened on her face. The car idled beneath them. He didn't move.

"You probably won't believe this, but I don't do that sort of thing. I mean, that never happened to me before."

His expression was unreadable. *Did* he believe her? Had it been the same for him, unequaled, unprecedented? She couldn't tell what he was thinking.

"Maybe it was because I was scared, maybe it was the fatigue from the trip, oh hell, maybe it was the moon. I don't know. But can't we just forget it?"

"Can we just forget it?" His voice was very soft.

Linn didn't respond. His eyes moved over her, hot blue, heavy, rendering her speechless. They harbored sensuality the way a scent-laden summer breeze suggests a coming storm. No, they couldn't forget it.

"I don't want you to think less of me," she finished miserably.

"Why should you care what I think of you?" he said neutrally. "The good opinion of the groundskeeper can hardly matter to the owner of the house."

Linn clasped her hands in her lap. They were shaking. "Shall we be off?" he asked curtly. The wall had formed again.

She nodded, swallowing.

He put the car in gear and they drove away.

Ballykinnon, County Clare, was nestled in the green rolling fields of southwest Ireland like the smallest jewel in a rich emerald tiara. The sea was not far distant, and on days when the wind was right there was salt in the air. Ildathach was located about four miles outside the town itself, and the estate was connected to the main road by a country lane, which wound through the trees up to the house. The entrance was guarded by a pair of wrought-iron gates. Clay stopped the car and got out to open them.

Linn studied him as he lifted the crossbar and swung back the heavy metal barriers. He was turned to the side. His nose, like Barrymore's or Redford's, was not quite straight, not quite perfect, and all the more distinctive for the slight arch at the bridge. She had noticed that he had a habit of inclining his head, which threw his chiseled profile into sharp relief, as if he knew the effect it created. Maybe he did. He was certainly aware of his physical appeal; he moved with the ease, the assurance, of a man at home in his body and accustomed to admiration. Linn watched the play of muscles across his back as he reset the lock, shoving the bolt home, and wondered where he had been wounded. She hadn't seen any scars last night.

Clay slid in beside her and gunned the motor, sailing out onto the dirt road in a cloud of dust. Linn sat up and craned her neck at her surroundings. This was her first sunlit view of her father's birthplace.

Farmland stretched in all directions. Sheep and cows and horses grazed in pastures the color of bottle glass and the rich texture of finest velvet. The sky above was an azure vault dotted with wisps of cotton clouds. Clay honked his horn as they passed a donkey cart on the road, and the man leading the animal doffed his cap. Linn was charmed. It was a picture out of another age. The twentieth century had made few inroads here. "Back of Godspeed," they called it, and so it was.

"It's all so beautiful," she murmured, and then stopped when she realized she had spoken aloud.

Clay shot her a measuring glance. "Isn't your country beautiful as well?" he asked innocently.

He was baiting her. "Of course it is," Linn answered sweetly. "From Malibu to coastal Maine, from the plains of Montana to the Gulf of Mexico. It's all beautiful."

"Every bit of it?"

"In different ways. 'From sea to shining sea,'" Linn responded with satisfaction.

To her utter surprise, Clay burst out laughing. It was a delightfully masculine sound, reverberating in the car. His white teeth flashed as he said, "What an American you are. 'Anything you can do, I can do better.' Do they still say that in the States?"

"They do, when the occasion warrants it."

"And is this such an occasion?" He was smiling. He had a dimple in his left cheek.

"I think it is." She sensed that he enjoyed this verbal jousting, and that was fine with Linn. She was good at it.

His eyes danced mischievously. "A curious thing I've noticed about Americans. All they do is criticize one another, on the telly and in the press, carrying on about this senator or that program, what's wrong with everything and what should be done about it. But the minute somebody else dares to say an unkind word, they turn on him with fangs bared. Now don't you think that's a bit odd?"

"No, I don't."

"Neither do I. I think it's wonderful. I've always had a great admiration for that spirit. We could use some of it in this country. We're divided here, and it will be the ruin of us."

Linn stared at him; this attitude was as unexpected as his laughter.

"I read something once," Con said, "about Baron von Steuben. He was working with the Americans at the time of your Revolutionary War. He said that he could tell one of his soldiers, 'Do this,' and he would do it, but to an American he had to say, 'This is *why* you should do this,' and then he would do it. I love that story. It's the key to your national state of mind."

"You seem to know a lot about that," Linn commented. "Were you ever in America?"

"I was," he replied, looking straight ahead at the road again. "I spent a year as an exchange student, from Trinity College in Dublin to Fordham."

His tone was flat, uninviting, and Linn got the impression she shouldn't pursue it further.

They arrived in downtown Ballykinnon, which consisted of one main street with a church at one end and a war memorial at the other. In between were various shops and several public houses, or "pubs," the largest of which was the Kinnon Arms. Clay skirted the World War I monument, turning toward the church. Linn looked back over her shoulder at the two men who sat on the base of the stone structure, sunning themselves.

"The town layabouts," Clay advised her, seeing the direction of her glance. "Both of them together not worth the powder to blow them up. The one on the right is Johnno Keegan. He was injured in an accident about twenty years ago and has been living off it ever since. If you should be so crass as to suggest that he might get a job, he has a sudden attack of limping and stumbling fit to wring tears from a stone. A sharp article, he is, too; you'd best watch out for him. He'd skin a flea for its hide and fat."

Linn coughed delicately, struggling not to laugh. He wasn't trying to be funny.

"The other is Seamus Martin, the *schanachie*. He must be taking a break."

"The what?" Linn inquired.

"*Schanachie*. Storyteller. This time of day he's usually in the pub, spinning yarns for pints of stout. He hasn't done a lick of work a day in his life, but of course one could not expect such a revered folk artist to soil his hands. At this point, the sight of him engaged in gainful employment would stun the population for a range of ten kilometers in every direction."

"What sort of stories does he tell?"

"Gaelic folktales filled with pookahs and dullaghans and witches ripe for burning. For an extra grog he'll throw in a heroic saga or two. He's a spellbinder, I'll give him that. His audience is rarely disappointed."

"What's a pookah, and a . . . dullaghan?" Linn asked.

"I see that your education is sorely lacking," Clay responded. "A pookah is a spirit horse with breath of fire and crystalline eyes. And a dullaghan is a headless horseman. He brings the death coach for a departing soul to take it on the journey to the afterlife. Rumor has it that he carries his head on the seat next to him."

Shades of Sleepy Hollow, Linn thought. "He knows all those stories by heart?" Linn asked.

"Hundreds of them, possibly thousands. His is an oral tradition, passed down from father to son. Seamus has an amazing repertoire; it's a wonderful thing to hear him."

Linn sensed that Clay admired the schanachie, no matter how he criticized his lack of ambition. She concealed her disappointment as Clay stopped the car in front of what was obviously Mr. Fitzgibbon's office. "Lawrence Fitzgibbon, Sol." was printed in gold letters on the window glass.

"There you go," Clay said. He took an envelope from the seat next to him and handed it to Linn. "Will you give this to Fitz for me? He'll know what to do."

Linn nodded and took it. They looked at one another.

Linn seemed to be having some difficulty getting out of the car.

"Shall I come back to fetch you?" Clay asked.

"That would be nice. I don't know how long this will take, though."

"I'll stop off at four. You can have a look around the town if you finish early. Not that there's much to see."

"I've already seen the town characters," Linn said, smiling.

"This town is full of characters," Clay answered. "You've only seen two of them."

Linn grinned, and Clay smiled back. He looked over her shoulder at the window.

"There's Fitz," he announced. "I'd have a care if I were you. He looks ready to pounce."

"Bridie said he was a blatherskite."

Clay chuckled. "Did she indeed? You must consider the source of that information. Bridie has a tendency toward exaggeration."

"What *is* a blatherskite?"

"Oh, a scoundrel, an opportunist. What you might call an operator."

"I see. Like a shyster lawyer."

Clay smiled sagely. "Very like."

Linn was getting worried. "Is that true?"

Clay waved his hand, dismissing the notion. "You must overlook a great deal of Bridie's blarney. She thinks silence is her mortal enemy; she'll batter your ears till they need a holiday. She had some sort of a romance with Fitz when they were young, and it ended badly somehow. She's never forgiven him. She takes every opportunity to blacken his name. He's not above a bit of fancy dancing, but in his profession that's almost a necessity. Just keep your wits about you, but don't be put off by Bridie's nonsense."

"She said that he'd taken the pledge at least ten times."

Clay grinned. "I've no doubt of it."

"What does that mean?"

"The pledge is a vow to give up strong drink. We've a grand lot of pledge takers around here. It's the national pastime, like your baseball."

Linn laughed. "I'd better go," she said, reaching for the door handle. She didn't want to leave him.

"Go on, then," Clay said softly.

Linn got out of the car and marched up to the door of Fitzgibbon's office. She didn't look back until she heard the roar of the departing motor behind her. She just caught a glimpse of Con's dark head as he drove away.

Inside, Mr. Fitzgibbon waved her into a chair across from his desk. "Have a seat, Dr. Pierce," he said.

"Please. Call me Linn."

Fitzgibbon smiled. "I will."

Linn looked him over as he rustled the papers on his desk. He resembled a greeting card illustrator's conception of a leprechaun. With his flaming red hair and apple cheeks, all he needed was a green felt hat and buckles on his shoes to complete the picture. Linn tried not to imagine him squatting on a mushroom as he recited a list of reasons why she should put the estate up for sale.

"Mr. Fitzgibbon," Linn interrupted, "I have told you before that I won't be selling Ildathach. I'm going to spend the next couple of months getting things organized there."

His eyebrows shot up. "Staying, are you? Well, I didn't know."

"Now you do. I would appreciate your help with any legal matters, of course, but the estate is mine and will remain so."

He shrugged. "Just as you say." He reached for another folder on his desk and said, "This is your grandfather's will and some of his other papers. We should go over all of this and get it out of the way. Have you the time to spend today?"

"Yes. Mr. Clay will be back for me at four."

Fitzgibbon narrowed his eyes shrewdly. "And what do you think of our Mr. Clay?"

"I don't know," Linn answered truthfully. "He was friendlier this morning, but when I first arrived he acted as though I were . . . intruding or something." She looked up. The lawyer was eyeing her intently. She handed him Clay's envelope. "That reminds me. He asked me to give you this."

"Ah, that will be his contract," Fitzgibbon said, taking it. "I must get right to it. It's already overdue, I'm thinking. His publisher will be haunting me."

"What does he write?" Linn asked, unable to stem her curiosity.

Fitzgibbon's eyes widened. "Did you not know? Con's our famous local hereabouts; won lots of prizes, Con has. He writes under the name of Trevor Drennan, his da's first name and his mother's maiden name. He's been published in the States, if I recall."

Linn sat dumbly, immobilized with shock. *Con* was Trevor Drennan? Linn had read everything he'd written, including his volume of Gaelic poetry in translation, *The Eden Tree*. It was her all-time favorite; she had whole passages from it memorized. Her Ph.D. adviser at Columbia had thought that Drennan was the best thing to come out of Ireland since William Butler Yeats. Clay was a bona fide literary prodigy living in the cottage on her grandfather's estate. His beautiful translations, published to critical acclaim, had established his academic reputation, but they had only a small readership. It was his novels, written in English, that were commercially successful in the United Kingdom and at home. They dealt with the Irish present and were praised for their insight into both human nature and political realities. The most recent, *A Terrible Beauty,* had been a best seller.

As she thought about his success, Linn began to get annoyed. "Then he has money," she said softly.

"He has a lot of money," the lawyer agreed.

"So he could probably buy Ildathach five times over if he wanted to, and have a fortune to spare."

"Like enough he could," the lawyer answered. "In point of fact, he's been waiting to hear if you would sell."

Ah. Did that explain Con's resentment? He wanted Ildathach for himself. But as soon as she thought it, Linn realized that there was more to it. Something else was bothering Con, something not so easily explained.

"Is that why he stays at the gatehouse when he could afford better?"

Fitzgibbon shrugged. "He has a sentimental attachment to it; he was raised there. And he wanted to help out old Dermot if he could. The man was kind to him. Con says that it's a good, quiet place to work, with few distractions." The lawyer sighed. "Of course that was before you came."

Linn let that pass. "That still doesn't explain why he was acting like the lowly servant about to be ordered off the property."

Fitzgibbon smiled. "That's an attitude that has nothing to do with money. His parents were servants at Ildathach, and he hasn't forgotten that. In his eyes you're still the daughter of the house, and he's the son of the help."

"That's nonsense."

"That well may be, but you forget where you are, Linn. Things change very slowly here. You may have noticed that the locals call him the 'keeper.'"

She nodded.

"It's an old term, from the days when there was game on the estate and a servant was appointed to care for the animals and keep out poachers. Now the game is gone and the poachers are extinct, but the title remains. Con may sell a million books and be world famous, but to the people in this town he will always be the child of Dermot Pierce's servants."

Linn considered her conversations with Con in light of this new knowledge. "He said something I didn't understand when we were talking about the estate. He said that he was 'the man by the wall.' Do you know what that means?''

''I do indeed. It's a phrase from the old language, meaning a servant or serf. You see, the property owner sat next to the fire, and the others had to crowd around as best they could. The lowliest, the man by the wall, was the furthest from the source of heat.''

Linn shook her head. ''I never heard such garbage. He can't really believe that.''

Fitzgibbon gestured to indicate ignorance. ''You'll have to ask him, lass. Now, shall we get on with this? There's a lot here, and it may take a while.''

Linn listened, but only partially, as the lawyer went on to talk about her grandfather's will. One corner of her brain was busily ruminating. Any hope she'd had of telling herself that her reaction to Clay was only a physical infatuation melted away like a dawn fog. He was Trevor Drennan. Through his writing, she'd greatly admired and respected him for years. How could she possibly resist him after this revelation?

Fitzgibbon handed her a sheet of vellum, and she cleared her mind to read it. She would have to deal with Connor Clay later.

The object of Linn's thoughts was thinking about her too. Connor sat before his typewriter in the gatehouse, staring into space. He could not get the woman off his mind. She was not turning out to be what he had expected. Her behavior this morning confused him. She'd been nervous, embarrassed, almost . . . ashamed. This was hardly the reaction of a worldly sophisticate to a casual encounter. On the basis of her looks, he had put her into a category, and it now appeared that she didn't fit it. It was a puzzle.

Con rubbed his forehead with the back of his hand. His feelings certainly weren't a puzzle. He could still taste her, smell her. She lingered like the savor of fine wine, like a tantalizing, exotic scent. She had been the most responsive woman he'd ever touched, there in the glen, and yet the next day she had withdrawn into herself and become another person. When he saw her in the morning, demure in her skirt and blouse, her hair primly bound, she was recognizable but different, as if the night had worked some magical transformation. But he had still been tortured by visions of her body as he'd seen it, by what he knew lay beneath her clothes. And that glorious hair—he'd longed to pull it free of its pins and spread it, like molten gold, over her ivory shoulders.

Con made a sound of disgust and ripped the blank sheet of paper out of the typewriter. He rolled it into a ball and threw it against the far wall of the cottage. There would be no work done today. He glanced at his watch.

Only three more hours before he could pick her up.

Linn was with Fitzgibbon until three o'clock. They had a working lunch of sandwiches supplied by his secretary, a middle-aged woman in a navy dress who appeared mysteriously and vanished the same way. By the time Linn took her leave, she had had enough of legal documents to last a lifetime. She strolled out into the street and looked around.

There weren't many people abroad at midafternoon in Bally, as the inhabitants called it. Even the monument was deserted now. She walked over to it and sat on the cool stone, propping her back against the column. What was good enough for Seamus Martin, schanachie of some note, was good enough for Linn.

She looked down the main street (named for Daniel O'Connell, as almost everything here was) and saw a man walking in the distance toward the church. Something in his gait reminded her of Rick. For the first time in a long while she allowed herself to entertain the memory. There was an air of nostalgia in this place, almost palpable, as if

the population lived half in the past. Linn stared unseeing-
ly into space, remembering her ex-husband.

She had met him when she was eighteen and married
him when she was twenty. Everyone said they were too
young, but they didn't care; they were in love. They were
both students, but Rick's family was wealthy and he had a
trust fund sufficient to support them both. They began
married life with the optimism which only the young and
innocent can achieve.

Linn's father had warned her of Rick's shyness, his
timidity, which the older man suspected of concealing
deeper problems. Linn would not listen; there was nothing
wrong with Rick that her love and understanding couldn't
fix. His reticence was a hint of frailty in a wonderful
person, and she could certainly help him to overcome
whatever was bothering him.

But it wasn't until after they were married that the true
nature of Rick's problem was revealed. He had never
pressed Linn sexually, never tried to take her to bed, and
she had been grateful. She was innocent and thought it
considerate of him to wait. Once they were together she
expected him to help her and initiate her.

It soon became clear that Rick couldn't even help
himself. He was inadequate as a lover, often unable to
perform, and their lovemaking sessions frequently degen-
erated into scenes with one or both of them in tears. Linn's
nerves suffered from the strain; she insisted that they go
for counseling, which Rick flatly refused to do. The
situation persisted until Rick's family got wind of it. His
parents maintained that the whole matter was Linn's fault:
If she couldn't make herself desirable to her husband,
what could she expect? Things came to a head when Rick
swallowed a bottle of tranquilizers Linn had been taking,
and was rushed to the hospital. There Linn learned from
his doctor that Rick had been in analysis for years before
he met her, confused about his sexual identity. He had
apparently regarded his marriage to Linn as some sort of

test, which he was failing. He couldn't face his failure and attempted to escape.

Linn was shocked and miserable, unable to believe that Rick and his parents had conspired to keep his background from her. The family wanted the whole matter cleared up as quickly as possible and arranged a fast divorce. Their main concern was the prevention of gossip. She would not have talked about the failure of her marriage anyway; it was as painful to her as it was to Rick and his family. So Linn followed her father's advice and made a career for herself. She refused all alimony and borrowed the money for school from her father. Linn even learned to forgive Rick, who wasn't a bad person, just desperate and confused. He felt deep regret about the way he had used her, and in the end Linn pitied him and absolved him in her heart.

Linn went back to her maiden name and spent the next five years immersed in the world of academe, avoiding entanglements with men at all costs. Once was enough. She was able to turn away even the most persistent with her aloofness and reserve, which had earned her the sobriquet of Ice Princess among the other graduate students. Once she completed her doctorate, she had found her present position and had remained there until she got the news of her father's death.

And now the Ice Princess was in severe danger of melting. Connor Clay had caught her at a vulnerable moment and had breached her wall of indifference when her defenses were down. He had awakened old desires, old longings, with such a vengeance that she feared she would be consumed before she knew what was happening. When she had maintained to her friend Anne that she would never become involved again, Anne had replied wisely, "It only takes one."

Anne was right. One was all it took.

Linn looked up from her reverie to see Connor leaning

against a building across the way, watching her. She jumped. She had no idea how long he'd been there.

When he saw that she was aware of him, he sauntered over to the monument and put one foot up on its base, folding his arms on his upraised knee.

"You were lost in the stars, my lady," he said.

"In the past," Linn replied, ignoring his form of address.

"Pleasant journey?" he inquired innocently, widening his eyes.

"No," Linn said shortly, making it clear that she did not wish to discuss it. Two could play that game.

A small smile danced about the corners of his mouth at her tone. Linn had the unsettling feeling that he knew exactly what she was thinking.

"Will you have some tea or a drop at the Arms?" Connor asked.

Tea here, as in England, was a meal. "I'm not hungry, but I'll have a drink," Linn replied, drawn to him in spite of herself. She craved his company and couldn't decline, though she knew she should.

He took her hand to help her stand, and Linn flashed on an image of his fingers enclosing her breast. She took a deep breath and withdrew her hand.

Conn led her to the pub, putting his arm above her head to open the old-fashioned wooden door.

The interior was dim and cool, and Linn had to wait a moment for her eyes to adjust to the light. She focused first on the bar that ran the length of the room, against the wall facing her, backed by an assortment of mirrors and framed posters, handbills and liquor advertisements. A banner proclaiming "Guinness is good for you" was draped along the top of the largest mirror. Several patrons sat on stools nursing drinks and conversing with the bartender, a rotund man with white hair who was using the bar mainly as a prop for his elbows while he talked. There were booths along two walls, and tables were scattered around the rest of the room at random. A dart board was tacked to the wall farthest from her, and a game was in progress, with two cronies desultorily throwing darts and arguing about their accuracy. At a table near the door four men were playing cards, murmuring their calls and slapping the table decisively with the cards as if each move carried earthshaking implications. With the exception of a slim, pretty woman in an apron wiping glasses behind the bar, Linn was the only female in the place.

All heads turned to watch their progress as Con steered her into a booth.

"They're all staring at me," Linn hissed under her breath.

"So they are," Con replied, amused. "It must be your fascinating beauty."

"Oh, shut up," she said, shooting him a furious look. He was enjoying her discomfiture, and she was wishing she had declined his offer. He had the advantage here, and she didn't like it.

"What's wrong, my lady?" he asked, smiling. "Not accustomed to so much attention?"

"Stop calling me that," Linn said angrily, keeping her voice down. "And you can knock off calling me 'girl' too, while you're at it. I don't like it. I'm a woman, and my name is Linn."

The smile vanished from his face, and his eyes took on that intimate, slumbrous look she was coming to recognize in her soul.

"I know you're a woman, Linn," he said. "I think no man knows it better than I." His voice was very low, but distinct.

He was standing in the aisle next to her, but she felt as if he'd touched her. She didn't answer.

"It's just that you're new here," Con added reassuringly. "The last interesting stranger we had here was the

Lord Mayor of Dublin when his car broke down in front of Saint Michael's on his yearly progress. That was in 1948."

Linn looked up at him and smiled. He knew that his comment had unnerved her, and he was injecting a note of lightness to allow her to recover. It was a nice thing to do.

"I don't think I'm much competition for the Lord Mayor," Linn said.

"You're prettier than he was," Con said. "He had a paunch and a great, ugly nose. I'll get your drink. What would you like? Our choices are somewhat limited here."

"What are you having?"

"Stout."

"What's that?"

"Dark beer, of a sort."

"All right." Linn watched him as he walked away. She felt a pair of eyes on her and looked up to see the woman behind the bar watching her. Her expression wasn't friendly. Con spoke to her briefly as the bartender filled two glasses, and the woman turned her back on him as he returned to the booth. Linn frowned. Trouble was afoot there.

Con sat across from her and put a glass of something on the table in front of her. It was an evil-looking brew the color of raw liver. Linn eyed it doubtfully.

"Go on and try it," Con urged.

"This is like beer?"

"Aye."

"Beer isn't brown."

"Lager, then."

"What's lager?"

"Will you give over and try it?" Con said impatiently. "It won't kill you."

Linn took a sip and made a face. "It's bitter."

Con half rose from his seat. "I'll get you something else."

Linn put her hand on his arm. "No, don't get up." She took a bigger sip and swallowed. "I think I'm getting used to it."

Con smiled slightly. "You're a good sport."

"Am I?" Linn asked softly, meeting his eyes.

"You are indeed," he answered, holding her gaze.

The moment was interrupted by the conclusion of the card game. The winner jumped up and danced a jig next to his chair.

"He's happy," Linn commented, glad of the distraction.

"Drunk, more likely," Con observed philosophically, setting his glass back on the table. "When the drink is in, the brains are out."

Linn watched him trace a circle of wetness on the table left by his glass. She glanced away. "Isn't Clay an unusual name for an Irishman?" she asked.

He looked up. "We're not all named O'Shaughnessy, you know. My father was Anglo-Irish. There's lots of Clays up Derry way. In a drought, it would rain Clays."

Linn resolved not to laugh. She had to get used to his colorful speech; what passed for wit at home was normal conversation here.

"Mr. Fitzgibbon told me your pen name."

His eyes narrowed, watching her closely for the effect of the revelation. He sighed. "Larry Fitz should shut his mouth. He'll soon be catching flies."

"It's not a secret, is it? Don't the people around here know?"

"Oh, aye, they know. But we're not much impressed with writers here, Linn. They grow wild, like shamrocks. We've more writers than potatoes, and we've got a lot of potatoes."

"Not writers like you. *The Eden Tree* is my favorite book of poetry. I think it's wonderful."

He didn't answer for a moment, and when he did his voice was very quiet. "Thank you," he said. "That's a fine compliment, coming from you, since you should know.''

Linn felt his eyes on her, moving down from her face to her throat and her breasts, scorching through the cloth. She couldn't look at him.

"What are you thinking?'' she whispered.

"I'm thinking I should have made love to you last night when I had the chance,'' he answered evenly.

The bartender appeared at the booth. "Will you have another, Conchubor?'' he asked Con.

"I will.'' He looked at Linn.

She shook her head, and the barkeep walked away. "What did he call you?'' she asked Con.

"Conchubor,'' he answered. "It's my name in Gaelic.'' It was pronounced "Con–a–hoor.''

"What does it mean?''

"Desire.'' Con's voice caressed the word.

Linn closed her eyes. She was definitely losing control of this conversation.

The bartender returned with Con's drink and paused to look at Linn. "So you're Dermot's granddaughter,'' he said.

"That's right.''

"You're a long way from home,'' he observed.

Linn smiled at him. "I don't know about that. From the moment I set foot in Ireland, I felt as if I belonged here.''

"And so you do,'' the bartender answered kindly, glancing at Con. He winked and ambled back to the bar.

"Is that true?'' Con asked. "What you said to him?''

"Yes. All my life I've had a feeling of . . . I don't know . . . displacement. The Germans have a word for it. *Weltschmerz*. It means—''

"I know what it means,'' Con interrupted softly. "Homesickness for a place you have never seen.''

The poet in him had put it very well. "Exactly. And now I know what I've been homesick for. This place.''

"And me?'' he asked.

The silence was deafening. Breaking it, Linn changed the subject by saying brightly, "Bridie told me that you were fighting in the North."

"I was."

"But you came home."

His gaze was direct, challenging. "I could bear it no longer."

"It must have been terrible."

"It was all of that, and more."

"And that's why you can't sleep."

He looked away. "I close my eyes and see the pavements running blood, hear the bombs exploding." He took a healthy slug of his drink. "It's easier not to sleep."

"Was it worth it?" Linn asked.

He eyed her speculatively. When he spoke, he didn't answer her question. Instead he said, "You are Irish and sympathize with those who wish to be independent?"

Linn gazed at him levelly and answered, "I am American and sympathize with those who wish to be free."

He smiled, a glint of admiration in his eyes. "You've been spending too much time with Larry Fitz. It seems his fancy dancing is a catching disease."

"I had it before Larry Fitzgibbon, Con."

"That I can believe," Con answered dryly.

"You won't go back to the North?" Linn asked, backtracking.

He shook his head. "I'm known now. I've been told that it would be unwise for me to return. No, I'm out of that now. Well out of it."

"But you're wanted?"

He put his head to one side and regarded her archly. "You've been watching too many of your Western films: Wanted—Dead or Alive. I'm considered an undesirable, which means my presence is not desired."

"Bridie told me that you were wounded."

"Bridie told you a great deal."

"I'm afraid I asked her," Linn admitted, not wanting Bridie to take the rap for her own curiosity.

"Did you now?"

"Yes. Where were you hurt?"

Con took her hand and pulled it under the table, placing it on his thigh. Linn resisted the impulse to snatch her hand back and left it there. The heat of his body seared through the denim cloth, branding her palm. "Just there," he murmured.

Linn stood abruptly, sloshing the remainder of her stout. "I'd better go," she said lamely. "It's getting late." She didn't wait for him to answer, but walked quickly to the door, feeling all eyes on her as she passed. She heard Con get up and drop some change on the table as he left.

"Wait a bit," he called after her, catching up to her just outside the door. His fingers closed around her upper arms, holding her fast. "Don't run from me." She could feel his warm breath stirring her hair.

"Connor, please," she said helplessly. She didn't even know what she was pleading for—mercy, perhaps?

"I'll not hurt you," he murmured. "Surely you know I'll not hurt you." He turned her around to face him, and she glanced down, unwilling to meet his eyes.

"None of that, now," he said softly. "Look at me."

Linn did so. His eyes glittered like aquamarines in the failing light.

"Will you walk with me?" he asked.

"Where?" she asked.

"Up to Cool Na Grena, above the town. It's a smashing view from there."

"All right, Con."

He smiled, and Linn didn't resist when he took her hand. Who was she fighting anyway, Con or herself?

The sun had set and it was almost dark. Dusk shrouded everything in gray shadow, and the first stars glowed like tiny candles in the sky. A crescent moon was rising, barely visible against the clouds that drifted across it, gathering into thunderheads. It would rain tonight.

Con led her to a path that wound up the mountain. The going was easy; he was surefooted and knew the way. Linn clung to his hand, glancing at him occasionally, trying to read his thoughts. He was absorbed, quiet.

"What does Cool Na Grena mean?" she asked, to break the silence.

"A Place in the Sun," he answered. "It's a natural clearing amidst the trees." He stopped walking and brought her up short. They were at a juncture in the path where two forks led upward into the woods. "Will you halt awhile in Bally?" he asked. "Do you plan to stay?"

Linn nodded. "I don't know what my long-range plans are; I'll have to work them out later. I only know that I wanted to get here as soon as possible." Linn dropped his hand and moved away toward a large stone at the edge of the woods. "I can't tell you how much it means to me to find someplace where I belong. Losing my father has made me feel so . . . lonely. Homeless. I hardly knew that Ildathach existed. My father never discussed it. But as soon as Mr. Fitzgibbon contacted me, I had to come here. It was like the answer to a prayer."

Con studied her for some sign of dissembling. He found none. "You know nothing of your father's reasons for going to America, then?" he asked.

"No. Only that he split with my grandfather and they never communicated after he left. It was a taboo subject in our house. He wouldn't talk about it, and I knew better than to bring it up."

Con absorbed this without comment. It was true; she was unaware of her father's past. He didn't quite know how to react to this realization. He couldn't quell entirely his resentment of her family and of her presence on Ildathach, but it was constantly at war with his overpowering desire for her. And desire was winning handily.

Linn glanced over at him. He was standing with his arms folded, regarding her thoughtfully. She turned her head, determined not to stare. She couldn't look at him without wanting to touch him. She shoved her hands into the pocket of her skirt, as if to prevent the thought from transforming itself into action. "What is this rock?" she asked, turning to a boulder that looked like some kind of landmark.

"A Druid stone," Con replied, coming to stand next to it. He put his palm flat on the surface of the gray slab. "Ireland wasn't converted to Christianity until the fifth century. This is called a *sarsen*. It was used by the ancient Celts in pagan rites. It's very old."

"Do you believe those stories of magic spells, bloody sacrifices?" Linn asked.

Con ran a forefinger along a vein in the rock. "It doesn't matter whether you believe or not. They were a fierce, proud people and they left their mark on the land." He glanced up at the crescent moon. "They had a spirit full of incantation."

And so do you, Connor Clay, Linn thought. They had left their mark on their descendants as well.

Con extended his hand to Linn again. "Come along. It's just a little further now."

They took the fork leading up to the left. As promised, after a short distance they came to an open field where the ruins of a temple took on an eerie quality in the moonlight. Only a few columns were left standing; the rest of the structure had collapsed into a heap of rubble.

"It looks Roman," Linn breathed, awed.

"It is. They built it after their invasion and left it behind. The local story is that Saint Patrick blasted it for a heathen house of worship on his way through, but I think it more likely fell down from lack of attention."

"The Romans invaded Ireland?"

Con snorted. "The Romans, the Vikings, the Danes, the Gauls, the Germans, you name it. Anybody who could

float a boat. We have here what you might call a bad
location. The intrepid navigators out seeking a path to the
New World—or merely some plunder for the old one—
sort of crashed into us on the trip. We're in the way, you
see.''

Linn laughed delightedly. He picked up a pebble and
tossed it at the temple. "Think I'm amusing, do you?" he
asked, with an undertone of irony. "Well, it wouldn't be
the first time I provided amusement for an American
lady.''

Linn was puzzled by his tone. Now what on earth did
that mean? He was driving her crazy with his cryptic
remarks, but she knew already that pressing him for
details would only make him more reserved. Anything he
told her would have to be his idea.

Con walked to the edge of the precipice that bordered
the clearing. "Come and see," he said.

Linn joined him and looked down from the height. The
town of Ballykinnon was spread below them, the houses
and the fields, the church tower and the ribbon of roads all
in miniature. The lights looked like the twinkling of
fireflies.

"Oh, Con, it's beautiful."

"Aye, it is." He turned to look at her. "Is your full
name Linda?" he inquired. "I recall that was a popular
name in the States."

"Aislinn," Linn answered. "My father said that it
meant a dream or a vision."

Con took her face between his hands. "So you looked
to me last night," he said huskily. "The embodiment of
every fantasy I ever had."

Linn gazed back into his beautiful eyes, trying to
maintain her sense of reality in this fairy-tale setting with
this storybook man. Was he really so different from other
men she'd known? He seemed so. The false, sophisticated
bar dwellers, the stuffy academics, all the men from the
past five years receded from her mind.

"Do you recall the flyleaf poem from *The Eden Tree?*" Con asked, tracing her lips with his thumb. A cloud passed over the moon and shadowed his features. "It was called 'To My Unknown Lady.'"

"I remember."

Con recited softly:

"So a woman made of moonlight, with amber hair
Will save me, and enslave me, but only if I dare
To join the dance
To take a chance
And love . . . "

Linn closed her eyes. Reality receded further into blackness.

"You see the way of it," Con whispered. His lips were almost touching hers. "I described you before I ever met you. Save me, Aislinn. Will you save me?"

The sound of distant thunder boomed in Linn's ears as Con kissed her. His embrace was so tender and so gentle that she felt the sting of tears behind her eyelids. Why should this man affect her so much? He was a stranger, and yet he was not. The previous night had been a searing introduction to the taut strength of his body, the taste of his mouth, the softness of his hair. People she'd seen every day, year after year, hardly left an image in her mind, but Connor was impressed upon her senses so indelibly that Linn knew she could never forget him.

Con moved his mouth to her neck. "God, I love the way you smell," he said thicky. "I could find you in the dark, my lady."

His tone told her that the mocking salutation had become a term of endearment. When he turned his head and sought her lips again, she responded eagerly, clinging to him. Con's gentleness fled in a surge of mounting passion. He ran his hands over her body, leaving a trail of fire where he touched. Linn was weak with hunger; her lifelong fast had not prepared her for this banquet. If Con had released her, she would have fallen.

The wind whipped through the surrounding trees, and lightning illuminated the heavens. Thunder cracked overhead, much closer now. Linn hesitated at the noise, but Con was oblivious. He lifted her against him, molding her to his hard contours. His body heat was rising; he was caught in the vortex of male need and he was carrying Linn into the whirlpool with him. In a moment she would drown.

Linn pulled away from him forcefully. He followed after, blindly.

"Con, the storm is coming," Linn moaned feebly.

He bent swiftly and slipped an arm underneath her knees, picking her up.

"Aislinn," he rasped in her ear, his hoarse voice barely perceptible over the rising wind, "the storm is already here."

He walked with her in his arms toward the stand of trees.

Chapter 3

CON CARRIED LINN TO A SMALL COPSE WHERE THE
interlocking branches above their heads, dense with foliage, protected them from the falling rain. Con's face was
wet with scattered droplets, his skin fiery hot, as he
pressed his lips into the hollow of Linn's shoulder,
lowering her gently to the ground. He pinned her the
instant she was prone, and she welcomed his weight,
caressing him wherever she could reach with eager,
searching hands.

"Aislinn," he breathed, drawing her knees up to settle
himself more closely against her. Linn arched to meet
him, moaning softly at the sensation of aching need that
overwhelmed her to the point of pain. She shifted restlessly, whimpering in protest when he pushed himself off
her with one hand, the other going to the neck of her
blouse.

"Shh, shh," he soothed, gentling her with his voice,
his touch. He murmured something she didn't understand,

unbuttoning her shirt, opening the front catch of her lacy bra with a nimble forefinger. His breath stopped in his throat as he looked his fill, his parted lips bearing the faint stain of her lipstick. Then he gathered her to him, rubbing his cheek luxuriously over her silky skin.

"The memory of you like this robbed me of sleep all the night," Con said huskily. "So sweet, so soft, as smooth as milk. I had the taste of you in my mouth and I couldn't forget. You're a witch, Aislinn. You cast a spell on me in the moonlight."

"If I did, it bewitched us both," Linn answered, stroking his hair as his mouth moved over her breasts. He paused, using his tongue, and she gasped, clutching him tighter.

He moaned, cradling her in his arms, fusing her hips to his. "Share your body with me," he panted. "Give me what I should have had last night."

The reference to the previous evening made Linn stiffen, and Con sensed the change immediately. His hold loosened and he raised his head.

"What?" he murmured, still drugged with passion. The screen of his lashes lifted, and his eyes, promising sensual delights, made Linn want to abandon all caution and do as he asked. He was so close above her that his blue gaze seemed to fill the world. Linn turned her head away from its heat.

"You want me," he urged. "What's amiss?"

Linn swallowed. "Con, I can't do this," she said miserably.

He didn't answer. The patter of raindrops on the leaves above them was drowned in a peal of thunder. Linn pressed her face into his shoulder, feeling the mist drift down and enclose them in a soft embrace. The storm was passing, but not for Linn and this ardent, impatient man.

"And why not?" he finally said, his voice calm, deliberately controlled. But the tension in his body had not relaxed; he was wound as tightly as a steel cable.

Linn moved to sit up, and Con released her. When she clutched her clothes to her bosom awkwardly, he reached over and expertly hooked her bra, settling the straps back on her shoulders neatly. Linn rebuttoned her blouse with shaking fingers, noting unhappily that he was very familiar with women's apparel.

"It's difficult to explain," she began.

"Try," he responded tightly.

He was angry and hurt, but too restrained to show it. It was amazing how well he could master his feelings. Linn wished that she had such command of hers. She pressed her hands to her flaming cheeks, trying to think of a way to make him understand. She was tongue-tied, and he was so good with words.

"I've been here little more than a day," she said, struggling, "and if I haven't been crying, I've been"— she gestured helplessly, close to tears yet again—"rolling around in the grass with you." She covered her mouth with her hand, shaking her head helplessly. "I hardly recognize my own behavior."

He was silent, crouched next to her, listening. The dripping from the leaves above suddenly seemed very loud.

Why didn't he help her, say he understood, tell her that everything would be all right? Instead he held his breath with unnatural stillness, his expression unreadable in the gloom, his dark hair curling about his head, the ringlets glistening. He looked like a creature of the woods that surrounded them.

"I'm ashamed of myself," Linn burst out, desperate to get through to him.

That got through to him. He stood abruptly, dusting grass and mud from his jeans smartly.

"I'd not realized that my lovemaking shamed you," he said evenly. "Thank you for explaining it to me."

Linn tensed with alarm. "Con, no," she began.

"Get up," he said tersely.

She remained as she was, staring up at him.

"I said get up!" he repeated, his calm facade cracking. He yanked on her hands and hauled her ungently to her feet. Linn stumbled against him and he held her off, steadying her with as little contact as possible. Then he turned away and stared into the distance, giving her a chance to collect herself.

Linn clasped her hands together, striving not to panic. In trying to make her feelings clear, she had only succeeded in alienating him.

"Connor, listen to me," she said flatly.

He whirled on her angrily, no longer trying to conceal his reaction to her tactless statement. "No, I will not listen to you!" he said vehemently. Then he took a deep breath, closing his eyes and shaking his head. "Why did I not learn? How did I get mixed up with somebody like you again?"

"Somebody like me?" Linn repeated numbly.

"An American *lady,*" he clarified, drawing out the last word with exquisite sarcasm. "One experience should have been enough."

"What are you talking about?"

He examined her with narrowed eyes, as if determining whether or not to tell her. Then he gestured with irritation. "When I was a student in the States, I met a girl. Her name was Tracy Alden. They all have names like that, don't they? Tracy, Stacy, Lacy, Candy, Sandy, Mandy. All those long-haired, long-legged American girls." He smiled mirthlessly.

"Not all," Linn answered pointedly.

He ignored that. "Anyway," he went on, "we became . . . involved. Isn't that the word? Very involved. She was rich, of course. Her family had homes everywhere: a townhouse in New York, where she was staying when I knew her; a vacation place in Florida; a ski chalet in Aspen. And I was," he chuckled bitterly, "much as you see me. Quite the primitive in her eyes, I should think.

Unpublished in those days, not a prospect in the world, a wild foreigner with an amusing accent.''

Linn listened, and she could tell by his tone that she wouldn't like to hear what was coming. A breeze blew through the trees, sprinkling them with an aftershock of raindrops. She shuddered as Con leaned back against a tree trunk and hooked his thumbs into his belt, continuing his tale.

''I don't know why I didn't realize that to her I was just an entertainment, a toy like the Corvette and the speedboats. That will tell you how green I was, grass green. I suppose I was something different, a breed apart from the usual stud service. A curiosity to be served up at cocktail parties along with the canapés. A romantic figure,'' he spat derisively.

Linn waited, her head averted now.

''Well, we went on that way for a while, I in my ignorance, she in her playful mood. We were happy enough until, as I recall, I brought up the subject of marriage. I was also foolish enough to suggest that I didn't want to live off her father's money.''

He sighed. ''What a clod I was. She laughed at me. Trying to separate that girl from her da's greenbacks was like trying to separate sunshine from summertime.''

Con straightened, frowning at the clearing night sky. ''And then I began to see myself as she had seen me all along, an uncouth bogtrotter totally unacceptable as a husband but desirable enough for . . . other pursuits. She wasn't paying me by the night, but she might as well have been for all the difference it made. It was quite a revelation, I can tell you.''

Linn could hear the old pain, buried but still present, in his words. She found her voice. ''Don't put that on me, Con, just because she hurt you,'' she said softly. ''She was thoughtless and cruel. I'm not like that.''

His eyes swept over her face. ''Are you not? I wonder.''

"No, I'm not!" she responded heatedly. "Just because she was American, you assume that I'm shallow and selfish too. That's ridiculous and totally unfair."

"You're Kevin Pierce's daughter!" he shot back.

So they were back to that again! "Why should that make a difference?" Linn demanded.

"It makes a world of difference to me. I mean to bear it in mind in future." He moved to take her arm. "Come along, I'll take you back to the house."

Linn snatched herself away from his grasp. "I'm not taking one step from this place until you tell me exactly what my father did to make you so bitter," she stated firmly.

"I'm not bitter," he replied, in a manner that belied his words. "I'm a madman to forget for a minute who you are."

"I mean it. I'll stay right here until you tell me."

He shrugged. "Suit yourself, my lady. The ruins are said to be haunted, but I'm sure the spirits are locals. Just tell them who you are and they'll trip all over themselves to bow and scrape before you." He started off down the slope.

Maddened beyond endurance, Linn ran after him and dodged in front of him, blocking his path. He stopped short to avoid plowing her down.

"How can you be so unreasonable?" she said, clutching at his hands. "You're blaming me for something, and I don't even know what it is. Please, don't I deserve an explanation? Connor, you owe me that much."

For just an instant his fingers returned her pressure, and she could see him relent. He inclined his head in his habitual way.

"So I do," he agreed. He stepped back from her and folded his arms. "Your father seduced my mother, and then abandoned her," he said.

Linn's eyes widened in shock.

"You did not know it?" Con asked.

Linn shook her head dumbly.

"I thought not. No doubt your father wasn't too anxious to reveal the reason for his departure from Ildathach. Nor would I be, in his shoes. You see, when my mother proved to be a problem, putting an ocean between him and the irritant was thought to be the solution."

Linn stood rooted, stunned.

"It's an old story, the lord of the manor using the servant girl and then making . . . other arrangements. I'm sure it was very effective for him, but it wasn't too helpful to my mother. She loved him to her dying day. She never got over him. Never."

Con's fists clenched at his sides. "Kevin ruined her life, and her husband's life as well. My father was a good man. He deserved to be loved. When I was a child, in bed at night, I'd hear them arguing long after they thought I was asleep. He would plead with her, ask her to give him a chance, beg her to try to forget the man who'd so easily forgotten her. She tried, I know she tried, but even I could see that she was not able to do it. The night my father died, he said to her, 'You never loved me, Mary. You've been Kevin's wife in your mind from the start. We've slept three in a bed all these years.' "

Linn's eyes filled with tears. It was a heartbreaking story. She could imagine Con as a little boy, desperately trying to alleviate the anguish of his beloved father, sensing that something was wrong between his parents. And when he got older, his growing understanding brought resentment toward the source of their unhappiness: Linn's father, Kevin Pierce.

Con saw her reaction. "Yes, it's a sad story. Sadder to me, because I lived it. Kevin was a shadow between them all their lives, the one that got away, the man she wanted but could not have. My father was a very distant second, and he knew it. He had to settle for Kevin's leavings, for the shell of a woman Kevin ditched after he was through with her and had taken off to new conquests across the sea.''

Linn swallowed with difficulty. She couldn't equate Con's description of the careless, callous seducer with the warm, loving father she'd known, but what reason would Con have to make up such a terrible lie? And it explained so much—his attitude toward her when she arrived, the undercurrent of suspicion and hostility which she'd sensed from the moment they met.

"What became of your mother after my father left?" she managed in a low tone.

"Oh, Dermot married her off to my father, sent her to England where my da supervised the mines. I was born ten months later. A husband and a family to help her forget, don't you know." His eyes were cold. "But my mother had a tenacious memory." He lifted his chin, his demeanor hard and unyielding. "I inherited mine from her."

"But you can't hold me responsible for what happened between them so long ago," Linn said softly. "You're heaping your memories—of Tracy, of your parents—on my head. I'm not Tracy, and I can't change now what my father did over thirty years ago." She spread her hands in appeal. "What else can I say? I have two strikes against me, and neither of them is my fault."

Con sighed. "That well may be, Aislinn, but it changes nothing. I'm sorry I let this go so far; nothing good can come of it. Let's give it up as a bad job, shall we? You look exhausted and should get some rest. Come with me now, we've been too long away."

His distant, resigned tone chilled her to the bone. Linn would have preferred his anger to this emotionless surrender to the insurmountable past. He clearly thought that the barriers between them were too strong, too high to scale and too thick to penetrate. He simply wasn't equal to the effort.

Linn let him lead her onto the mountain path, and she walked down with him in silence.

Everything was wet from the rain. Con picked his way carefully, supporting Linn, catching her once when she slipped on a patch of mud. The beauty of her surroundings, the washed-clean sky and the gleaming leaves splashing her with cool, crystalline droplets, was lost on Linn as she trod in Con's footsteps. They retraced the route they had taken and were back to Con's car too soon.

Bally was quiet. Linn glanced at Con's set profile as he handed her into the front seat and slammed the door next to her. She felt something like despair. He had been reminded again of his reasons to hate her; she knew he wouldn't forget a second time.

Con drove efficiently back to Ildathach, concentrating on the road and saying nothing. He walked Linn up the steps to the door of the house, waiting while she fiddled nervously with the lock.

The door swung inward. Linn looked up at Con inquiringly.

He towered over her, his face inscrutable.

She put a tentative hand on his arm. "Con . . ."

He shook his head. "Best to leave it. No more tonight. I've said more than I ever meant to already." He looked at her a moment longer, and then turned and ran lightly down the steps.

Linn went inside in a dreamlike state, trying to absorb all the information she'd just acquired. It was too much. She shut the door behind her and leaned against it, lost in thought. A movement to her left caught her eye, and she jumped. It was the cat, Ned. He was perched on the entry table, staring at her and swishing his tail.

Linn exhaled noisily. "That's the second time you've scared me," she informed him, picking him up and smiling into his little foxy cat-face. He blinked and purred loudly.

Linn carried him into the kitchen, where he expressed

an interest in the plate Bridie had left in the icebox. Linn had little appetite and wound up feeding her dinner to Ned, who appreciated it greatly. She left him with the remains of his feast and went to her room, where she undressed in the dark and crawled into bed.

A thud jarred her awake in the middle of the night. Ned had arrived and remained. She awoke in the morning to find him draped over her like a fur piece, fast asleep.

It seemed she had lost one friend and found another.

After breakfast, Linn began the process of going through the house and examining its contents, determining what to keep, what to sell, what to throw away. Precious little fit into the latter categories. She couldn't bear to part with most of the mementos of her family's past, and simply repacked pictures and books and silver and china, storing them for an uncertain future. Bridie assisted her, grumbling that Linn wasn't accomplishing anything, merely redistributing the clutter. The older woman followed her from room to room, commenting on each piece Linn handled, filled with stories about the grandfather Linn had never known. They removed sheets and dust covers, rummaged in drawers and chests trying to create some order out of the chaos that had surrounded the eccentric old man. He had been a pack rat, hanging onto artifacts that had far outlived their usefulness, but Linn was fascinated by the hidden treasures contained in the old house. She spent several days, covered with grime, crouched on the floor amid piles of her grandfather's knickknacks, while Bridie snatched them up and wrapped them in newspaper. Bridie complained loudly that they would never finish if Linn insisted on examining them all as if they were priceless museum pieces. In this fashion they made slow but steady progress, until most of the items were put away in crates and boxes. The rooms were aired, the rugs beaten, the windows washed. Linn did most of the heavy work; Bridie leaned on brooms and dust mops and talked. Linn didn't mind. She was good company, and her chatter took Linn's mind off her preoccupation with Con's conspicuous absence. She saw him, but only from a distance. He never came to the house. She would watch him from a window as he worked around the grounds, mowing the lawn on a tractor, cutting the weeds along the drive with a scythe, whitewashing the stucco facing on the barn, which adjoined the gatehouse. Once she saw him walking at night; he stopped under a tree and stood looking up at the house, his shadow long and dark in the moonlight. But he didn't approach Linn, and she waited in vain for him to do so. As she had feared, her double burden of being Kevin's daughter and Tracy Alden's countrywoman was too heavy for him to shoulder. He had decided to stay away.

As the days passed and Linn watched him from afar, grooming the property as he'd been doing all his life, his antagonism toward her upon her arrival became understandable. He'd been here for years and years, caring for what was not his, and then she had arrived on a plane from a distant somewhere, a stranger descending to take it from him. It was more than his memories of a self-indulgent American girl that separated them, more still than her father's behavior toward his mother; as he had said, she was the owner and he was the employee. For a man of his pride and sensitive nature, that was a distinction impossible to dismiss.

A week went by, and Bridie was making tea in the kitchen one afternoon when there was a knock on the front door. Linn's heart leaped into her throat. Was Con ready to break the silence?

Not so. When she answered the door, it was a pleasant-looking young man with a clipped moustache and a rough thatch of brown hair who greeted her.

"How do, miss," he said, grinning. "You must be the new lady. I'm Sean Roche; I have the milk route. That's my truck beyond."

Linn looked past him to the van that stood in the drive. It was emblazoned with Roche Dairy, Ltd, on the side.

"Yes? What can I do for you?" she inquired.

"Will you be carrying on with the same schedule as before?" he asked. "I've not received any new instructions since the old man passed on."

Bridie walked into the hall. "Is that you, Seaneen? What are you after, boy?"

Sean looked uncomfortable. "Hullo, missus. I was just checking about the deliveries. Will you have the same as always?"

Bridie shot him an arch glance. "And why not? Wouldn't I have called you if there was to be a change? You wouldn't be using that as an excuse to snatch a peek at our young lady here, would you?"

Sean turned red, confirming Bridie's suspicions.

"As I thought," Bridie said airily. "Be off with you. And tell your father that it will be two quarts of milk, a pint of cream and a pound of butter every other week, the usual order, thank you very much."

To his credit, Sean stood his ground even though he was burning under Bridie's condescending treatment. He ignored the older woman and said to Linn, "I'll not deny I wanted to meet you, miss. Will you be coming to the festival?"

"What festival?"

"It's a fair in the town. I thought if you came in to Bally, you might spare me a few minutes. I'd like to talk to you about the States."

"Sure, I guess so," Linn answered, mindful of Bridie hovering in the background, her ear on a stalk. "I suppose I'll go, if everyone else plans to be there."

"Grand." Sean beamed. "I'll look for you, then. Good day for now."

"Good-bye," Linn called after him as he trotted back to his truck. He roared off in a cloud of dust as Linn turned back to face Bridie's disapproving stare.

"What's wrong with you?" she asked Bridie irritably. "If there's a local fair, why shouldn't I go? And why shouldn't I talk to him if I want to? I've been cooped up in here all week listening to you lecture me on what an amazing collection of junk my relatives managed to amass."

"Don't get testy with me, my girl, just because he hasn't come by."

"Who?" Linn demanded, pretending ignorance.

"Him you were hoping for when the knock came at the door. Him that you watch through the window with your tongue on the floor."

Linn winced at Bridie's graphic description. She didn't answer.

"He's a good lad," Bridie said quietly.

Linn knew she wasn't referring to Sean. She still kept silent, not knowing what to say.

"I said, Connor is a good lad," Bridie repeated louder, as if Linn were partially deaf.

"I heard you. I never said he wasn't."

"Fine figure of a man, too," Bridie added.

Linn was not about to debate Con's obvious attributes with Bridie. "I suppose so," she replied mildly.

"You've done more than suppose, Aislinn Pierce," Bridie stated tartly.

Linn turned on her. "What do you want me to say? He obviously isn't interested in me, so it doesn't matter what I think of him, does it?" Even as she spoke, she resented Bridie's ability to waltz her expertly into a corner and force her to admit her feelings. Bridie's talents were wasted dusting furniture in Ballykinnon. She could be making a fortune dissecting hostile witnesses.

Bridie smiled wisely. "Oh, he wants you; any fool can see that. But something is holding him back. What might that be?"

"I haven't the faintest idea."

"Indeed?" Bridie wasn't convinced.

"Indeed no. And in case I haven't told you, it's none of your business."

"It is my business when the two of you tiptoe around here circling one another like a mare and a stallion at the Bantry Fair. What's up with you, girl? If you keep dragging your feet, you're going to lose out. The man has a way with him, and you've no lack of competition. That Mary Costello down at the Kinnon Arms has been after him for years. Are you going to stand about like a chess piece and let her snatch him from under your nose?"

"And what do you suggest I do?"

"Stop mooning through the rooms like a love-sick calf, for a start. Why *hasn't* he been back? Did you have a tiff?"

"Not really. He thinks there are reasons why it . . . wouldn't work out between us, that's all."

Bridie snorted. "That boy always did think too much. If he just followed his heart he'd be a lot better off, I say. He's all the time trying to cover his feelings, putting on that mask."

"I wish I could tell what he was thinking," Linn mused, almost to herself. "Sometimes it seems I can, but other times he looks at me out of those cool blue eyes . . . " She let the sentence hang, unfinished.

Bridie watched her closely. "Think he's a cool customer, do you?" she asked, picking up on Linn's metaphor.

"Not always," Linn answered vaguely. She'd seen him flash very hot on a number of occasions.

"Well, you'd be wrong," Bridie stated flatly. "He's got a temper on him like a volcano, and you don't want to be around when it erupts. Don't mistake control for lack of feeling. He just keeps himself in rigid check, is all."

Linn sighed. "Bridie, I know you're trying to help, but there's nothing I can do once he's made up his mind. If you know him as well as you say, then you know how stubborn he is. Now let's have the tea and then get on with the list of repairs. I want to order a new refrigerator and get an electrician in here to rewire the house. We'll never be able to handle the new appliances with the old fuse box.'' Linn made for the kitchen with a determined expression. The subject was closed.

Bridie followed with the restrained air of a woman who meant to have her say at a later date.

The next day Linn was scrubbing the tile in the front hall on her hands and knees when Con walked through the door. She scrambled to her feet, flustered.

He handed her a stack of mail. "I've brought the post from the village," he said shortly.

"Thank you." Their fingers touched briefly as he withdrew his hand.

He nodded, looking around at the interior of the house. "How are you getting on?"

"Fine. Bridie's helping me with the housework. We're almost finished."

As if on cue, Bridie appeared from the parlor. Linn closed her eyes for a second in silent prayer. If Bridie said anything to indicate the subject of their recent conversation, she wasn't going to live long after Con left.

"Connor," Bridie said briskly. "Been busy these past days, have you?"

"Aye. There's a good lot to be done."

"And you're writing as well?"

"I am."

"Then that explains why we haven't seen much of you. We've been wondering how you've been keeping."

"Have you?" Con asked, glancing at Linn.

"I've been meaning to ask you to take a look at that drain out back. It's stopped up again, and you were so clever about fixing it last time. Would you give it a go? There's a good son."

Con shared a half smile with Linn that indicated he wasn't taken in by this blarney. "You can spare the speech; I'll have a look at it." He went through the hall and out the back door. Linn followed his progress with her eyes.

"Bridie, he's limping," she said when he was out of earshot.

"Oh, aye, he does that off and on. There's a piece of metal left in that leg yet. I've seen him drag it before, when he was tired."

Linn's face was shadowed with concern. "But he must be in pain much of the time," she murmured.

The older woman's face softened at Linn's anxious tone. Why, she's in love with him, Bridie thought, and she doesn't even know it yet.

"Go and talk to him, lass," Bridie urged gently. "You've missed him so."

Linn didn't need any further encouragement. She brushed her hair back off her forehead and glanced into the hall mirror as she passed. She'd pinned her hair up on top of her head that morning, but it was half down from her exertions. There was a smudge on her nose, and her blouse had a wet stain from the cleaning rag she'd been using. This didn't even slow her down. Bridie was right; she'd missed Con far too much to waste this opportunity.

Linn found him digging out the cairn next to the well, removing the debris which had been clogging it. He looked up at her, his hands covered with muck.

"Lovely job," he said, commenting on the task at hand. "It's no wonder she always gets me to do it."

Linn smiled. He bent over with his back to her, and she let her eyes dwell lovingly on the perfect symmetry of his body. It was cooler out than usual, and he was wearing a charcoal gray Aran sweater that made him look as though he belonged on a travel poster from the Irish Tourist Board. His mink-colored hair caught and reflected the bright sunlight. Linn tore her gaze away. She wouldn't be caught staring.

Con straightened. "There. That's done. Let me have something to wipe off on, will you?"

Linn got him a rag from the house. When she returned, he took it from her gratefully and cleaned his hands. He met her eyes.

"Why do you put your hair up like that?" he asked softly. "It looks so beautiful down about your shoulders." He reached out with a slightly grimy forefinger and loosened one of the pins that held it. The flaxen mass cascaded over his hand.

"Ah," he murmured. "That's better. Aislinn with the amber hair. You should always leave it just like that."

Linn caught his hand and held it to her cheek.

"I'm dirty," he protested, making no move to pull away.

"I don't care," she whispered.

He took a step closer. "Aislinn, why do you encourage me?" he muttered harshly. "I'm the man you said no to on the mountain."

"I don't care about that either."

"Then why did you refuse me?" he demanded, agonized. "Do you wish so much to hurt me?" He whirled away from her, incensed again at the memory. He strode rapidly around the house, and Linn ran after him, almost crashing into Bridie as the housekeeper brushed past Con on her way out. Con continued on his path, not looking around.

"What ails him?" she asked Linn. "What did you say to him?"

"I don't know, I don't know; I can't seem to do anything right," Linn wailed. "He blows hot and cold by turns; he's got me spinning like a top." They both looked up as Con vanished into the distance, walking as fast as his halting gait would permit across the lawn. Linn sagged against the doorjamb, exasperated to the point of screaming.

Bridie put a sympathetic hand on her shoulder. "He's not easy, lass. I know he's not easy. But he's worth far more than a dozen like young Sean Roche who tease and play but never put themselves on the line. Con works straight from the heart. If you win him, he'll be yours forever."

Linn turned her head to meet Bridie's intent gaze. Then she nodded slowly.

"Yes, I know that," she said quietly. "I think I've known that from the beginning."

There was a pause before Bridie cleared her throat and said briskly, "Now take yourself back into the house and finish that floor. You can't leave it half-done; it looks like the before-and-after pictures in a magazine advert."

Linn smiled wanly and went inside, Bridie's words repeating themselves in her mind.

If you win him, Bridie had said.

Linn picked up the bucket of soapy water and moved it to a new spot on the tile.

She wanted very badly to win him.

The weekend came, and Bridie stayed with her family in town. Linn spent Saturday going through the books in what was laughingly known as the library. This was a back bedroom with a massive fireplace and books stacked from the floor to the ceiling in a haphazard fashion that would have sent any self-respecting librarian running for the bottle. There was also a black-and-white television, which received three stations, RTE (Radio Telefís Eireann) 1 and 2, and BBC Wales. Linn spent Saturday night trying to start a fire and watching an old British war movie on the Welsh channel. When she finally got a blaze going, she switched to RTE 1, which was giving the weather report. She watched in fascination as the "news presenter," as they were known in Ireland, gave the forecast in English and then switched smoothly into Gaelic, repeating what she had just said in the native language. The Irish were valiantly trying to resurrect their dying tongue, and all signs and public notices, as well as broadcasts, were done in both English and Gaelic. All media personnel had to be bilingual. Linn listened to the liquid syllables of the poetic tongue, the spoken version of which was musically beautiful, and wished that she could understand. She felt that a treasure chest of literary and cultural delights was at hand, but that she didn't have the key to unlock it. When the presenter went back to English for the wrap-up, Linn was almost disappointed.

The forecast was for "bright intervals" the next day. She had to smile at the difference from the weather reports back home, which predicted "patchy clouds." Here the assumption was that the sky would be overcast; at home it was just the opposite. She switched to RTE 2, but it had ceased broadcasting for the night. The test pattern featured a large clock with the minute hand sweeping serenely around its face, telling the current time. At the bottom was the Gaelic legend *Nos Da*. "Good night." *Nos da* to you too, Linn thought, and shut off the set.

The telephone rang. She had a wild moment of hope, but it was Sean Roche, trying again when he knew Linn would be alone. She put him off with some feeble excuse about getting the house in order and hung up the phone. She walked to the front door and looked out across the yard.

Where was Con? Down in the pub getting chummy with Mary Costello? Wandering aimlessly around the grounds, tortured by grim memories? Working, thinking, asleep? She forced herself to march back to the den and pick out a book. Mooning around, as Bridie put it, was getting her nowhere.

She drifted off to sleep with the book still in her hand.

On Sunday Linn decided on a more aggressive approach. She got dressed early and took a walk, skirting the gatehouse carefully, making sure that she wasn't seen.

She had a right to stroll around her own property, didn't she? Of course she did.

The trip was wasted. The gatehouse looked deserted, and the Bentley was gone from the barn, which Con used as a garage. He wasn't home.

He didn't come home for the rest of the day.

Bridie returned on Monday, but Linn didn't mention Con's absence until Wednesday, when two more days had passed without a glimpse of him.

"I haven't seen Con around, have you?" she asked, in what she hoped was a casual manner.

"I have not."

"His car is gone too," Linn persisted.

"Is it?"

Bridie's stilted responses were significant. Her customary manner was more voluble.

"Do you know where he is?" Linn asked directly.

Bridie surprised her by fidgeting with her dish towel nervously. Linn paused with the teapot in her hand, alarmed now.

"Answer me," Linn demanded. "Do you know where he is?"

"I'd only be guessing," Bridie hedged.

"Guess, then," Linn said impatiently. "Where?"

"In the past when he disappeared of a sudden like this it was because he was called north."

Linn set the pot on the stove, afraid that she would drop it. "He told me he wouldn't go back there," she whispered. "He said he was through with all of that."

Bridie shrugged. "The boy doesn't lie. If that's what he said, he meant it at the time. Something must have happened to change his mind."

Linn swayed unsteadily, gripping the edge of the sink for support. "He was shot once before," she said fearfully. "He could be hurt."

"He could," Bridie agreed.

"I've got to do something," Linn said wildly.

Bridie turned to her, astonished. "And what do you propose to do, my lass? Tear off after him up to Belfast and get killed yourself? They don't ask for citizenship papers before they throw the bombs."

"But we can't just sit here and wait to see if he comes back in one piece," Linn wailed.

"We can do no other," Bridie said quietly. "Now you know what it feels like to be one of us, waiting for the phone call, the knock on the door. Waiting to see if the loved one will come back maimed—or come back at all."

"Maybe he just took a vacation or something," Linn said, grasping desperately at straws.

"Maybe," Bridie said. She didn't sound convinced.

Linn picked up her sweater from the kitchen chair. "I'm going to walk over to the gatehouse and see if he's there."

"Go on if you like."

Linn paused in the hall. "I don't suppose there'd be any way to trace him if he did cross the border."

Bridie shook her head. "They vanish into the hills like the mist. You'll just have to learn patience."

"I've never been very good at patience," Linn muttered, heading for the door.

The gatehouse was still empty, and the barn housed nothing but stale air. Dust motes danced before her eyes in a shaft of sunlight as she closed the wooden door.

Linn kept up her vigil for the next couple of days, checking the cottage frequently, but it remained deserted. Her anxiety increased with each passing hour. By Friday night she was frantic, certain that Con lay dead somewhere, unidentified, his body burned beyond recognition. Just after sundown she walked out to the gatehouse for the third time that day, practicing a ritual which she no longer expected to yield a result.

The car was still gone. Forlorn, she was walking past the door of the cottage when she noticed that it was ajar. While this was not unusual in itself ("What is there to steal?'' Bridie said), Linn was certain that it had been closed earlier in the day.

Her heart pounding, she edged up to the door and pushed it inward. She gasped at the sight that met her eyes.

Con was sprawled across the single bed, unconscious.

His leg from crotch to knee was covered with blood.

Chapter 4

LINN RUSHED INTO THE ROOM AND FELL TO HER KNEES beside the bed. Con was sprawled on his back, the uninjured leg bent at the knee, one hand trailing to the floor. He was waxen, his forehead beaded with sweat, his lips dry and chapped. His face was covered with coarse black stubble, and his eyelashes were matted with rime like a child's. He looked as if he'd been tossed on the bed like a discarded handkerchief, crumpled and very still.

Linn touched his clammy forehead with a trembling hand. Con stirred, mumbling, his lashes fluttering. Linn sobbed aloud with relief.

"Con, it's Linn. It's Aislinn. You're hurt; what happened to you?"

He continued to mumble, slurring his words so badly she couldn't understand what he was saying. She stroked his cheek gently, and his eyes opened, then widened in recognition.

"Aislinn," he whispered.

"Yes, I'm here," she said softly. "Oh, Con, how did you get hurt like this?"

"Leg opened up," he answered hoarsely.

"You mean where you were shot? It's bleeding badly. You need a doctor."

"I'm all right," he rasped. "Be all right."

"Don't be ridiculous," Linn snapped. She was frightened for him and in no mood for macho theatrics. "I'm going to get help."

His fingers curled around her hand. "Bind it," he said.

"You need a doctor!"

"Cut the pants," he gasped, "and bind it. Aislinn, do as I say. Get the scissors from the drawer there." His head fell back in exhaustion from the effort of speaking. When she remained unmoving, he added, "Please."

"Please," from him, she couldn't refuse. Linn got up and rummaged through the dresser next to the bed. She came back with the scissors and knelt again next to the bed.

She was afraid to touch his wound. Avoiding the injured area, she cut the jeans away from his ankle and worked her way upward to his knee. From there on the cloth was soaked with blood and fluid, the skin below it parched and hot.

Con was watching her through slitted eyes. Linn's fingers pressed onward to his thigh, and he gripped the sheets, twisting them, his knuckles white. He didn't make a sound, but his mouth was contorted with pain. Linn hesitated, close to tears, unwilling to hurt him.

He saw her reluctance. "Go on," he directed, his teeth clenched around the words.

Linn took the severed material in her hands and ripped it apart. When she saw the wound, she made an involuntary sound, closing her eyes and taking a deep breath.

"Bad?" Con asked.

Linn couldn't speak. His thigh was a gaping hole filled with pus and blood and surrounded by the ragged edges of torn flesh. Linn could see the glint of a metal fragment embedded in the lumpy scar tissue.

"Talk to me, girl," Con said weakly, with some of the old amusement in his voice. "I've never known you to be at a loss for words."

Linn found her voice. "Con, I can't handle this," she said, striving to sound calmer than she felt. "You must let me call a doctor."

He sighed. "Book next to the phone," he said. "Neil McCarthy. The number's there."

Linn went to the phone, which was on his desk next to the typewriter. She pushed aside several stacks of papers and found a leather-bound notebook underneath them. Dr. McCarthy's number was scrawled in Con's bold, angular hand.

She glanced over at Con while she got the operator to ring the number. Bally was still on the antiquated system which made every phone call an involved project. Con was peering down at his leg, trying to see what it looked like without moving.

McCarthy's wife answered, and then put him on the phone.

"Dr. McCarthy, this is Aislinn Pierce."

Uncomprehending silence.

"Dermot Pierce's granddaughter. I'm at Ildathach for the summer, straightening out his estate."

"Yes, Miss Pierce?" His voice indicated that her identity had registered.

"I wonder if you could come over to the gatehouse on the property. Connor Clay is . . . injured."

"Connor, eh?" the doctor answered. "Well, I'm not surprised. What is it this time?"

Linn tried to think of a way to explain, and then just plunged into it. "He was shot in the leg a while back, and somehow he managed to reopen the wound. It looks like there's a piece of metal emerging from the skin or something. I'm afraid I really don't know what the problem is, but it looks . . . I really wish you would come," she finished lamely.

"That will be the piece of bullet casing left in when they sewed him up. A botched job, but it was an emergency. Tell me, is he conscious?"

"Yes, but feverish."

"Best not to move him. Keep him warm and I'll be there as soon as I can."

"Thank you, doctor. Thank you very much." Linn hung up and turned to face Con, who was resting back on the pillows, watching her.

"He's on his way," Linn said. She folded her arms and surveyed him critically. "Are you going to tell me how this happened?"

"Do I have to go into it now?" he asked wearily.

He looked so beaten that Linn relented. "All right. You can tell me the details later, but you went north again, didn't you?"

"I did. And don't look at me as if I were demented. I had to go. You know nothing about it."

Linn felt a surge of anger so intense it almost made her ill. "Fine, Mr. Independence, just great. I think I'll leave you here to bleed to death; how would that be?" she flared at him.

Con's eyes closed. "You won't leave me, Aislinn," he said. His voice was quiet but full of certainty.

He was right, of course. "I should," she said. "You take off without a word to anybody and show up again in this condition. I never heard of anything so inconsiderate."

His lips twitched. "Why, lass, I think you were worried about me," he said without opening his eyes.

"Bridie and I were both worried. And with good reason. Look at you. You have to be insane to keep going back up there for more of this."

Con's eyes flashed open. "They were putting my friend

in a camp," he said heatedly. "No hearing, no trial, just off to the camp, which is a jail, if you don't know."

"Well maybe he belongs in a jail," Linn fired back. "Those people are terrorists."

"Christy Dugan is not a terrorist. He doesn't hold with the violence and neither do I. But his brother is a different sort, and Christy got hauled in along with him. Could I sit back and do nothing?"

Linn could see that she was getting nowhere; he was only becoming incensed and weaker. This was an argument she would never win. He had been shaped by different forces and was pulled by different tides. She went over to him and pushed him back on the pillows. He had risen to his elbows in agitation, and he subsided reluctantly, wincing as the movement disturbed his leg.

"You're ill, and I'm not going to fight with you," Linn said. "It's no concern of mine if you want to trifle with your life."

"I'm not trifling with my life," he answered, his voice low and losing volume. "I'm here, as you see. I got out."

"This time."

"Every time. I'm lucky. I've always been lucky."

"Oh, I can tell that just by looking at your leg," Linn said sarcastically. "You were lucky when you took that bullet, I suppose?"

"Certainly. Anyone else would now be guarding the entrance to a harem." He smiled slightly and closed his eyes, drifting off.

Linn smiled too, in spite of herself. She discovered again that she couldn't remain angry with him. She unfolded the blanket from the foot of the bed and spread it over him, pausing to wipe the perspiration from his forehead with the back of her hand. His eyes opened.

"I'm glad you're here, Aislinn," he whispered. He reached up and took her hand, drawing her to the edge of the bed. "Sit with me," he added.

Linn sat gingerly, careful not to jostle him. He closed his eyes again, still holding her hand. She was in the same position, watching the rise and fall of his chest, when McCarthy came to the door.

Linn got up and let him in. He was a tall, heavyset man in his fifties with graying blond hair and a small moustache. His direct gaze swept quickly over Linn and then took in the patient, prone on the bed.

He brushed past Linn and pulled over a chair, depositing his bag on the seat of it. He examined Con's leg and shook his head.

"Will you look at this, now?" he said to Linn. "Do you think the wild man here will ever learn? Six months ago he stops a bullet that nicks the femoral artery, and he damn near bleeds out before they slap a tourniquet on him and rush him to hospital. Once there it takes enough blood to float the Armada to get him back on his feet, and yet here he is, up to his old tricks again. He *will* mix it up with those hooligans in Ulster, and this is what it gets him."

Con's lashes lifted. "Will you skip the oratory and patch me up, Neil?" he asked faintly. "She doesn't need to hear the sordid history of my life."

"Be still," the doctor said sharply, picking up his bag. "You're a sick man." He took a probe from his case. "This one, now," he said to Linn, continuing his monologue, "I've been making a career out of stitching him up since he was fourteen. That time he jumped off the roof of Saint Michael's, if you please, and broke the other leg. He's been trying to kill himself creatively ever since."

"Can you help him?" Linn asked anxiously.

McCarthy sent her a measuring glance. "Have you a strong stomach?" he asked.

Linn swallowed. "I think so."

"Yes or no?"

"Yes."

He nodded. "Good." He removed forceps, a pair of thin rubber gloves and a tin of antiseptic powder from his case. "I'm going to take out that scrap that's causing all the trouble. It had to come out sooner or later. This really should be done under sterile conditions in hospital, but I don't want to move him. Now, you keep him still, lass. This will smart a bit, and I can't have him jouncing all over the place. Get up there with him and hold him fast."

Linn climbed onto the bed and cradled Con in her lap. He was losing consciousness again, his head lolling, his breathing shallow. She looked away from the wound when she saw McCarthy packing it in gauze and sliding a wadded sheet under Con's leg. That done, he uncapped a flask he'd brought with him and held it to Con's lips.

"Have some of this, son; it will ease the pain."

Con came around a little and sipped, choking on the strong spirits.

"That's good Jameson's, boy; don't waste it," the doctor said kindly, giving him some more and wiping away the spillage. He waited until Con swallowed and then put the flask aside.

"Let's get to it," he said to Linn, picking up the forceps.

Linn couldn't look. She bent her head over Con's, holding him close, pressing her lips to his hair. She felt his fingers close around her arms as the doctor went to work.

Con gasped and stiffened as the instrument probed his flesh. He writhed in silent agony, his hands gripping her like a vise. Linn murmured to him, hardly knowing what she was saying.

"It's all right," she said, her voice breaking. "Almost over now. Just about done." His body relaxed, and she knew that he had lost consciousness. She went on talking to him anyway, kissing his head, his shoulders, anywhere she could reach, unaware that she was crying.

"You'll be fine, my darling, you'll be fine. I know it hurts, and you're so brave, not a sound. It's wonderful to be so strong."

She continued that way, holding his limp body, babbling nonsense, until McCarthy said triumphantly, "Got it. Now let me sew him up, and there's an end to it."

Linn raised her head, blinking through her tears. "He'll be okay?" she whispered. "He doesn't need a transfusion?"

"Of course not. He'll be fine. No doubt of it. This looks a mess, a lot worse than it actually is." He saw Linn's death grip on his patient, and he added gently, "You can let him go now. Help me clean him up."

Linn settled Con carefully on the bed and wiped her face with the sleeve of her blouse. She crawled around to the doctor's position and assisted him silently while he cleaned and dressed the wound.

"There," McCarthy said, taping the gauze in place. "Done, and done." He glanced at Linn. "You look like you could use a drink yourself."

Linn tried a smile. "I guess I could."

McCarthy raised his flask. "Neat, from the jug?" he asked.

"Yes."

He handed Linn the bottle. She bolted a large swig and gasped, more tears springing to her eyes.

"That'll set you up," the doctor stated, then took a substantial pull of his own. He eyed Linn worriedly. "Are you all right, girl?"

"Yes, I think so. I guess I didn't realize that it would . . . hurt him . . . quite so much."

The doctor nodded thoughtfully. After a moment he said, "Does he know how you feel about him?"

Linn stared at him, stunned.

The doctor shrugged. "I'd tell him, if I were you. Con's a smart lad about most things, but he can be a bit thick when it comes to women."

Linn couldn't think of a suitable reply to that observation, but McCarthy didn't seem to expect one. He set about washing his things in the sink at the other end of the cottage, humming cheerfully. Linn had composed herself by the time he returned. He loaded a syringe from a bottle and injected Con with the solution.

"This will hold him till morning," he said. He gave Linn a paper packet with a handful of pills inside it. "Give him one of these every four hours. The shot was a pain killer and these are antibiotics." He looked at Linn. "You'll stay with him?"

"I'll stay."

"He's a tough character, you know. Terrible strong-minded. He has to stay quiet, and he may take a notion to get out of bed when he wakes up."

"I can handle him," Linn answered with grim determination.

McCarthy turned away to hide his smile. "I believe you can," he said evenly. "Now he may spike a fever, which is normal under the circumstances; just keep him warm and off that leg. Call me if he becomes agitated or if anything seems wrong. I'll be back to check on him tomorrow."

"All right. Thank you, doctor. I'm so grateful that you came to take care of him."

"Oh, Con's a favorite of mine. He's trouble on wheels, to be sure, but he has a great heart."

That's just what Bridie said, Linn thought.

"By the way," McCarthy said as he was packing to go, "do you know how he got back here without his car?"

"No, I don't. I don't even know how he was hurt, except that it happened while he was trying to spring some friend of his who was picked up for internment."

The doctor nodded. "A familiar story. Those boyos stick together." He picked up his bag and glanced around to see if he had left anything.

"I think that's all," he said with finality. "Good-bye, then, Miss Pierce, and take good care of our patient."

"I will. And thanks again for coming."

He made a deprecating gesture. "Not at all." He

saluted Linn with two fingers and slipped through the door.

Linn glanced at her watch. It would be a long night. She settled down in the chair next to the bed and decided to take a rest.

Later, while Con slept, she would tidy up the cottage.

Linn fell asleep in the chair and woke an hour later. The moon had risen and shone through the window above the bed, casting a shaft of light across Con's face. He was sleeping peacefully, and Linn pulled the cover up under his chin. She put the back of her hand to his forehead, and it felt cool. Satisfied, she got up and went to the kitchenette, putting the kettle on to boil. She thought with a mental sigh that she could kill for a cup of American coffee, but she'd found that it was scarce in this country. They were all passionately devoted to tea.

She had the opportunity to examine Con's home for the first time since she'd arrived. He had converted the interior of the stone cottage into a sort of bachelor pad. There was a small modern kitchen in one corner next to the brick fireplace, which was obviously original. A combined leisure and work area consisted of twin couches in front of the hearth and a sturdy work table, which contained the telephone and typewriter. Three of the four walls were lined with bookshelves, which were crammed with everything imaginable, including a small Japanese television set and a stack of clean shirts. He had a dresser and a chest of drawers in the alcove that housed the bed. Chintz curtains that matched the print on the sofas covered the windows. Linn looked around curiously for the bathroom and saw a door leading off from the rear of the kitchen. He had added that, as well as the many electric outlets which dotted the walls. He must have rewired the whole place to accommodate his appliances, a process that Linn was just beginning at the main house.

The kettle whistled, and Linn went to turn it off,

glancing at Con, who slept undisturbed. She turned on the small lamp on the bar portion of the kitchen and looked around for tea bags. In one of the cupboards she found something better: a jar of instant coffee. It was a British brand and didn't compare favorably with her beloved ground roast, but it was better than nothing. Mug in hand, she wandered over to the bookshelves and investigated their contents.

He had an Irishman's taste in books. He had many volumes of poetry, including a copy of Yeats's original notes in the writer's own hand, which must have cost a fortune. There were selections on Irish, American and British history and a wide range of contemporary fiction. Quite a few were in Gaelic, which is written with a runic alphabet and read from right to left. Linn flipped through a volume, thinking that the writing looked like Hebrew. Con seemed particularly interested in the Celtic folktales, which were Seamus Martin's stock-in-trade; Linn examined a book on Deirdre of the Sorrows, which featured lovely pen-and-ink sketches of the principals in her tragic story.

There were some textbooks he'd saved from Fordham, and a Trinity yearbook in which she found his picture. Linn checked on the patient guiltily; he might not like her inspection of his library. You could learn a lot about people from the books they owned. Linn felt that this tour was the best insight she'd had into his character, providing information he would never volunteer himself.

There wasn't a single copy of his own books. She thought this odd; if she ever had anything published, she intended to wallpaper her rooms with the cover proofs.

Linn drained her cup and set about putting the large room in order. The cottage wasn't dirty, just cluttered. She put Con's papers into neat, organized stacks and resisted the strong temptation to read the manuscript pages she found on top of the typewriter. She washed the dishes in the sink and put away a bag of groceries he'd left to

decompose on the countertop. Most of the stuff was
salvageable; she poured the soured milk down the sink and
tossed out the rock-hard loaf of bread. He had evidently
left in a hurry.

She was crouched before the mini refrigerator, putting
things away, when she heard a sound from Con's direction. She hurried to his side. He was whimpering,
muttering under his breath, bunching the bedclothes in his
fists. Alarmed, she felt his forehead, but he was still cool.
He wasn't delirious; he was having a bad dream.

She touched his arm lightly, but he continued to talk,
louder now. He spoke in Gaelic, and she couldn't understand a word. He was becoming more upset, and she was
just about to shake him when he sat up with a loud cry,
shocking himself awake.

"Con, you're all right," Linn said soothingly, putting
her hands on his shoulders. "You had a bad dream."

He looked at her and around at the room. Relieved, he
sank back on the bed. "It seems I did," he answered
hoarsely.

"You were yelling in Gaelic," Linn said.

He nodded. "We use it for a code. The tans can't
understand it."

The tans. He used the old word, with the old bitterness.
"Is that what you were dreaming about, the trouble?"

"Aye." He swallowed. "I was trying to warn someone, but he couldn't hear me. I've dreamt the same
before."

"Do you want to talk about it?"

He shook his head. "It doesn't bear repeating." He
took her hand. "Will you get me a drink? I've the mother
and father of a thirst." He glanced at his leg. "I see Neil
patched me up."

"I'll get you a drink of *water*," Linn replied. "You're
full of drugs; no booze for you. It's time for your pill
anyway."

"Who died and left you boss?" he said grumpily.

"Dr. McCarthy left me in charge."

"Neil has no mercy." He sat up and tried to slide his injured leg off the bed.

Linn paused in her path to the sink. "And where do you think you're going?" she demanded.

"I have to use the lavatory," he said uncomfortably, flushing faintly.

"You can't go by yourself. I'll take you."

"The devil you will!" he roared. "I'm not a cripple yet."

"Dr. McCarthy said you were to stay off that leg. You can use me for a crutch." Linn went to him and helped him stand, propping up his bad side by slipping her arm around his waist. "Don't be afraid to lean on me," she said to him. "I'm strong."

Con looked down at her. "You are that," he said softly.

Linn pulled him closer, trying to get a better grip on him. He was still holding back, reluctant to let her take his full weight. "Con, you must let me help you," she said, glancing up at him.

His blue eyes held hers. "You have helped me," he murmured. "I'd be in a bad way if it weren't for you."

Linn dropped her eyes, acutely conscious of his muscular body pressed against hers. He turned her chin up with his free hand, forcing her to look at him.

"I'm afraid I've given you a rough time," he said quietly. "I'm a notoriously nasty patient."

"Anyone in pain can be forgiven for being nasty," Linn answered evasively.

"Am I forgiven then?" he asked.

"You know you are."

"Show me."

"Con, you shouldn't be standing this long and—" Her words were cut off by the pressure of his mouth. His lips touched hers briefly, warmly, and then he raised his head, leaving her aching for more.

"Aislinn aroon," he whispered. "You're a treasure."

Linn allowed herself the luxury of turning her face against his chest and hugging him for a second. Then she straightened and said briskly, "I believe you wanted to take a walk."

"That I did." Linn led him to the lavatory in a lurching duet as he hopped on his good leg and she did her best to keep up with him. She opened the door and handed him inside, then leaned against the wall to wait. There were water sounds and muffled curses followed by a loud, splintering crash.

"Con!" she called. "Are you all right?"

"I am not," he answered in a tone that indicated he wasn't at death's door, either. "I just broke this bloody bottle of mouthwash."

"Will you forget that stuff and come back to bed before you trash the whole bathroom?" she asked.

The door was yanked open, and he faced her. "I just scared myself with a glance in the mirror," he announced. "I look like I'm coming off a five-day drunk."

"I can stand it," she replied dryly, slipping her shoulder under his arm again.

"Mind the glass if you go in there," he said. "The floor is strewn with shards."

"I'll clean it up later."

They struggled back to the bed, and Con settled on it with a heartfelt sigh. Linn lifted his bad leg gingerly and laid it on the coverlet.

"How do you feel?" she asked him.

"Like my leg has a separate existence," he replied. "I'm here with you, and my leg is in a baker's oven."

"I know it hurts," she said soothingly. "I'll get your pill." She returned with it and a glass of water. He swallowed it obediently.

"I'm sorry about all this, Aislinn," he said. "You've better things to do than babysit me."

No I don't, Linn thought. Aloud she said, "Are you hungry? I could fix you something to eat."

He made a face and shook his head. "No. All I want is you up here next to me." He held out his hand.

Linn hesitated.

"Oh, come on, girl, I'm in no shape to threaten your virtue," he said wearily. "I just need to feel you close."

His use of the word "need" decided her. She moved up next to him, being careful not to jar the bed. He lifted his arm and she curled into his body, resting her head on his shoulder.

"Ah, that's better," he said, satisfied. Then, after a pause, "I missed you."

So he'd been lonely too. After their explosive meeting, his indifference had been terrible. It was good to know that it had been feigned.

She felt his lips brush her forehead. "I finally get you into bed with me, and I can't move," he said grimly. "A fine thing."

Linn shook with silent laughter. "I'm sorry."

"Not as sorry as I am," he answered. "You're a beautiful armful, my lady."

"I'm not beautiful," she said before she thought about it.

There was a moment of silence, and then he said, "Indeed you are. How can you think otherwise?"

"My husband didn't want me," she blurted. Why was she telling him this? Was it the warmth, the closeness, the dark? She had never trusted another person with this painful memory.

"You were married?" he asked, his voice deep and very near above her head. She felt the rumble in his chest beneath her ear.

"Yes."

"I wondered . . ." he said, his words thoughtful. "You didn't seem very . . ."

"Experienced?"

"Aye."

"He wasn't very good at it."

There was a stunned pause. Then, as if he couldn't believe his ears, "What?"

"He wasn't interested," Linn said miserably. Why had she begun this confession? She felt humiliated.

"Then he was a fool!" Con spat vehemently. His hands moved over her back, caressing. "And have you carried that around with you ever since?"

Her silence was his answer.

"Was he a poofter?"

"A what?" She half laughed at the Irish slang.

"A nancy boy, one of those who don't like women." He stirred slightly. "I don't understand them myself," he added, sounding genuinely puzzled.

"He was confused."

"He must have been," Con replied violently. He turned her in his arms to face him. "Come here to me and I'll show you how confused I am." He pushed her down and rolled her under him, shifting to favor his injured leg. He moved his mouth over her face and then took her lips with his.

"Con," she protested weakly, turning her head, "don't. You're sick."

He bent his head and his mouth seared her throat. "I'm never that sick," he murmured.

"Your whiskers are rough," she moaned, not caring at all.

"My hands are gentle," he replied, sliding them along her body. He mouthed her breasts through her clothes. "I'll make you forget him. I'll make you forget everything but me."

He had already accomplished that. Linn held his head as he kissed her everywhere he could reach without moving, awkwardly trying to undress her.

"Help me," he finally ground out in frustration.

"Con, no," she whispered. "Dr. McCarthy said—"

He yanked on her blouse, popping the top button, and tongued the valley between her breasts. "The hell with

Neil McCarthy,'' he muttered. "I want you. Now." He pushed aside her chemise, seeking her soft flesh.

"But . . ." Her protest was lost in a sigh as he took a sensitive nipple in his mouth and sucked, running his hard palm down her back underneath her loosened blouse. Linn moaned and closed her eyes, succumbing to the exquisite sensation. He lowered his head and left a trail of kisses down her body to the waistband of her skirt, encircling her waist with his hands and nudging the material covering her skin.

"Take this off," he rasped. "Get up and take this off."

Linn stood quickly and shrugged out of her blouse, then slid her skirt over her legs to the floor. She lay back on the bed and reached for him, wearing only her camisole and pants.

"Those too," he growled, pulling the top over her head in one smooth movement. Linn tensed to object, but when he saw her creamy nakedness he forgot everything else and bent, pulling her swiftly into his arms, caressing her with his hands and mouth until she was sobbing aloud.

"It's not enough," he said thickly. "Tell me it's not enough."

Linn whimpered in reply. The soft, helpless sound of passion inflamed him. He pushed her down and slid along the bed, pressing his burning cheek to the skin of her stomach, his face rough with stubble, his arms and shoulders knotted with the strain of self-discipline. He wanted desperately to plunge lower; when her fingers slipped from his hair to the back of his neck, he shuddered wildly, his whole body trembling.

"Aislinn," he moaned, gripping her hips and running his mouth over her abdomen and thighs, never lingering, teasing her with feather touches that drove her mad. When he knew that she was past the point of resistance, he reached for the wisp of lace that covered her.

"Let me love you in the only way I can tonight," he panted. "I can wait no longer."

Neither could Linn. She shifted to accommodate him, moving her leg, and her foot jarred against his thigh. Con doubled up in pain, rolling away from her. He was silent, but she saw the beads of sweat forming on his forehead with the effort of not crying out.

Mortified, Linn seized the opportunity to break free. She stood unsteadily, slipping into her blouse, ashamed of her weakness. How could she do such a thing? The man was practically a hospital case, and she was such a pushover for him that she'd almost let him . . . Her face flamed at the thought of what she'd almost let him do. What she'd *wanted* him to do. In her entire life she had never lost control like that; he was a drug, an aphrodisiac that turned her into a needy, hungry stranger.

"I hurt you," she said quietly. "I'm sorry."

"I'm all right," he responded quickly. "Don't fret."

"It's just as well," she continued in a restrained voice. "I don't know what I was thinking about. . . . I guess I just wasn't thinking at all." Linn paused to take a deep breath. "I'm going to go in and clean up the mess in the bathroom, and you need a chance to recover your strength. Go to sleep."

"Go to sleep!" Con yelled, his voice incredulous. His fist crashed against the wall next to the bed. "Woman, you are driving me to distraction!"

"I must be making progress," Linn said tartly. "I've gone from 'girl' to 'woman' in one evening."

Con's eyes closed, his lips moving. Then he opened his eyes and said aloud, "Aislinn, I'm warning you—"

"Go to sleep," she cut him off. "You can warn me in the morning." Before he could answer, she fled to the bathroom and shut the door.

Once inside, she listened intently, half-afraid that he would try to follow her. But all was silence. She made a great project of cleaning up the glass, taking twice as long as was necessary. When she finally emerged he was sleeping, as she'd hoped.

Linn went to his bedside and stood looking down at him. His clothes were in tatters, one pants leg cut off at the knee, the stained gauze bandage bound awkwardly below the ragged edge of the material. His hair was disordered and wild, and the dark beard obscuring the lower half of his face blunted the effect of his strong jaw. He looked like a highwayman out of a Victorian melodrama, and she loved him beyond belief.

Linn brushed back a lock of his dark brown hair, and he stirred slightly. Why am I resisting him, she thought, when I want him so badly and care so much? But she knew the answer. He was the one she had feared for five years, the man who would force her to stop running and face herself. There were no half measures with Con; he wouldn't allow her to hide and dodge the emotions he had aroused in her. She would be vulnerable again, open to the hurt she had managed to avoid since Rick. Linn kissed her fingertips and pressed them to his mouth. She loved him, but she was terrified.

Linn remembered Bridie as she was wrapping the pieces of shattered glass in an old newspaper she'd found. She called Bridie at home and told her what had happened. She reassured the housekeeper that Con was fine, though she couldn't make that same statement about herself. She told Bridie that she would see her the next day and hung up.

Linn curled up on one of the sofas and tried to go to sleep, but it was no use. She wanted to be with Con. Stealthily she slipped onto the bed next to him, and when he didn't stir, she allowed her head to move onto his shoulder. He sighed in his sleep and pulled her close.

Linn listened to the steady rhythm of his breathing and drifted off thinking that she hadn't felt so comfortable in a long time.

Chapter 5

LINN WOKE FIRST IN THE MORNING AND SLIPPED OFF THE bed, taking care not to disturb Con, who slept on peacefully. His beard was even darker now, but the blue shadows of fatigue under his eyes seemed less pronounced. Linn was afraid to touch the dressing on his leg, but she convinced herself that the skin surrounding the wound looked better.

She went to the kitchenette and made a light breakfast, eggs and toast, brewing instant coffee for herself and a pot of tea for Con. The smell of the meal roused him; he stirred and propped himself up on one elbow, obviously feeling improved enough to express an interest in food.

"Good morning," Linn said brightly. "How are you feeling?"

"Grand, thanks to you," he replied.

"And Dr. McCarthy."

"Neil had less to do with it than you," Con said. "What have you there?"

"Something for you to eat."

"Smells good."

"I hope it tastes good," Linn said doubtfully. She plugged in the can opener to open a tin of peaches, and as the appliance began to hum the lights dimmed. She had noticed the same thing the night before when she used the electricity. She looked up, puzzled.

Con smiled slyly. "Think you're going blind?"

"You've noticed it too?"

He waved a hand in the air. "I rewired the place myself and didn't know what I was doing. If you plug in too many things at once, the lights go dim. It's like living in the *Addams Family* house."

Linn chuckled. His reference to the American television show reminded her of the time he'd spent in the States.

"Thank you for telling me," she replied, dishing up the fruit. "I was beginning to feel like Ingrid Bergman in *Gaslight*."

He laughed delightedly. Linn joined in, idiotically pleased with herself for having amused him. She had noticed that, although he had a finely tuned sense of humor, he didn't laugh all that much.

"I can think of pleasanter ways to drive you crazy," he said lazily, his voice heavy with remembered passion.

Linn ignored that. She walked to his bedside and set the tray she'd prepared on the night table, then propped his pillows behind his head and helped him to sit up. She put the tray in his lap.

Con watched her fixedly all the while. When she wouldn't meet his eyes, he said with resignation, "I see. We're going to pretend that nothing happened last night."

"I don't want to talk about it," Linn said. She looked up defiantly. "You know, the way you don't want to talk about how you hurt your leg."

He eyed her narrowly. "Quite the saucy little item, aren't you? As fresh as paint."

Linn stared him down. She wasn't going to back off on this one.

Con pressed his lips together and bent his head, conceding defeat. Linn felt a flash of triumph. He must care about her to accede to her wishes like this. He was not a man to give in so readily.

"All right, Aislinn," he sighed. "As they say in the States, let's make a deal. I'll tell you what you want to know, and then we'll discuss what's happening between us. Fair do?"

"Fair do," she replied, smiling slightly at his idiom.

He took a huge gulp of his tea. "I was called in to spring Christy from the truck taking him to Mountjoy," he said simply. "We ambushed it and set him free."

"And how did you open up the leg?"

He looked uncomfortable. "I had to jump off the transport while it was moving," he explained. "I landed on my bad side, and the next thing I knew it was bleeding. I just managed to hitch a ride back here."

"Where's your car?"

"With friends. I'll get it back when the heat's off."

"Oh. And is the heat on?"

He glanced at her quickly. "No one is after me, Aislinn. This is a different country, you know."

"I understand. You run up north and do your dirty work, and then scamper to safety back here."

"It isn't dirty work to help a friend."

"The finer points of your scruples escape me," she said sarcastically. "All I know is that you are involved in that awful situation."

"I've never hurt anyone, Aislinn," he said quietly, putting down his cup. "Believe me on that. There are things that can be done to help without tossing grenades."

"Why do you have to help at all?" she burst out. "Why did you have to do this to yourself?"

He had picked up a piece of toast, but he set it back down again. He pointed to the bookshelves behind her.

"Over there," he said, "is a book on the American civil rights movement. One of the marchers was asked why she felt she had to get involved. She answered, 'You have got to stand up. Freedom is not something which is put in your lap.' "

"But you're dashing back and forth across the border like a child playing snatch-the-wallet, just asking to be picked off!"

He shook his head. "No more. I told you once that I was done with that. But I had to help Christy. He'd have done the same for me."

"That's very noble," Linn said. "Greater love than this no man has, that he lay down his life for his friend."

"I didn't lay down my life. You needn't be so dramatic."

His implacability was infuriating. "Con, I don't care about noble sentiments or the cause of freedom. All I care about is you!"

He froze in the act of raising his fork. It clattered to the tray and he pushed the dish aside.

"Do you, Aislinn?" he asked. "Do you?"

"Oh, how can you ask me that? Isn't it obvious?"

He put the tray on the floor. "Come here to me."

Linn stood her ground. "No. You'll just get me all . . . confused."

"What is there to be confused about?"

Linn's mouth fell open. "You tell me! I'm still an American *lady;* I'm still Kevin's daughter. Those factors seemed very important to you not too long ago."

Con dropped his eyes. "They become less important every minute," he said quietly.

Linn held her breath, afraid that he would say something else to qualify that statement. But the silence lengthened in the room. What did he mean? He had changed his mind?

"Do you trust me now?" she asked in a small voice.

He looked up. "I'm trying."

"Well, that's not good enough!" she blazed, furious that he could have even the slightest doubt about her after what she'd done for him. "I'm so terribly sorry that I don't have the right father, and that I wasn't born in a thatched hut down the lane. Too bad about you and your delicate sensibilities, Connor Clay."

"Wait a bit," he began. "You can't expect . . ."

"Oh, *cahn't* I?" she demanded, imitating the broad '*a*' of his accent. "I can damn well expect plenty. I didn't come here to take care of you because I'm a volunteer for the Red Cross. I came because . . ." She stopped and shut her mouth. She wasn't going to say it.

Con watched her in silence. Then he said, "I didn't mean to upset you."

"Of course you didn't," she answered evenly. "You never do."

Con glanced around the room. "You needn't stay any longer," he said, not meeting her eyes. "Neil will be here soon. You can go."

"And you can go straight to hell," Linn responded without inflection. "I'll wait for him to arrive. If I leave you alone, you'll probably trip and split your head open before he gets here."

Con bit his lip reflectively. "Well, as long as you're going to stay, will you help me to the bathroom? I need a shower. These clothes I'm wearing are about to get up and walk away—and I'll hear no arguments."

Linn shrugged, walking to his side and helping him to stand. She held herself stiffly away from him as he hobbled to the bathroom. She released him at the door and was about to turn away when he put his hand on her shoulder.

"You didn't let me finish before," Con said. "You have a wonderful facility for misunderstanding what I say."

"I think I understand very well. You've made your

position clear, and I have my own reservations about our . . . relationship. So why don't we just drop it, okay?''

He remained as he was. ''But . . .''

''I said to drop it,'' Linn repeated wearily. ''Take your shower.''

Con moved on reluctantly and shut the door. Linn picked up his tray and started to clear away the breakfast, which he'd barely touched. She heard the rush of water begin behind the door, and she carried the dishes to the sink with a heavy heart.

This will never work out, she thought. He wants me, but he doesn't love me. He still can't forget the past and my father. And I can't afford to take a chance on a man who might hurt me again. I won't recover a second time. She made herself another cup of coffee and sipped it slowly, a sense of loss spreading through her like a slow poison.

The cascading water stopped, and then after a short silence the door opened a crack.

''Will you get me a shirt from the shelf there and some pants from the drawer next the bed?'' Con asked. ''Anything will do.''

Linn selected the clothes and handed them through the door. She pushed it open to reach him and saw him standing just inside.

He was still wet from the shower, his hair in damp, glistening ringlets, droplets clinging to his lashes like crystal beads. Rivulets ran on his arms and chest. A towel was knotted around his waist. He had removed the bandage from his leg, and a freshet of blood stained the towel above his wound.

''Con, your leg,'' she said. ''You shouldn't be standing so long.''

''Help me, then,'' he said softly. ''Come here.''

Linn moved up next to him, and he put his arm across

her shoulders. His skin glistened wetly, an invitation she couldn't refuse. Before she knew what she was doing, Linn bent her head and licked a trail of droplets from his chest, slitting her eyes like a purring cat.

Con sucked in his breath and pulled her tight against him. His hand slid beneath her hair and closed around the nape of her neck, pressing her close as she kissed him wildly, lost in a tumult of desire.

"Oh, Con," she whispered, "you can hardly stand up, and still I can't keep my hands off you."

"Keep your hands on me," he said thickly, pulling on her hair to raise her head. "I've thought of nothing else for so long." He sought her lips with his, backing her up against the tiled wall, and Linn ran her hands over his almost naked body. His muscles bunched and flexed beneath her fingers in response to her loving touch. Her mouth opened under his, and then her head fell back as he moved his lips over her throat, pausing to fit her hips to his and surge against her powerfully with a force that made her gasp aloud.

His towel did little to conceal his arousal, and Linn's hands, which seemed to be acting of their own accord, moved to caress him. He groaned, and his arms loosened to allow her access. The towel fell to the floor.

Con shivered as Linn's fingers closed around him and he pulsed strongly in her hand. She encircled him and moved with deliberate slowness, prolonging his pleasure. Con's fists clenched.

"You torture me," he moaned. His chest and shoulders were flushed red, his breath coming in shallow gasps. His eyes were closed, as if he feared that she would be too shy to continue if he looked at her.

Linn's eagerness to please him overcame her ignorance; guided by instinct rather than technique, she put her face against his damp shoulder and stroked him, clasped to his body in the curve of one strong arm. His soft sounds of gratification made her bold; she nipped his skin with her teeth and felt the answering pressure of his palm in the hollow of her back. He made a deep noise in his throat, almost a growl, and she hesitated.

"Don't stop," he begged. "Please don't stop." He opened his eyes, and his gaze was so blurred with passion that he looked drugged.

There was a knock on the outside door.

"Oh, no," Con groaned. "Not now. Ignore it."

"Con, I can't. It's sure to be Dr. McCarthy, and he knows we're in here."

Linn stepped away from him, and he slumped backward, raising his arm to cover his eyes. She could see that he was still shaking. She averted her gaze from his nude form, picking up his clothes from the floor.

"Get dressed while I let him in," she said. Then she saw a terrycloth robe hanging on the back of the door. "On second thought, you'd better put the robe on so he can have a look at your leg."

Con didn't respond, and after waiting a moment she closed the door quietly behind her and hurried to answer the persistent knocking, which was getting louder and more enthusiastic.

"Hello, Dr. McCarthy," she said breathlessly, stepping aside to let him walk past her into the room. "We were expecting you."

"Were you indeed?" he asked mildly. "It seems to me I might have interrupted something."

Linn could feel her face flaming and knew she was blushing wildly. "You said you would be back," she replied meekly.

"So I did. Where's the patient?"

"In the bathroom. He'll be out in a second."

"I hope he hasn't been running any marathons on that leg."

"I couldn't stop him from taking a shower."

McCarthy nodded sourly. He glanced at the sink full of dishes. "Charming domestic scene," he commented dryly.

"I made breakfast," Linn answered, growing tired of the doctor's tart observations. "Doesn't he have to eat to keep up his strength?"

"It would take more than a short fast to deplete his strength," McCarthy stated. "That boy's a bull."

Linn turned away so that her companion wouldn't see on her face the effect of that last remark. She busied herself rinsing dishes while McCarthy folded his arms and watched her as a scientist might survey an insect specimen. She glanced at him, and then away. The man's face was impassive; she couldn't tell what conclusions he was drawing about her relationship with his patient.

The bathroom door opened and Con emerged, clad in the terry robe.

McCarthy looked him over. "Just as I suspected, a miraculous recovery. You're amazing, boy. As often as you're knocked down, you spring back up like a jack-in-the-box."

"You should know, Neil," Con replied, looking at Linn.

"Come here and let me have a look at that leg," the doctor ordered.

Con walked to the bed with the doctor's assistance and sat on the edge. McCarthy crouched on the floor in front of him, and then threw him a dirty look.

"Who told you to take off that dressing?"

"I got it wet in the shower."

"And strained the stitches as well. It's oozing blood."

"Is it? I thought it was oozing ink. Will you leave off talking and just bandage it for me? You charge a high price for your services, Neil; I have to listen to all this drivel before I receive treatment."

"The drivel is part of the treatment. You can't expect to go getting yourself torn up without hearing a lecture or two from those who care about you." The doctor glanced slyly at Linn. "Isn't that right, Miss Pierce?"

Linn didn't know what to say.

"I'll bet this young lady here has been telling you to stay out of those donnybrooks up north, has she not?"

"She has," Con responded tightly.

The doctor removed a package of gauze from his bag and began unwinding a piece of it. "Well, then, we're in perfect agreement. She sounds a sensible lass to me." McCarthy looked up from his work and met Con's eyes. "Not like some who'd send you into danger for their own selfish reasons."

Con's mouth became a grim line, but he said nothing.

Linn watched this interchange, bewildered. What was McCarthy talking about? Was someone encouraging Con to resume his former activities? She carefully placed a cup on the drainboard, lost in thought.

McCarthy finished bandaging Con's leg, patting the last length of tape into place. "Well, I hate to admit this, but despite your best efforts to cripple yourself, this looks like it's healing fine. You should be back up to snuff in no time." He replaced his things in his bag and glanced around at Linn. "Might you have a cup of tea for me, Miss Pierce?"

"Linn. Certainly. It may be a little strong, but I'll add some hot water to it."

"Leave it. I like it strong enough to walk on, with lots of sugar." He turned back to Con. "I'll help you to the loo, son; you'd best get dressed."

Con's eyes flashed between Linn and the doctor, as if he suspected some incipient conspiracy, but he went meekly enough when McCarthy offered his help. The doctor returned for a chair and left it in the bathroom.

"He's sitting down to shave," McCarthy informed Linn as he emerged to join her, taking his cup of tea and dropping onto a sofa with it. Linn was nursing another cup of coffee, and they sipped in companionable silence for a while before the doctor broke it to say, "So don't you think it's time you told me what's going on here?"

Linn shut her eyes briefly. Were all these people as nosy as Bridie and this man, or had she been cursed with unfortunate luck? She felt as if she and Con were performing on a stage, with McCarthy and the housekeeper and half of Ballykinnon a rapt audience.

"I don't know what you mean," she said evasively.

"I think you do," he replied. "There's so much tension in this room, I feel as if I'm sitting in the middle of an electrical storm."

"Well, we did have a bit of an argument earlier." God, she was even starting to talk like them. Pretty soon she'd be nattering about hooligans and donnybrooks too. The vernacular was seductive.

"That's not the only kind of tension I feel," the doctor responded archly, eyeing her over the rim of his cup.

Linn would have to be a dunce to mistake what he was implying, and he knew she was no dunce. "I didn't realize that it was so obvious," she replied.

The doctor choked on his tea. "Obvious! It's as plain as the whitewash on Paddy's pig. It may interest you to know that after your grand appearance in the pub with young Conchubor, some of the lads started taking odds, you against Mary as works in the Kinnon Arms. Word has it you're winning, hands down."

Linn stared at him, horrified, speechless with shock.

"Aye," McCarthy went on, entranced with his own narrative, "since you appeared on the place, Con hasn't been seen about the town with Mary. Or any of the other hopefuls, I might add. You're the front-runner, to be sure."

Linn slammed her cup down on the bar. "I'm very glad to hear it! It's comforting to know that everybody in town thinks I'm yards ahead of the local barmaid in capturing that exalted prize, that man among men, the incomparable

Connor Clay!'' Furious, she grabbed up her purse and sweater, then whirled to confront the astonished doctor.

''If and when he comes out of the inner sanctum, you can tell him that I'm through playing nursemaid. If he gets stabbed or shot, clubbed or beaten, or falls down a well, tell him to call Mary Costello. I'm sure she'd appreciate the chance to improve her standing from number two.'' Linn stalked out of the cottage and slammed the door behind her so hard that it rattled on its hinges.

Linn charged back toward the house at breakneck pace, burning with humiliation. So she'd been providing free entertainment for the townspeople with her fascination for Bally's most interesting resident! Newly arrived from America, a pretty young woman sharing the estate with the virile local celebrity was sure to arouse comment. And she had given them plenty to talk about, Linn reflected miserably. She wasn't good at hiding her feelings; her behavior with Con during their visit to the pub had been enough to establish her as a contestant for Mary's erstwhile boyfriend. What a fool she'd been making of herself! She felt ill when she considered what everyone must think of her.

The phone was ringing when Linn opened the front door of the main house. She considered ignoring it, but she had never been able to dismiss the summons of that insistent bell, no matter how much she wished to be left alone. Ned curled about her legs in greeting as she picked up the receiver.

''Hello,'' she said resignedly.

''It's Bridie, dear. How are you?''

Linn responded to this question by bursting into tears.

Bridie's heartfelt sigh came over the wire. ''I thought as much. When I didn't hear from you this morning early, I knew you two would be mixing it up. Is Con all right?''

''Yes.'' Linn sniffed.

''Then what ails you?''

Linn picked Ned up from the floor and buried her face

in his fur. He purred, making a sound like a miniature outboard motor. "Everything," she responded dramatically.

"Ah, well, in that case, you'd best come and have dinner with us this day," Bridie stated, her kindly voice tinged with amusement. "We'll have a chat and you can tell me all about it."

Linn hesitated. "I don't know . . ."

"Yes, you do," Bridie replied firmly. "I won't be back until Monday morning, and by that time you'll be floating away on a river of tears. It's no good feeling sorry for yourself, I say. Now get yourself ready and my Terence will be by with his cycle to pick you up. I'm sending him off right now."

The suggested method of transportation sounded vaguely suspect, but Con and his car were out of the question, each for its own reason.

"All right," Linn said.

"Good girl. And don't forget to feed that cat, now; he'll be terrorizing the birds." The line went dead.

Linn went to the kitchen. She opened two cans of cat food and placed the contents of both tins into a bowl. She refreshed the water in Ned's other dish and watched as the prospective diner marched up to the food, sniffed it disdainfully and stalked off with his tail in the air. Linn shrugged. He would get hungry later.

Bridie's Terence turned out to be a handsome, silent teenager who roared up the drive on a motorbike and waited with the patient detachment of a royal servant while Linn clambered up behind him. She put her arms tentatively around his middle, and then clung tighter when he suddenly surged forward. They flew down the path, spraying gravel, and traversed the four miles to downtown Bally with Linn hanging onto Bridie's offspring for dear life, absorbed in mental prayer. Trees and buildings passed in a blur; Linn finally closed her eyes and abandoned herself to fate.

The bike lurched to a stop, and Linn opened one eye cautiously. They had halted in front of a row of attached stone residences fronting Bally's main street. Though all of the houses were actually one long, low building, the individual apartments had been painted different pastel colors to separate them into distinctive little homes. Terence locked his bike to a rack outside a flat that was painted daffodil yellow and shoved open the front door.

"Ma," he bawled, so loudly that Linn jumped. It was the first word she'd heard out of him.

No answer from inside.

Terence put his hands on his hips and tried again. "Ma," he yelled, "your lady's here."

Bridie appeared in the doorway, wiping her hands on her apron. "That'll do, Terry; you needn't wake the dead." She smiled at Linn. "Come in, lass. We'll have a cup of tea."

Terence, who apparently felt himself dismissed, flashed Linn a grin of dazzling beauty and loped off down the street.

"Be back for dinner at half three," his mother called after him. "Miss the time and you'll starve. I'm not scouring the countryside for the likes of you."

Terence continued on his way, undaunted.

"That one," Bridie said in disgust, leading Linn inside. "He likes to pretend he's deaf." She pronounced it "deef," as Linn's father had.

"He's an attractive boy," Linn commented.

"And well he knows it," Bridie answered with asperity. "He thinks he's the catch of the town."

"He must be doing some damage to the female population under twenty." Linn chuckled.

"That he is," Bridie answered, not without a note of pride. "But he'll get his comeuppance one day, as we all do."

"I think I've gotten mine," Linn said, following Bridie down a narrow central hall that ended at the back of the house in a large kitchen. All the rooms opened off the middle passage; Linn had walked past a parlor and a dining room, as well as two tiny bedrooms.

"Sit yourself down and tell me what happened," Bridie ordered, removing the cozy from the teapot, which sat in the center of the deal table.

Linn recounted her night taking care of Con and her conversation with Dr. McCarthy that morning. Bridie's face filled with compassion at Linn's obvious embarrassment concerning McCarthy's comments.

"Neil McCarthy is a gossip; he was a gossip in the sixth form. He should be wearing a flower print dress and a veiled hat like my great aunt Catlin, God rest her soul."

Linn grinned at the mental image of Dr. McCarthy so attired.

"Pay him no mind," Bridie advised, pouring Linn a cup of tea. "He finds his life a little dull, so he likes to liven it up by getting mixed up in Con's adventures."

"It sounded to me as if he was scolding Con to keep out of them."

"Hah. Don't you believe it. If he wasn't patching Con up for one thing and another and lecturing him, Neil would have nothing to do."

Linn ran her finger around the rim of her cup, which she'd noticed was Belleek china and probably Bridie's best. "But do you think what he was saying about the town is true? Do you think everybody's watching me and Con to see what will happen?"

Bridie delayed answering by taking a large swallow of her tea.

"Bridie," Linn prompted. "Tell me."

"Well, I won't say there hasn't been talk. That's to be expected, you must admit."

"I knew it," Linn said unhappily. "Oh, this is awful. Well, I'm going to stay away from him from now on, you can bet."

Bridie nodded sagely. "And how do you propose to do that, with you half mad in love with him the way you are?"

Linn was past the point where she was going to deny the obvious to Bridie. "I don't know," she said. "But I'm going to do it. I have to. I've behaved so badly already that it has to stop."

"Oh, what do you care what a bunch of old sob sisters are saying?" Bridie demanded. "You want him, go after him."

"I would, if I were sure he wanted me."

Bridie rolled her eyes. "He wants you. Take my word for it."

Linn shook her head. "You don't understand. It's more complicated than that. He harbors a grudge against me because of my father, and he can't quite forget that, as well as the difference in our backgrounds."

"What about your father?" Bridie asked quietly.

"He was once in love with Con's mother and left her to go to America. Did you know that?"

Bridie looked down at the table. "I had an idea."

"Con's very bitter about that. He says it ruined his mother's life and his father's, too, because he couldn't compete with a memory. Do you believe that?"

Bridie thought a moment before answering. "I don't know as to the exact reason, but something shadowed Mary Clay's face with grief all her life. That was not a happy woman."

"Then I guess Con is right," Linn replied softly.

"But what does that matter now?" Bridie demanded. "You're not to blame for your father's actions, or for what happened in the past."

"Tell that to Con," Linn said sadly. "Sometimes he does put it out of his mind, but then I see it come back to haunt him. I can't fight that. He has to accept me, *everything* about me, or it won't work."

"But then, what will you do?"

"Stay away from him, as I said."

Bridie sighed. "Easier said than done."

Linn swirled the floating tea leaves in her cup. "If only he weren't so . . . difficult."

"Difficult?"

"Stubborn, opinionated, suspicious, wild . . ." she recited.

"Tender, sexy, witty, kind?" Bridie suggested.

Linn folded her arms on the table and bent her head. "Those too," she whispered. "Those too."

Bridie drained her cup. "So, as I see it, you've convinced yourself there are two reasons to avoid Con: one, the town is talking; and two, he's resentful toward you because of your da. As to the first, the hell with it. As to the second, if he loves you, he'll get over it. Con is opinionated, to be sure, but he's far from stupid. He does hang on to an idea, but when he sees that it's wrong, he lets it go. Give him time."

Linn looked up. "I don't know if I can, Bridie. I love him so much, and his distrust is breaking my heart."

"Give him time," Bridie repeated.

Linn examined the older woman. "Bridie, you know him."

Bridie shrugged. "As much as anyone can get to know that lad. He always had a head full of ideas and a soul full of secrets."

"But you've seen him grow up, observed him all his life. What chance do I have against a grudge he's harbored since he was a child?"

"You've a powerful chance, my girl, if only you would realize the fact. That boy can't take his eyes off you. The change is already working, but you'll halt the process if you give up too soon." Bridie nodded her head to emphasize her point.

The conversation was interrupted by the return of

Terence, who entered the kitchen through the back door, which led to the small rear yard.

"Back on time, for a wonder," his mother greeted him. "Couldn't find anybody to get up to mischief with?"

Terence grabbed a biscuit off the sideboard and Bridie slapped his hand. "Put that back, you devil; wait for dinner."

Terence tossed the biscuit to Linn, who caught it by reflex. He flashed her another lady-killer smile and then dropped his eyes seductively. Linn was riveted. The kid's panache was amazing; he was all of about sixteen and already he had the sexual confidence of James Bond.

Bridie glanced at Linn as the boy strolled through the room and down the hall. "That's what God sent me for a cross in my old age," she said. "Five others, and all together not the trouble of that one there."

"You have six children?"

"Aye, all gone and out of the house now except Terry."

Linn took a bite of the biscuit, vaguely ashamed. She'd been so wrapped up in herself during her conversations with Bridie, dwelling on her problems with Con, that she had never even inquired about the housekeeper's personal life.

"Where are they?" Linn asked.

"My two girls are married, one living in the Gaeltacht up near Donegal, the other out on the Dingle Peninsula. My three boys are scattered. Dennis is in the merchant service, Johnny works in the Belfast shipyards, and Michael is in the Waterford glass school, training to be a cutter."

"And Terence?"

Bridie smiled. "Oh, I have high hopes for my Terence. He has the brains and the charm to go far, if I can keep him out of the hands of the garda long enough."

The garda were the police. "Has he been in trouble?"

Bridie's lips tightened. "Only on the fringes so far, but he has to be watched. He has more will than sense at this age."

The front door opened and Linn heard the sound of footsteps coming down the hall. Mr. Cleary entered the room. He was a wiry man of medium height, several inches shorter than his youngest son, who was on his heels.

He nodded at Linn. "How do, miss?" he said, and glanced at his wife. She silently handed him a cup of tea, which he took, seating himself at the table and unfolding a newspaper, which had been tucked under his arm. He proceeded to read it without another word.

Bridie and Linn got the meal together, over Bridie's protests. She at first insisted that Linn was a guest but finally allowed that she could use a little help. Terence hung around grabbing samples of the various dishes and flirting wordlessly with Linn. He was as quiet as his father, but in his presence there was an undercurrent of sensuality that was unmistakable. Linn could well believe that he'd been in trouble with the garda and a number of others too.

They ate in the dining room, which featured an ancient cherry table covered with a handmade lace cloth, and an assortment of family photos on the well-worn sideboard. Mr. Cleary left the conversation to the women, and Linn wondered whether his reticence was natural or an adaptation to thirty years of Bridie. Linn avoided the subject of Con in the presence of the men, and so relaxed enough during the meal to feel recovered from her earlier upset. She and Bridie washed up while Mr. Cleary watched a hurling match on the television and Terry occupied himself in the yard. The Cleary men weren't a very liberated bunch; the preparation and disposition of food was left to the women.

Linn insisted on leaving right after they finished in the

kitchen. She had cried on Bridie's shoulder enough and had things to do back at the house.

She was treated to a whirlwind return journey on the back of Terry's bike. As they rounded the curve of the drive, they saw a figure half reclining on the front steps of the house. Linn's heart sank. It was Con.

Terry halted the bike and Linn slipped off, not meeting Con's eyes. He sat in silence and watched her say good-bye to the boy, who smiled into her eyes in farewell, never looking at Con. He took off in a cloud of dust and displaced gravel.

Linn turned to meet her visitor. Con was dressed in the track shorts and shirt she'd selected earlier, the gauze bandage visible beneath the hem of his pants. He was leaning against the stone banister, a cane propped up next to him.

"Con, what are you doing here?" Linn asked wearily. "You should be home in bed."

"I talked Neil into dropping me off on his way into town. He'll be back to fetch me shortly." He adjusted his position slightly, favoring his bad leg. "I've been calling the house all day, trying to reach you. I finally tried Bridie, and she told me you were just after leaving, so I thought I'd wait for you here."

"I'm surprised Neil went along with this scheme."

"I promised him I'd stay put and not walk about. He knew if he didn't bring me I'd find another way here." He raised his chin and eyed her suspiciously. "What are you doing riding around with that crazy Cleary kid?"

"Bridie wouldn't like to hear you say that."

"I'm as fond of Bridie as you are, but that doesn't make her boy any less crazy. He tools about on that instrument of destruction like a madman." His jaw tightened. "I didn't like the way he was looking at you."

Con's implication was clear. "Don't be ridiculous," Linn replied. "He's sixteen years old."

"Old enough at that."

Linn folded her arms. "I'm not going to dignify that with an answer. What do you want?"

Con surged forward and grabbed her wrist. "I want to know what Neil told you that made you dash off like that. What did he say to cause this change?"

Linn was silent, meeting his blue gaze directly.

"Answer me, Aislinn. That man runs off at the mouth like an overfilled glass. What did he tell you?"

Linn tried to shrug free, but Con held her in a grip of iron. "He didn't tell me anything I shouldn't have figured out for myself," she finally said.

Con gritted his teeth. "I'm going to beat him senseless when he gets here."

Linn made a disgusted sound. "That ought to be a good trick, since you can't even walk. Besides, won't you need him to stitch you up after your future skirmishes?"

Con tried to pull her closer, and Linn resisted. "There aren't going to be any future skirmishes!" Con fumed. "How many times must I say it?"

"Save your breath. It seems to me I've heard that song before. I'm going in. I trust your ride will be here soon."

Con didn't release her, searching her face.

"Let me go," Linn said calmly. He was stubborn, but she knew he would never hurt her. "Neil will look after your leg. Leave me alone."

Con's fingers opened, and she stepped away. She ran lightly up the stairs and unlocked the door, not looking back. Once inside, she closed the door and leaned against it, listening.

She knew he couldn't climb the stairs, but she wanted to make sure that Neil did come for him, that he wasn't left out there alone. It wasn't long before she heard the noise of a car's motor, doors slamming and the sound of raised voices. She winced, glad she didn't have to witness the reception Neil was getting.

The car departed, and silence descended. Linn was sure

Con's friendship with Neil would survive this incident, but she felt a little guilty about it nevertheless. Maybe she shouldn't have made her response to the doctor's recital so obvious, but it was too late now.

Linn went into the kitchen and boiled water for tea. She sank dispiritedly into a chair and contemplated her unhappy situation.

How had she, cool and careful Dr. Pierce, managed to wind up in this predicament? She was hopelessly in love with a man whom she feared for his power to hurt her, a man who distrusted her for reasons which were beyond her control.

What on earth was she going to do?

Chapter 6

LINN SPENT THE WEEK ORGANIZING WORK ON HER grandfather's house; it was still difficult to think of it as hers. An electrician arrived from Limerick, thirty miles to the south, to do the wiring. Delivery trucks brought a new refrigerator and stove, and a washer and dryer to replace the wringer model and clothesline Bridie currently used. Linn tore down the stained, wine-colored crushed velvet drapes in the parlor; they'd given the whole room the atmosphere of a funeral home. She contracted painters from nearby Ennis to redo the rooms in a light cream color and selected airy, finely woven curtains from the Dunne's catalog. As things began to take shape she felt better, but nothing could remove the slow dull ache of longing for Con, which never left her for a moment. It was always there, just below the surface, like a chronic pain she had to tolerate.

Mr. Fitzgibbon effected the release of Dermot's bank accounts, which provided enough cash for her renovations with plenty to spare. Linn arranged to continue Bridie's wages through direct payment from the lawyer's office and gave her a healthy raise. She also called Limerick to inquire about a car rental. Linn didn't know if Con's Bentley had been returned, but even if it had, she felt that the situation precluded requesting him to act as chauffeur.

She saw Con from a distance several times. On the first two occasions he was walking with a cane, and then later he was walking on his own, slowly but steadily. Neil had evidently prescribed exercise as part of Con's recovery regimen. From what Linn could see, Con was making almost supernatural progress. McCarthy was right; Con rebounded like a boomerang.

In his walks, Con never came close to the house.

Saturday night was the Fleadh Ceoil na hEireann, or summer music festival, celebrated throughout Ireland in each town and village. Just in case Linn had forgotten about it, Sean Roche called to remind her. He suggested that he pick her up at the house at seven that evening, and Linn was feeling just perverse enough to agree. She had no interest in Sean, but as Con was having difficulty making up his mind about her, it might be nice to be in the company of a man who had no such problem.

Linn dressed carefully, though she didn't know what was appropriate for such an occasion. Bridie had told her that everyone turned out for this event, and everyone included a certain someone from the gatehouse who was sure to be there. She told herself severely that she wasn't childish enough to dress for him, but she selected a flattering skirt and a peasant blouse, which showed her creamy shoulders to advantage. And when the evening promised to be warm, she was tempted to put her hair up, but she left it down. Linn stared at herself in the mirror and insisted silently that this decision had nothing to do with Con's expressed preference. Her hair really did look better down, and that was all. She added a small print scarf and was ready.

Sean arrived on the dot of seven, beaming with his own good fortune. Ned hissed at him and slunk away into the parlor.

"That animal doesn't like me," Sean said sadly, settling Linn's lace shawl about her shoulders.

"Ned is neurotic," Linn replied. "If he were human, he'd be seeing an analyst."

Sean laughed. "Surprised I was that you accepted my invitation," he said, standing by while she locked the front door. "I thought you might have made prior arrangements."

"Is that so? With whom?"

Sean colored faintly and dropped his eyes. So he had heard the talk about her and Con too. This should prove to be an interesting evening.

Linn dropped the key in her purse. Sean smiled.

"Why do you lock the door? There's nobody here who wants Dermot's trophies."

"American habits are hard to break," Linn said dryly. "When we leave the house, keys spring into our hands automatically."

"So I've heard," Sean replied, opening the door of his mini rover and handing Linn inside. As they drove out the lane toward the main road, Linn glanced at the cottage. It was dark.

"Have you ever been to one of these?" Sean asked, driving through the iron gates, which stood open. Con hadn't left yet; he always closed them.

"No. This is my first time in Ireland."

"Ah, ye'll have a grand time. We all do. This was started to revive the *Sean-Nos* singing, the old-style unaccompanied chanting songs passed down in Gaelic. But it's grown to include the ballads, which are arranged for folk instruments like the tin whistle and drum, and dancing as well. We love our traditions here, you know; they were very nearly taken from us."

"Yes, I know," Linn answered quietly.

"I do a newspaper for the Siamsa Tire, the national folk theater. We've established two cottages for the performance of the music, one in North Kerry, near Listowel, and the other at Carraig, at the western tip of the Dingle. So I'll be a working journalist tonight, gathering information for the paper. We're doing a series on the celebration of the Fleadh in the small towns."

"I don't mind," Linn said. "Take notes, if you want."

Sean grinned. "I may at that."

The four miles to Bally passed quickly, with Sean chatting about his work for the folk theater as well as his job with his father's dairy. The former was his true love, but the latter paid the bills. His artist's soul was clearly at odds with his mundane occupation, and Linn almost felt sorry for him.

Linn heard the music before she saw its source. The tin whistle had an eerie, flutelike sound, which carried through the night air, haunting and elusive, like the notes from Pan's pipes, not meant for human ears. Sean held up a finger, listening.

"'Mairin de Barra,'" he said, naming the tune. "Beautiful, is it not?"

"It certainly is," Linn agreed. The plaintive air reminded her of "Greensleeves." She smiled. "I'll bet it's a sad love song."

Sean laughed. "That's a safe bet. They all are."

"Not so. My father sang a lot of rousing battle songs."

Sean nodded as he drove into the square, looking for a parking space. The street was crowded with cars; people had come into town from miles around. "But the war songs don't sound like that. They're loud and rhythmic, like marches."

"Yes, I see what you mean."

Sean parked the car and they got out. Linn craned her neck down the street. All the activity was taking place at

the other end of the main thoroughfare, in the field around
Saint Michael's. She could see a raised wooden platform
on which people were dancing, and a group of musicians
seated on folding chairs. The doors to the Kinnon Arms
stood open wide, and a steady stream of patrons flowed in
and out, laughing and talking. A few danced along to the
music, which carried down the street; they were all as
graceful as careless children caught up in a game.

As they approached the platform, the music changed to
the steady drumbeat of the "Garry Owen," and in the
blink of an eye, the dancers fell into a wild jig, arms at
their sides, feet flashing in intricate patterns. Linn
stopped, fascinated. It looked like a Hollywood produc-
tion number, as if they'd been practicing for weeks.

"What do you think of that?" Sean asked, seeing her
reaction.

She shook her head slowly in wonder. "Surely some of
you must be clumsy," she said.

Sean laughed. "Not hereabouts. We run them out of
town."

"You'd better not get me dancing, then. I won't last
long at Ildathach."

"I'll show you the steps. You'd be amazed how easy it
is."

"I certainly would be amazed if that turned out to be
easy."

Linn walked into the crowd with Sean, looking around
at the participants. She saw Neil McCarthy with his wife,
a wispy blonde who clung to his arm, and Bridie with her
husband. She caught Linn's eye and waved. A few
minutes later Linn spotted Terry Cleary, hoisting a glass
of contraband Guinness, surrounded by a bevy of teenage
girls. Sean touched her arm and she turned to him.

"Will you have a drop?" he asked, pointing to the
wooden kegs set up on a table nearby.

"Yes, I think so. What's available?"

"Stout and porter, beer maybe."

"American beer?" Linn asked hopefully.

Sean shrugged. "I'll try." He made his way through the crowd, and Linn turned back to view the dancers. Bridie was standing behind her.

"Where's himself?" Bridie asked. "Have you seen him?"

"If you're referring to Con, I haven't seen him, and I don't care to."

Bridie nodded. "Tell it to the Scots. I don't believe a word of it. I'll save you the trouble of asking; he's with Mary Costello."

Though this hardly qualified as a surprise, it still stung. Linn did her best to hide her reaction, but Bridie wasn't fooled.

"Don't look like that, my girl; you've no room to talk. You're here with that blatherskite, Seaneen Roche."

Oh, dear. Another blatherskite. They seemed to be multiplying. "Sean is very nice," Linn replied. "I'm having a good time."

"Hmmph," Bridie responded. She looked into the distance. "Here comes my man. I'd better get back." She took Linn's arm. "Don't do anything foolish. I happen to know that Con came alone and Mary just attached herself to him like a barnacle."

Linn's spirits rose, though she remained impassive.

"He's over by the players, just forninst the drummer," Bridie hissed in farewell as Sean arrived with their drinks. Linn stood on tiptoe but could see nothing.

"No beer, but I got you a shandy," Sean said, handing Linn the glass.

"That's fine, Sean. Thanks."

They sipped in silence, and then a drumroll called attention to the platform. Larry Fitzgibbon was approaching the microphone.

"What's he doing?" Linn asked.

Sean raised his eyes to the sky. "He's the mayor, God help us. Did you not know?"

"No, I didn't."

"Well, he is, and long-winded as well. He'll make a speech now; I hope we're all still standing when it's over."

Linn scanned the crowd while Larry droned on, and then her eyes settled on their target. Con was leaning against the makeshift bandstand, his back to the speaker. She found him because he was looking at her.

He was wearing a stretched and faded Fordham sweat shirt with equally well worn jeans. His clothing didn't matter; to Linn's hungry eyes he couldn't have looked better if he were wearing a tuxedo.

His gaze held hers for a long moment, and then he bent to hear what the woman at his side was saying. Mary, damn her, looked very pretty in a flowered shirtwaist that made the most of her tall, slender figure. Linn watched briefly, then turned away.

Larry tried to prolong his big moment, but even he took the hint when people began conducting individual conversations. He gave up and surrendered the mike to a tenor who began "Kathleen Mavourneen" in a high, reedy voice. Dancers gathered on the platform and the festival resumed.

Linn tried to forget about Con in the next couple of hours. Sean taught her a simple jig and she practiced it on the grass before venturing up with the group. They were very generous and helpful, tolerant of her mistakes and lavish with praise. Her moment of triumph came when she joined in a reel and was able to follow the flow of the dance and complete it without an error. Flushed and laughing, she spun into Sean's arms at its conclusion, then looked up to find Con's eyes on her. He was standing at the edge of the crowd among the onlookers, and his expression was grim. Mary was gone.

Linn stopped short and turned in the other direction.

"Could we take a walk, Sean? I'd like to get away for a while."

She didn't have to ask twice. Seizing what seemed to be a golden opportunity, Sean took her arm.

"Would you like to see the churchyard?" he asked. "Some of the stones are very old."

"Fine."

They were strolling away from the crowd and had made it to the stand of evergreens that fronted the yard when a voice called out to Sean from behind them.

"Sean, may I have a word?"

Linn turned to see a priest approaching. He smiled at her.

Sean, dismayed at this interruption, looked on unhappily. "What is it, father?" he asked.

"Introduce me to the young lady, Sean. Have you no manners?"

"Miss Pierce, this is Father Daly. Father Daly, this is Linn Pierce, Dermot's granddaughter."

"So I've heard," the priest responded. "How are you, my dear?"

"Fine, father. It's nice to see you."

"What do you want, father?" Sean asked impatiently.

"I need to borrow you for a moment, if the lady doesn't mind. I've got Mrs. Cudahy waiting, and if you want that donation for the music cottage, you'd best come and talk to her now."

Sean was clearly torn. He didn't want to leave Linn, but he didn't want to miss the chance to romance Mrs. Cudahy and her money.

"Go on, Sean," Linn said. "I'll wait right here."

"Are you sure?" he asked anxiously.

"Yes. I'll look around while you're gone."

He nodded and walked away with the priest. Linn watched them go and then wandered over to the small churchyard, which was enclosed by shrubbery and tucked into the shadow of the masonry wall. The oldest markers

were stone slabs flat on the ground; the newer ones were
upright Celtic crosses or angel wings or plain square
monuments. She read the inscriptions, thinking of all the
lives represented there. This was all that was left when
the toil was done, when the laughter was silenced and
the tears ceased to flow. "Dearest wife," she recited to
herself. "Beloved mother." She knelt and traced the
letters on one limestone slab, so old that the date was
rubbed out and only the name remained. "Purcell," she
read. "Child Helen, aged three years." Child Helen had
not had much of a life.

A sound behind her made her whirl, startled. Con was
watching her, his arms folded across the top of one of the
tombs.

"What are you doing here?" Linn demanded. "Are
you following me?"

"Somebody should be," he replied, straightening and
coming toward her. "If only to prevent you skulking
about in the bushes with Seaneen Roche."

"Skulking! I was not skulking! I was merely taking a
walk."

"Can't you find better company than that milkman?"

"Sean is good company, and he's much more than a
milkman. He's a journalist."

Con sneered. "He's a milkman. He's a milkman with a
typewriter."

Linn confronted him angrily. "Well then, I guess that
makes you a caretaker with a typewriter, doesn't it?"

Con stiffened. "I've never denied it."

"And while we're on the subject of companions,
where's your girlfriend? She's the one Neil was talking
about, isn't she, the one who wants you to go back north
and get yourself killed?"

"That's none of your business."

"Which means I'm right. What is it, Con? What's
worth your safety to Mary?"

"Her father's in a camp."

"Oh, fine. Listen to her and you'll be in one too, if you're lucky, dead if you're not."

Con closed the gap between them and seized her shoulders. "And would you care, Aislinn? Would you?"

Linn could feel herself melting at his touch, and she deliberately went rigid, unyielding. "You'd better let me go, Con. Sean will be back in a minute."

Con released her so suddenly that she rocked back on her heels. "You tell him something for me," Con said, his voice deadly quiet. "You tell him that if he touches you, I'll break his back. You're mine."

Linn stared at him, aghast. "I'm not your property!"

He reached out with one hand, his fingers curled into a fist, and ran the edge of his knuckles over her throat from the underside of her chin to her collarbone. She shivered violently in reaction, and he smiled.

"My property, no, but mine just the same." His fingers opened, then closed about her neck. "You burn for me," he said huskily. "I've felt the heat."

Linn stood rooted, unable to speak. Then with a mixture of disappointment and relief, she heard Sean returning. Con's hand fell away and he stepped back.

Sean halted when he caught sight of Con. His eyes moved from the man to the woman; it was clear that something had happened, but he didn't know what.

"Seaneen, will you be singing later?" Con asked conversationally.

"I suppose," Sean answered, still puzzled by the charged atmosphere. "I usually do."

"Will you favor us with 'Fainne Geal an Lae'?" Con asked. "I think Miss Pierce would especially like to hear that one."

"I will," Sean answered.

Con nodded, glanced at Linn, and left. Sean regarded Linn thoughtfully. "There's been talk about you and him in the town," he said.

"Has there?" Linn said mildly.

"Any truth to it?"

"Sean, you don't have the right to ask me that question."

Sean stared at the ground.

Linn regretted her nettled response. "Sean, forget it. Let's go back and see what's happening." She tried to walk past him, and Sean put his hand on her arm.

"I cannot compete with him, Linn."

Although this was perfectly true, Linn was touched by Sean's defeated expression. "I said to forget it. I want to see the rest of the festival. What did Con mean about the singing?"

"Oh, at the close, some of us take turns and sing, sort of in a round robin. Whoever feels the urge will take the floor. Everybody's half down the well by then; it makes for some interesting performances."

Linn laughed, and Sean's good humor was restored.

When they returned to the group, the singing was already underway. They joined the listeners, and when the young girl who had the mike concluded, Sean got up and took her place.

The crowd applauded enthusiastically. Sean was evidently a favorite.

"I've had a request for 'Fainne Geal,'" he said. "For those of you who haven't the Irish, the title means 'The Dawning of the Day.'"

Sean left the mike and walked around the circle, singing in a well-modulated baritone. He sang first in Gaelic, and then repeated the verses in English. It was then that Linn understood Con's request.

> *"No cap or cloak this maiden wore,*
> *her neck and feet were bare,*
> *Down to her breast in ringlets fell*
> *her glossy golden hair. . . ."*

The song described Linn on the night she'd met Con, when she'd dashed from the house in the grip of her dream and come across a man stacking wood in a moonlit glen. Slowly she raised her head and met Con's eyes across the crowd of listeners. His blue gaze locked with hers and he knew that she had received the message.

Sean finished to appreciative applause. No one rose to take his place. The pause lengthened until a feminine voice said, "Perhaps our American visitor will offer us a tune. We'd so love to hear something from the States."

It was Mary, speaking up from her position next to Con. Con flashed her a deadly glance, which she ignored. She was determined to put Linn on the spot.

Linn's first instinct was to decline, but then she recognized Mary's overture for what it was: a challenge. She was trying to make Linn look bad, either by forcing her to back down, or by making her sing and perform badly. Either way, Mary would win. Only by accepting and doing well could Linn beat her at her own game. The gauntlet had been thrown down. She looked around at the expectant group. Well, she was Dermot's granddaughter, and she wasn't going to turn tail and run away. She would pick it up.

Linn smiled with forced brightness. "I'll give it a try." She walked over to one of the musicians, who was playing an instrument that resembled a guitar. "Would you strum the chords for me?" she asked. "It goes like this." She hummed a few bars, and the boy was able to pick out the chords. Linn nodded. "Good enough."

She turned to face the villagers and heard a murmur of appreciation run through the crowd. Irishmen loved courage better than anything; whatever else one could say about the Pierce girl, she had guts.

Linn began to sing softly, and then her voice got stronger as she gathered momentum. She had chosen one of her favorites, very meaningful but easy to sing.

"And I love you so, the people ask me how,
How I've lived 'til now, I tell them I don't know . . ."

Linn walked around the circle, her accompanist following, and it seemed the most natural thing in the world to
stop in front of Con. She gazed into his eyes and sang only
for him.

"I guess they understand, how lonely life has been,
But life began again, the day you took my
hand. . . ."

Con didn't move, but the look on his face said everything. Without uttering a word, he encouraged her, gave
her the strength to continue. Give them hell, Aislinn, his
expression said. Show them your stuff.

Linn moved into the chorus. She reached for the scarf
around her neck and untied it. As she sang, she lifted her
hands. Con's lashes drifted downward as he bent his head.
Like a lady bestowing a favor, or a king granting knight-
hood, Linn knotted the scarf around his neck. When Con
raised his head, his eyes blazed into hers with such ardor
that she almost stumbled over her words. Oh, Con, she
thought as she struggled to go on, there's a look to take
my breath away.

"And yes, I know how lonely life has been,
The shadows follow me,
and the night won't set me free,
But I don't let the evening get me down,
Now that you're around me."

The onlookers were riveted, unable to believe what they
were seeing: the Pierce girl making love to Connor Clay
with a song. Linn's voice sounded loud in the hush, but
she was beyond noticing anything but the man to

whom she was singing. She went on to the last verse.

> *"And you love me too, your thoughts are just for me,*
> *You set my spirit free, I'm happy that you do.*
> *The book of life is brief, and once a page is read,*
> *All but love is dead. That is my belief."*

Linn couldn't bear not touching him any longer. She swayed toward him, and he caught her about the waist to steady her. Linn put her palms flat against his chest and finished the song, repeating the chorus. She lingered on the last line, almost whispering, "Now that you're around me." As the last notes faded away, she stood on tiptoe and kissed him.

For just an instant Con's mouth remained still under hers, and then, as she began to move away, he pulled her close, kissing her deeply, his hands moving in her hair, binding her to him. When he finally released her she was reeling.

There was no applause for this performance. The villagers remained in stunned silence. Linn looked at Mary Costello; she was staring ahead at a point in space, unable to meet Linn's eyes. Linn felt a stab of triumph. You can't pull that garbage on me, sweetheart, Linn thought. You see what you'll get for it. Linn had taken a situation earmarked for defeat and turned it into victory.

She did not, however, feel particularly victorious. She was trembling from head to foot and, as she walked away from the crowd and into the field, was beginning to realize what she had done. If the people in town had been in any doubt about her feelings for Con, they speculated no longer. Skywriting would have been as subtle as her torch song. She leaned against a tombstone and pressed her cold hands to her burning face. You've done it this time, Linny, she thought. She was embarrassed, chagrined, and

yet proud at the same time. She would doubtless be
drowned in tears of mortification at her own behavior in
the morning, but the impression that overpowered all the
others was the desire in Con's eyes. He had wanted her,
right there in front of everybody, and he hadn't been
ashamed to show it.

Bridie stepped into her path. "You're coming with
me," she stated in a tone that brooked no argument. "I've
already told Seaneen we're taking you home."

"Bridie . . ."

"Be still. He didn't object, poor boy; but then, how
could he, after that spectacle you just made of yourself?
Saints preserve us, what a night."

She was dragging Linn by the hand toward the road.
Linn noticed Sean's lightning transition from "blatherskite" to "poor boy" but decided not to mention it. No
one had ever accused Bridie of being consistent.

"You were the one who told me to go after Con," she
said meekly to Bridie, who was now flagging down her
husband.

Bridie turned on her. "I said to go after him, not assault
him in public. And him undressing you with his eyes the
whole time, I've never seen the like of it. Father Daly
watched the entire thing; I'm surprised he didn't have a
heart attack."

"You heard what Mary said. What was I supposed to
do?"

"Sing 'God Bless America' or 'Home on the Range.'
I'll tell you one thing true: Dermot Pierce is revolving in
his grave this night."

"Come off it, Bridie. I didn't do a striptease. All I did
was sing."

"Holy mother. All you did was sing indeed. That lad
was one blink away from tossing you over his shoulder,
and well you know it." She addressed her husband.
"Jack, go and get Terry to take Miss Pierce home, will
you? I can't find that boy anywhere."

Mr. Cleary went to search. "Why couldn't I go home with Sean?" Linn asked reasonably.

"Are you daft, girl? I was trying to spare you both that painful trip. Can you imagine how he feels?"

Linn imagined it and felt pretty bad herself. An apology to Sean was definitely in order. Linn kept her eyes down, feeling crestfallen.

They were standing waiting for Terry when Father Daly walked past. He looked at Linn with an odd expression; he showed not the disapproval she'd expected, but alarm, almost fear. It shook her, and she stood in thoughtful silence until Terry roared up on his bike.

"Go on now," Bridie said to her. "Get yourself home."

Linn paused, looking at the older woman. "Bridie, do you know where Con went? I haven't seen him anywhere."

"He's crawled into a hole, if he has any shame. Now will you forget that lad and go home to bed?"

Linn stared at her, waiting for an answer.

Bridie sighed. "He left when you did, and I haven't seen him since. Be off with you."

Linn climbed on behind Terry and he shot off down the road.

All the way back to Ildathach she replayed the scene with Con in her mind. Bridie was right; it must have looked bad to the people watching her. Linn had been so caught up in the man and the moment that she had disregarded everything else.

Terry stopped in front of the house and watched Linn as she disembarked. "Shall I come in for a while?" he asked.

Linn glanced at him sharply. "What?"

"I thought you might be wanting some company."

Linn sagged against the stone balustrade, dumbfounded. This teenage lothario had witnessed her performance with Con, and it had given him ideas about his passenger. She wanted to smack him.

"Now you listen to me, sonny, and you listen good. I know what you saw tonight, but that was a very special situation with a very special man. I have no interest in you, or anybody else. Go home and drink your milk, and if you're a nice little boy I may not tell your mother about this, you get my drift?"

Terry got her drift. Undaunted, he flashed her another thousand-watt smile and gunned his motor, sailing forth into the night in search of easier game.

Linn let herself into the house, profoundly depressed. Terry's reaction painted all too clear a picture of the effect her behavior had created. While it could be argued that Terry required only minimal encouragement, it was still plain that she had given the impression she was some sort of femme fatale, when nothing could be further from the truth. She just wanted Con so badly that she forgot everything else in his presence. While she had been singing to him, she hadn't even remembered that the others were there.

Linn trudged wearily into the bathroom and headed for the tub. It was laughable, in a way. The Ice Princess, who'd been running from men for five years, was now regarded as a shameless temptress, the Delilah of County Clare. It could only happen to Aislinn Pierce.

Ned was asleep in the bathtub. He blinked groggily as Linn lifted him and transported him to the bed, where he stretched, rolled over and conked out again.

As Linn passed the dresser she saw the letter she had received from her godmother, Karen Walker, who'd been her mother's best friend. When Linn's mother died in childbirth, Karen had stepped in as unofficial aunt and quasi stepmother, serving as Linn's adviser and friend all her life. The letter was chatty and full of news of home, but in Linn's current emotional state it had seemed frivolous. She longed to call Karen and tell her what was happening, but it was hardly the subject for a transatlantic phone call. Linn sighed and reminded herself to answer the letter in the morning with something bright and cheerful that would successfully conceal the true state of her beleaguered heart.

She returned to the tub and turned on the taps. This antique was one of the few original appointments in the house that Linn liked. Most of the other fixtures were out-of-date and hopelessly inefficient, but the tub, deep and wide, afforded the opportunity for a good soak and ample reflection. You practically needed a ladder to climb into it, but Linn made do with standing on a footstool. She stripped and sprinkled bath salts liberally over the water and under the gushing flow from the taps. The powder foamed like the crest of a wave, enriching the air with its delicate scent. Linn waited for the tub to fill, remembering that Con had liked this blend. "I could find you in the dark, my lady." She closed her eyes, the scented steam rising about her, reminding her of that night at Cool Na Grena. His mouth had been so hot, and his touch so deft, so skilled, reducing her to a river of sensation. She sobbed in frustration and swayed, gripping the edge of the tub. This would never, never do. She climbed into the tub and sank into the warm water, letting the bubbles rise to her chin. Through the small window set above the vanity she could see the rising moon. She looked at it and wondered, as she often did, what Con was doing.

Would he walk tonight? Would he be restless, tormented, unable to sleep, as Linn certainly was?

Linn sat bolt upright, creating a swell that cascaded onto the floor. He would be in the glen tonight. She was certain of it, in a secret part of herself that knew things by intuition and not by reason. He would be drawn there by the memory of a barefoot girl in a dressing gown, the same girl who had kissed him in front of the townspeople at the end of her song.

Linn's heart began to pound. She rinsed off quickly and

stepped from the tub, drying on the curious Irish towels that felt like lint-free dishcloths, flat and ribbed. She padded to the open shutters and looked out across the fields.

Was he there, or on his way? Could she be so wrong? Maybe. But she knew she had to find out.

Her mind made up, Linn went to the closet and took out a thin robe of Chinese silk, a gift from her father on her last birthday. It was a lovely salmon color, exquisitely made, just the thing she wanted. She slipped it on over her naked body and belted it at the waist.

She picked up her hairbrush with trembling fingers and drew it methodically through her hair. One part of her couldn't believe what she was doing, preparing to meet a lover who might not even keep the unplanned rendezvous, but another part accepted her actions as perfectly sane. If she knew her man—and she thought she did—he would be there.

Linn picked up her cologne bottle and splashed some of the fragrant liquid on her wrists and throat. The crystal flagon flew out of her hands and smashed on the floor. She sighed, pressing her fingertips to her temples. Calm, calm, she had to be calm. But the thought of what might await her sent her blood pulsing through her veins. She glanced at the night sky, visible beyond the wooden louvers, and picked out a star. A half-forgotten rhyme from childhood surfaced in her mind. She recited it to herself, concluding with, "I wish I may, I wish I might, have the wish I wish tonight."

Then she squared her shoulders and strode from the room.

Con flung himself off the bed and stood up, wincing slightly as he felt a stitch in his thigh. The leg had healed quickly and well, and most of the time he forgot about it, except when a sudden move or a quick turn in the wrong direction produced a twinge to remind him. He straightened and shook it out, bending his leg at the knee. As good as new.

Would that he could say the same about his state of mind. He had given Mary the bum's rush, depositing her on her doorstep in town and taking off without a word. She had tried to do a hateful thing to Aislinn, and he couldn't forgive her for it. Cattiness in women disgusted him.

He took the scarf from his neck and held it to his nose, inhaling the heady mixture of Linn's perfume and her own warm, feminine scent. Then he wadded it into a ball and threw it on the floor. Damn the woman, she was tying him up in knots. If she was staying, then he would have to go. He couldn't take any more of this. The raw hunger for her was gnawing at his guts, making him distracted and useless at work. He was getting pointed inquiries from his editor about his manuscript, long overdue and going nowhere. The last chapter was incomprehensible; it read like jabberwocky nonsense. And all because of that amber-haired witch whose kiss still lingered on his lips. He groaned and thrust his hands through his hair.

He would go up to the house and show her who was boss. He would force the door if he had to, and then he would . . .

Con kicked the bedpost. He didn't want that; he didn't want to press her in any way. He wanted her willing and eager, clinging to him, fitted to him like a glove. He wanted her as on fire for him as he was for her. He wanted her to love him.

He swallowed hard and licked his dry lips. Perspiration beaded his forehead as he thought about her song at the Fleadh, the beckoning look in her wide dark eyes, the light teasing touch of her sweet mouth, the way she had melted against him when he drew her into his arms. She had seemed to want him then . . . but if so, why had she left him the morning Neil had paid his call? Why hadn't she been back since? Why, in short, was she dangling him on the end of this intolerable, agonizing string?

If he went to the house, he risked being rebuffed again. Another rejection from her would ruin him. His eyes moved to the open door of the cottage. But if he went out to the glen and waited, maybe, just maybe, she would come.

Con pulled his sweat shirt over his head and tossed it on a chair. He wouldn't sleep tonight; he might as well keep watch, and remember, and hope. He took a broadcloth shirt from a hanger and slipped into it, leaving it unbuttoned in his haste.

On his way out the door he bent and picked up her scarf, putting it in his pocket.

Linn stepped from the screen of trees, her heart pounding, and scanned the field before her.

The glen was empty.

Linn swallowed disappointment like a bitter medicine. Had she been sure, or just fervently hopeful? She shook her head, biting her lower lip to forestall tears. When was she going to grow up and learn that wishing didn't make it so? What had made her think for a moment that there was some sort of mystic communication between them, that she would want him and he would know? Slowly, sorrowfully, she turned back to the house.

Con came around the side of the large oak that bordered the property, retracing the same path he'd already paced many times that night. In the distance, a figure clad in peach silk with bright, loose hair was walking away from him.

Con dropped the scythe he was carrying and began to run.

Chapter 7

CON DIDN'T FEEL HIS INJURED LEG AT ALL, AND IT
didn't slow him; he ran like the wind, his feet as light as
his heart. She had come to him. She had come to him after
all.

He caught Linn in several steps. She halted when she
heard him behind her, and in the next instant his arms
closed about her, pressing her back against him.

"I knew you'd be here," she whispered.

"I wished that you would come," he replied.

Linn relaxed into him with a luxurious sigh, reveling in
the hard warmth of his body, the feel of his bare chest
against her back through the thin robe. Con drew his hands
up from her waist and cupped her breasts in his palms.
Linn quivered with delight, raising her arms and locking
her hands behind his neck, stretching along the powerful
length of him like a cat. The abandoned sensuality of the
gesture inflamed Con beyond control; he gripped her hips
tightly and pulled her against him, letting her feel his

143

arousal. Linn moaned as his lips moved through her hair and found her neck, covering her nape and exposed shoulders with kisses. His mouth was moist, hot, everywhere, sending shivers rippling down her spine, making her knees so weak she needed his support to stand.

Con spun her around in his arms, and she waited longingly for his kiss. Instead he held her with one arm and, brushing aside her robe, bent his head and took a nipple between his lips. The sudden, unexpected sensation was unbearably erotic; Linn lay back in the curve of his muscular forearm, her hair trailing almost to the ground, as he laved first one ripe bud and then the other with his tongue. He sucked and nibbled, caressing her tender flesh until she was stimulated to an exquisite, aching sensitivity. Then he straightened suddenly, embracing her, cradling her as if she were the most precious treasure in his world.

"I love you, Aislinn," he said, his deep voice hoarse with emotion. "I always have. I was lost from the moment I saw you."

Linn closed her eyes in absolute relief, absolute happiness. This was what she'd been waiting all her life to hear. But a tiny doubt remained. "And my father?" she said faintly, clutching him, afraid to remind him and afraid to let it pass.

"I don't care," he said fiercely, tightening his arms around her. "I can't make myself care anymore. All I can see, all I can think about, is you."

Linn raised her head to look at him and saw the truth of it in his face. The past was forgotten; it really didn't matter to him any longer. She put her hand up to touch his cheek.

Con turned her toward the cottage. "Come inside," he whispered, his eyes brilliant in the shadows. "I'll not let you get away again."

"No," Linn said, resisting. "I want it to be here, where it all began."

Con sucked in his breath sharply. "You'll stay with me, then?" he asked, as still as a statue.

"Yes, darling, yes. Don't you know by now I want you just as much as you want me?"

"That isn't possible," he muttered as his lips crushed hers, his tongue probing deeply, his hands drawing the silken robe down her arms. It fell to her waist, where it was held by the knotted belt. He worked the tie loose with one hand while he slid the other through the fold, caressing the softness of her belly, her thighs, until she trembled with heightened awareness, unable to believe she could be so eager for the touch of rough, work-hardened fingers on her skin. His hand searched, probing, and she gasped against his mouth as the kimono slipped unnoticed to the grass.

Con picked her up in one smooth movement and lowered her to the ground, spreading her robe beneath her and setting her gently on this makeshift blanket. He paused to shrug out of his shirt, and then flung himself down beside her, gathering her to him instantly.

"I will be gentle," he said shakily, as if instructing himself to maintain control. He shuddered as she explored the broad expanse of his chest, planting a row of kisses along his collarbone, then tonguing his nipples in tantalizing imitation of what he had done to her. Con clenched his teeth and rolled onto his back, pulling her on top of him. "But it won't be easy," he groaned.

Linn molded her body to his big frame, winding her arms around his neck. In her own wonder, her own delicious discovery, she was only half-aware of his agonized response to her slightest movement. He was still wearing his jeans, but she felt him as if he were naked, powerful and ready between her thighs. She sat up and moved astride him, and his hands slipped down her back and cupped her buttocks, guiding her. His eyes closed and his lips compressed, his chest heaving, and Linn was thrilled at her ability to please him. When his lashes lifted, she arched her back and rocked, her breasts lifting as she saw his reaction to the picture she made.

"Enough!" he ground out, pulling her down to him and reversing their positions so quickly she lost her breath. He stretched her arms above her head and pinned her, moving over her, kissing her until she was unconsciously wrapping her legs around his hips, asking without words for the fulfillment he could give. When he finally released her to stand and remove his pants, she never took her eyes from his, holding out her arms to welcome him back.

Con stripped quickly and returned to her, enfolding her tenderly, stroking her hair, keeping his flooding desire in check with an effort. This was his Aislinn, his vision come to life, his dream come true, and he wanted everything to be perfect for her. He was desperate with the need to take her, but he forced himself to slow down and enhance her pleasure. She had had a bad experience with her husband; Con wanted to erase the unhappy memory and replace it with this one of him. There was no rush, he told himself; he would have her in the end.

But he felt the rush in his throbbing loins, in the surging primal compulsion to bury himself in the woman he loved. When she sighed and pressed herself against him, her hands moving to caress him intimately as she had done once before, he forgot his prior intention and pushed her down roughly, his awareness of his own strength lost in the tumult of the moment. Con kissed her body feverishly, his mouth so consuming, so demanding, that Linn writhed beneath his sensuous assault, swept up in a hurricane of feeling. Con half sat, holding her firmly with one arm around her waist, and stroked the damp warmth between her legs until he could no longer contain himself and bent hungrily to put his mouth where his hand had lately been.

Linn tossed her head from side to side on the cushion of her robe, her fingers tangled in his hair. When he knew that her need was as great, as urgent as his, he knelt and pulled her legs around him. Before she had time to feel the loss of his lips, she was awash in a new sensation as he entered her slowly, pausing on the threshold of her womanhood to withdraw slightly and then ease in a little more, giving her the barest taste of what she wanted.

"You're teasing me," she moaned, clutching the folds of the robe beneath her with one hand. Her eyes locked with his and she watched the waves of pleasure, almost akin to pain, transform his features.

"I'm loving you," he answered thickly, rotating his hips, sinking into her further but stopping just as she was arching blissfully to meet him. Linn groaned in frustration.

"Do you love me?" he gasped.

"Yes, oh yes."

"Say it. I want to hear you say it."

"I love you, Con. I love you so much."

His control gone, Con drove into her wildly, making her cry out. He raised his head, searching her face anxiously.

"I've not hurt you?" he said hoarsely.

Linn kissed his parted lips. "How could you ever hurt me? It's just . . . I never knew it could be like this."

Con clasped her close, lifting her off the ground and holding her against his chest. Her head fell back and he rained kisses on her exposed throat.

"I want you so badly," he rasped. "I just can't hold back any longer."

"Don't," Linn whispered. "Don't hold back. I want to feel everything with you."

This was all he needed to hear. He surged into her repeatedly, catching her up in his rhythm, until Linn was panting, clutching him tightly, willing him not to interrupt his intoxicating cadence. Just when she thought she would explode into a thousand tiny particles of light, he paused, lowering her to the silken mat of her robe.

"Don't stop," she begged. "Con, please don't stop."

He had no intention of stopping. His eyes gazed into hers as he put his palms flat on the ground on either side of her, pushing himself up to the length of his arms. He thrust into her powerfully, penetrating more deeply than he had before. Linn whimpered and lifted her hips to engulf him, seeking the exquisite sensation.

"Aislinn," he said in her ear, "look at me."

Linn's eyes were squeezed shut. She opened them and gazed at her lover.

Con's skin was bathed in perspiration, his hair in damp ringlets, his mouth bruised and wet from her kisses. He caught his lower lip between his teeth as she moved slightly beneath him and intensified his pleasure.

"Promise me you won't leave me," he said.

"Oh, darling, I won't. I don't want anyone but you. I would die if I couldn't have you."

Con lowered his head and pressed his hot, flushed face into the soft curve of her shoulder.

"Then you shall live, my lady," he murmured, "because you have me, and always will."

Linn ran her hands over his strong, muscular back, delighting in his beautiful body. She held him close and listened to his harsh breathing, felt the ragged pounding of his heart and the wonderful fullness as he moved inside her. This is it, she thought, ablaze with emotion and physical hunger. This is the love I've searched for all my life. She felt cheated that she'd lived so long without it, grateful that she'd found it at last. She dug her fingers into his hips, moaning helplessly, burying her lips in his hair. Everything about him was a marvel: the hardness of his flesh, the softness of his mouth, the effortless strength and sureness of his movements. He quickened his pace again, then went rigid.

"Stay . . . with me," he gasped, barely able to talk.

Always, Linn thought, abandoning herself to the jour-

ney, spiraling upward with him. Her mind spun out to
blankness as, fused in white heat, they became one.

Con's voice broke into Linn's dreamy lassitude. "Are
you all right?" he asked softly.

Con hadn't withdrawn, but merely shifted to the side so
as not to crush her with his weight.

"Never better," she replied, "though you *are* a little
heavy."

"I didn't notice any complaints before," he responded
with a wry, very Con-like smile.

"Pleased with yourself?" she asked.

"And with you," he answered, kissing her nose. "I
knew from the start you were a Roman candle."

Linn groaned. "If you're referring to our first meeting,
I'd rather not discuss it. When I had to face you the next
morning, I was mortified."

"I'd love to discuss it. It was the premier experience of
my life, until tonight."

She punched him lightly on the shoulder. "You're a
beast to tease me about it. You know nothing like that had
ever happened to me before, and if you're going to razz
me about it, I'm leaving."

He grunted as she moved. "You'll have to take me with
you," he said, holding her down.

Linn inhaled sharply, feeling him growing inside her.
"Again?" she asked.

"Still," he muttered as she locked her legs around him
once more. "I'll never get enough of you."

This time he was easier, more gentle, soothing her with
soft words and lingering kisses, and when it was over, she
found that her face was wet with tears.

"No crying, now," he said, wiping her cheek with his
thumb. "I won't have it."

"It's just that I'm so happy," she said, snuggling into
him.

"Don't get too comfortable, my lady," he warned. "I'm taking you inside. You'll get sick from the damp and I'll be the cause of it."

"Oh, can't we stay? It's so lovely here."

"All right, for a few minutes," he agreed, lying back with his hands behind his head. Linn settled against his shoulder, gazing up at him. She traced the line of his jaw with her finger.

"Do you look like your father?" she asked.

"Not much, nor my mother either. I seem to be a throwback. What about you?"

"Oh, I've seen pictures of my mother; I look like her. My father was dark, like you."

He smiled. "Think I'm handsome, do you?"

"I think you're conceited. As far as your looks go, you've a bit too much jaw for some people."

"But not for you." He closed his eyes contentedly.

"And your nose looks like it was once broken."

"Twice," he corrected her without opening his eyes. "I suppose it spoils my beauty."

Linn kissed his cheek. "Nothing could spoil your beauty for me, Con."

He wrapped one arm around her shoulder, hugging her. "Is that so, my lady?"

"That's so."

"I'll wager that means you'll have to tell Sean he's out of the running," he said slyly.

"Sean was never in the running. I'm ashamed to admit it, but I'm afraid I was using him to get to you."

"A tactic which met with admirable success," he admitted ruefully. "Poor Seaneen. I actually like him, if you can believe that, but when I saw him with you it drove me wild."

"You said he was a milkman with a typewriter."

Con winced.

"Why do you call him Seaneen?" Linn asked.

"Oh, it means young Sean, little Sean. His father is Sean as well, you see."

"I see. I always thought that was a terrible thing to do to a boy, call him after his father. He's 'little somebody' all his life. He winds up a fifty-year-old man who's still Little Jim because his father, Big Jim, is still alive."

Con laughed. "Is that your charming way of telling me our first son won't be named Connor?"

Linn held her breath. Their first son? But he went on smoothly. "It's a famous name in the sagas, you know, Conchubor."

"Yes, I know. 'Young subtle Conchubor.' Whose line is that?"

"Yeats, the nonpareil. He's my religion, that man."

"He's everybody's religion over here. I couldn't believe it when I saw that his picture was on the twenty-pound note."

"Certainly."

Linn giggled. "Only the Irish would put a poet on their money."

"And why not? He's just as important to us as Jefferson or Lincoln or any of those bloody politicians you put on yours."

"I wouldn't call Lincoln a bloody politician," Linn said, outraged.

Con waved his hand, dismissing The Great Emancipator. "Shakespeare is on British money," he pointed out.

"Now there's a genius," Linn said, needling.

"To be sure."

"And an Englishman."

"I forgive him."

"That's very generous of you." Linn pressed his left nipple with her thumb.

He glanced down at her. "What are you doing?"

"I'm testing your erogenous zones."

"I think we've discovered that they all work," he said.

He shook his head. "I've created a monster in a single night."

She smiled at him. "That's what you get for taking on a wild American lady."

He cupped her chin in his hand. "The only thing wild about you is your response to me," he said tenderly.

Linn dropped her eyes. "That's not what everybody in town thinks," she said unhappily. "I made a fool of myself at the Fleadh."

He sat up. "You didn't make a fool of yourself; you just showed how you feel about me, and I'm glad you did. It gave me the nerve to try again, to come here and wait for you. And as for what they think, ten of them together *might* have one brain between them to think anything."

Linn chuckled wickedly. "Con, that's an awful thing to say. I know you don't mean it."

He frowned mulishly. "Perhaps not, but if any of them say a word against you I'll have their hides."

"Oh, come on. You'd have to admit I asked for it. My behavior even gave Terry Cleary ideas."

Con glanced at her sharply. "Oh, aye?"

She saw that she shouldn't have brought it up. "Well," she said uncomfortably, "it wasn't much actually . . ."

He waited, eyeing her narrowly.

"He just said something a little suggestive," she hedged.

Con's jaw tightened. "I may have to give him a clout in the mouth next time I see him," he said tersely.

"Con! You can't be serious. I'm sorry I mentioned it. Terry's just full of himself, that's all. He's sexy, and he knows it." She put her hand placatingly on his arm.

He shrugged it off. "Oh, he's sexy, is he?" he inquired archly.

"Con, you can't be jealous of a sixteen-year-old boy."

"I'm jealous of anybody who looks at you, including a sixteen-year-old boy, especially one you think is sexy."

"I think you're sexier."

"That's comforting."

"I think you're the sexiest man in Bally."

He snorted. "That's not saying much, and well you know it."

"The sexiest man in Ireland, then, and that's a significant statement."

He tugged on her hair. "I don't know about that, but I've decided that you *were* right about one thing."

"What's that?"

"Since you came here, if you haven't been crying, you've been rolling about in the grass with me."

Linn flung herself on him as he collapsed in laughter. "You're going to pay for that!" she yelled.

"Oh, I hope so." He grinned, pulling her across his body.

Linn clasped her arms around his waist and rubbed her cheek on his stomach. A cool evening breeze swept across her back and she shivered.

Con sobered, propping himself on an elbow. "Let's go in, Aislinn. You're cold; you'll have pneumonia by morning."

Linn ignored him, trailing her tongue across his navel, darting it along his hipbone down to his thigh. He caught his breath, moving his hand to her hair to massage her scalp. Linn raised her head.

"What was that you were saying?" she asked sweetly.

"Perhaps we'll stay a while longer," he whispered, pushing her down again.

Linn fondled him, and then touched him experimentally with her tongue. Con made a guttural sound deep in his throat and closed his fingers around the nape of her neck. When she saw the intensity of his response, her courage faltered.

"Con," she said, kissing him lightly, "I want to make love to you very much, but I've never . . . I'm not sure . . ."

He shushed her gently. "You love me, Aislinn. That will teach you what to do."

And he was right.

They didn't make it back to the gatehouse until three in the morning, by which time Linn was chilled to the bone. Even in midsummer, the nights were cool.

Con grabbed an afghan and draped it about her shoulders once they were inside, rubbing her arms briskly.

"Scoot up on the bed there and cover up while I light the fire," he directed. "Cuddle inside that and you'll be warm soon enough." He tossed his shirt on a chair and began to shift logs from the brace against the wall onto the hearth.

Linn drew the blanket around her and watched him work in quiet contentment. Relaxed, replete, she curled up drowsily, admiring the play of muscles across Con's arms and back as he built the fire. Finally he bent to light it, and then stood by to make sure it caught and drew well. Satisfied, he joined her on the bed.

"That should do it," he said, pulling her into his arms.

"What accounts for the weather here?" Linn asked.

"The Gulf Stream," Con replied. "It gives us our climate and makes the country green. The current encircles the whole island like a ring of bright water."

Linn smiled at his fanciful description; he talked the way he wrote. That reminded her of something.

"Con, why don't you have any of your books here?" she asked.

"Checked, did you?" he replied, a smile in his voice.

"Yes."

"Well, I did have some, but I gave them away," he said. "People always ask me for them."

"You'll never get rich that way, Connor," Linn stated dryly. "The idea is for people to *buy* them."

"Oh, they buy them, never worry," he answered.

"They all did well, except *The Eden Tree*. That just broke even."

"Poetry never sells that well. It has a select but appreciative audience."

"Just as you say," he agreed, nuzzling her neck.

"Where did you get the title?" Linn asked.

"Oh, that. I was trying to get across an idea from the Gaelic which wouldn't translate literally. The original phrase meant something forbidden, something or someone that you desire passionately, to the point of distraction, but can never, ever have. So I called it *The Eden Tree* because that seemed to sum up the situation."

"I see. It sounds like a perfect choice."

"I'm glad it meets with your approval." He pressed Linn closer and ran his hands lightly over her from her shoulders to her hips. "Aislinn," he breathed. "Nothing, nothing, has ever felt as wonderful to me as your soft warm body in my arms."

Linn closed her eyes and melted into him. "Oh, Con, I love you so. I was wretched when I thought you didn't want me."

He hugged her tighter. "Not want you? I've been consumed with wanting you, destroyed by it, since I met you. When you sang to me at the Fleadh, I was so . . . hot. . . I wanted to throw you down and take you right there."

Linn giggled. "That would have caused even more of a stir than my performance did." She paused thoughtfully. "You don't suppose anybody saw us tonight in the glen?"

She felt his mouth form itself into a smile against her skin. "If so, there'll be more talk about you in Bally tomorrow."

Linn burrowed into his chest. "Don't even suggest it. My reputation is in shreds already. You'd think the locals would have something better to do than revile me."

"They don't," Con said with a laugh. "And besides, they're not reviling you. You're interesting, and that's the truth of it."

Linn stroked his soft hair, drying now in the heat of the room. "Con," she asked softly, "how did you know I would be there tonight?"

"Oh, that's simple. I put the come-hither on you."

"What's that?"

"A spell to summon a person to your side. Very effective."

"You're full of baloney."

"Blarney," he corrected. "Here we call it blarney."

"Whatever you call it, it still sounds suspicious to me."

"Ever the practical American," he said, rolling her under him and framing her face with his hands. He kissed her lingeringly, raising his head finally to gaze into her eyes.

"I'm going to take you everywhere," he said. "I want to show you everything there is to see, from the Cliffs of Moher to the Dingle Peninsula to Sligo Bay in the Northwest. Yeats lived there, as you know, and you can see the places he wrote about, not much changed from when he knew them."

"It sounds wonderful," Linn said dreamily.

"You can see Ben Bulben from the road as you approach, always shrouded in clouds hanging low about the bare head of the mountain. And right at the foot of it, in the shadow of the cliff, is Drumcliff Churchyard, where he's buried. The grave has a limestone marker, as he requested, and the inscription is carved into it—"

" 'Cast a cold eye on life, on death. Horseman, pass by,' " Linn recited.

"That's my girl," Con said. "And just across the road is a tavern where you can get pub grub, where the work crews come in for a glass of stout and a bite to eat. Oh, you should hear them talk, Aislinn. It's like music, those lyrical voices; it's a wonderful thing to hear."

"You love it very much, don't you?" Linn asked, her voice misty with emotion.

"What?"

"Your country, its people."

He shrugged. "I don't think about it; it's just something that is always there."

"I know what you mean," Linn whispered, so full of love for him that she didn't trust herself to say more. She held him as he relaxed against her, and was almost asleep when he stirred and sat up.

"Where are you going?" she asked.

"To stoke the fire. Go back to sleep."

"You won't leave?" she asked, her words blurred with fatigue.

"Never," he said soothingly. "Where would I go?"

He slipped off the bed, and she heard him adding logs to the blaze. When he returned, she murmured quietly, "Do something for me?"

"Anything," he answered.

"Take off your pants."

He chuckled softly. "Certainly, my lady. I shall in all my best obey you." He discarded the offending garment and gathered her into his arms.

"That's better," she purred. She fitted herself against him, curling up like a sleepy puppy. "I love you, Con," she whispered before drifting off. "I can't seem to stop saying that."

"I love you too, mavourneen," he replied. "Sleep now, and when you wake, I'll be here."

She did, and he was.

Chapter 8

IN THE MORNING LINN EMERGED FROM THE BATHROOM TO
hear Con rummaging loudly in the kitchen area of the
cottage, muttering to himself. She belted the sash of the
silk robe around her and padded over to him. Dressed in a
pair of jeans, barefoot, he was on his hands and knees on
the floor, shifting canned items around on the lower shelf
of one of the cupboards.

"What are you doing?" she asked.

"I'm looking for something to eat," he replied. "So far
I've found a tin of sardines and three cans of stewed
tomatoes."

"Sounds like a charming breakfast," Linn said with a
smile, going to the open door. The morning was fresh and
cool, with a fine mist that threatened to become rain at any
moment. This did nothing to dispel Linn's newly acquired
view that the world was a wonderful, even magical, place.

"Everything is coated with dew," she said dreamily.

Con looked up from the perusal of his meager larder.

"Aye, a soft day," he answered, glancing out at the glistening trees.

"What is that?"

"A day that seems to hang between a fog and a drizzle, like this one, but pleasant just the same," he explained. "We have many such; there's even a song about them: 'A soft day, thank God, when the wind from the south with a honeyed mouth blows a secret through the trees.'"

"That's lovely."

Con stood, dusting his hands on the thighs of his jeans. "So are you." He jerked his head back in the direction of the pantry. "That's the lot," he said, referring to his stock of food. "Unless you've a yen for fossilized chocolate-covered peanuts. I also have those."

"Is that all you keep in the house? What do you live on?"

He shrugged, gesturing vaguely. "I usually have stuff delivered, but lately I . . ." His eyes slid away from hers. He looked up again. "Sort of lost interest," he concluded.

Me too, Linn thought. It had to be love. They were exhibiting the same symptoms.

"We'll have to go up to the house, or in to town," Con added.

"We'll have to go up to the house to get me something to wear," Linn replied, "but there isn't much to eat there. Bridie is supposed to do the shopping today. And I don't think an early-morning tête-à-tête in Bally is advisable. After last night, the sight of us having breakfast together would certainly stimulate conversation."

Con made a disgusted sound. "Nosy beggars, all of them. None of their damn business, anyway."

"Con . . ."

He held up his hand. "All right, Aislinn. You've made your point." He thrust his hands into the pockets of his jeans and cocked his head. "I'll take you to Ennis; there's a place there that serves American coffee."

Linn stepped into her slippers. "I'm on my way."

Con sprinted after her and caught her from behind, enclosing her in his arms and dropping his face to her shoulder. "I can't believe you're here with me," he murmured. "When I woke up, I thought for a moment that I dreamed it all, but then I felt you, warm and snug against me, and I knew that it was true."

Linn leaned back into him, sighing with pleasure. "Sometimes dreams do come true."

He straightened and spun her around to face him. "I told you I was lucky," he said, planting a kiss on her forehead.

Linn reached up to touch his face. "And now you've made me lucky too," she said softly.

Con turned his head to kiss her fingers, and then pushed her playfully away from him. "None of that, now," he said. "Don't get me started; I'll never be able to last the course without food. You wouldn't want me to die of starvation in your arms, would you?"

"Certainly not," Linn said dryly, watching him remove a shirt from the stack on his shelf and shrug into it. He got a pair of socks from a drawer and pulled them on, searching for his shoes on the floor. He crawled around for several moments and then looked up, exasperated.

"Aislinn, where are my shoes?"

"I'm not wearing them, Con," she said, amused.

"Bloody hell," he swore, peering at the four corners of the cottage. "This place is a mess. Infinite chaos in a little room."

Linn laughed at his paraphrase of Marlowe's famous line. "You're a slob, Conchubor," she said.

"I am not," he replied defensively, spying the pair of loafers under the bed and reaching out one long arm to retrieve them. "I try very hard to be neat, but I swear everything I put in its place grows legs and walks away." He put the shoes on and turned to face her.

"Are you ready?" Linn asked with exaggerated patience.

"I am."

"Lead on." Linn followed him out to his car, which had been returned by his ubiquitous "friends," and got in beside him. It seemed strange to be riding around in the Bentley at this hour wearing nothing but the Chinese bathrobe, but Con seemed oblivious to her reaction. He talked easily, outlining the revisions he wanted to make in the book he was working on, and Linn thought that she had never seen him so relaxed. His rigid reserve was gone as if it had never existed, and she was filled with tenderness at the change in him. He trusts me now, she thought, and knew that it was true.

Con pulled up outside the house and walked around to open Linn's door. He lifted her out of her seat and into his arms.

"Hurry along, now," he whispered, nuzzling her. "I'm perishing for lack of a decent meal."

"I get the message," she answered, laughing. "I'll be quick." She ran up the steps and unlocked the door as Con came more slowly behind her. He lingered in the hall while she changed into slacks and a blouse, which fastened at the back. She couldn't do all of the buttons and went out to seek Con's assistance.

"Would you button those last two I couldn't reach?" she asked, standing in front of him.

Con pulled her closer and kissed the exposed skin of her back. "I'd rather unbutton those you did reach," he said huskily, running his lips up to the nape of her neck.

Linn shivered, squirming loose from his hold. "I thought you were going to drop dead if you didn't fill your empty belly," she said archly.

As if to emphasize her point, Con's stomach growled ominously. Linn's eyes widened.

"That sounds serious," she said, awed. "We'd better get you to the breakfast table immediately."

Con took her hand and pulled her after him out the door and down the steps, pausing only to let her lock up and put the key in her pocket. "I agree," he replied, "but I intend to pick up where we left off as soon as we've eaten." He hustled Linn into the car and slammed the door after her, sliding in beside her seconds later. "If I faint before we get to Ennis, you'll have to take over the wheel," he said.

"Try to stay conscious," Linn replied. "I don't think I'm equal to the challenge of driving with your countrymen."

"Best drivers in the world are in Ireland," Con said smugly. "I don't know what you're talking about." He started the car and drove off smoothly.

"Oh, really?" Linn answered sarcastically. "The only problem I've noticed is that they seem to think the posted speed limits are roadside decorations. You know, the sort of thing that adds atmosphere but that no one really pays much attention to."

Con grinned. "God made us fast. We don't like to let anything slow us down."

Anything, or anybody, Linn thought. She snuggled closer to Con and closed her eyes as he pulled out onto the main road.

Con glanced down at her. "Still tired, are you?" he asked.

"I didn't get much sleep," she said, smiling.

"Take a nap, then," Con answered. "We'll be there before you know it."

Linn took him at his word, drifting off as he drove along and coming to as he slowed to a stop in downtown Ennis. She stretched and sat up, yawning.

"There's the place," Con announced, pointing down the street toward a shop which displayed a sign above its door reading The Coffee Bean. Traffic in and out of the restaurant was brisk.

"It looks promising," she commented, trying to wake up as they emerged from the car and strolled down the road. Linn looked around at the buildings they passed: a

Bank of Ireland branch, a Dunne's store, a butcher's shop (known as a victualler's) and a pharmacy (known as a chemist's). Ennis was an old town, and the streets rose away from the center of commerce into a winding warren of stone houses and brick walls that branched out from the business district. The thoroughfare was thronged at this hour by people on their way to work, and quite a few of them were stopping off at The Coffee Bean for a "cuppa."

Con led Linn inside. A buffet ran along one wall, and the single large room was filled with picnic benches. The patrons picked up their food, cafeteria style, and then sat where they liked. Two chefs stood at a grill ready to prepare dishes while they waited. Con rattled off an enormous order for himself and filled two cups from the urns at the end of the line while Linn asked for scrambled eggs and toast. When everything was ready, they took their trays to a long table near the window and sat.

Linn watched in fascination as Con ate two fried eggs, sausage, bacon, an order of porridge and a plate of fresh fruit. He washed all this down with tea. He looked up, munching happily on a bran muffin, to see Linn transfixed with her coffee cup in her hand.

"What's the matter?" he asked. "Coffee not good?"

"It's heavenly," she said. "May I have some more?"

He got up and returned with a whole pot of it. "Keep it," he said, placing it on a ceramic plate the cashier had given him. "Drown yourself in caffeine."

"I intend to." She eyed him warily. "I'm really concerned that you may not have had enough to eat."

He grinned and took her free hand, raising it to his lips. "You worked me fearful hard last night, woman," he said. "I have to replenish my strength."

"How can you drink all that tea?" she asked. "It tastes like hot water."

"It is hot water," he replied, holding her hand against his cheek. "Wonderful stuff, the backbone of the nation."

Linn shook her head, smiling. "I thought that was whiskey."

He released her hand. "That's the soul of the nation," he stated. *"Uisce beatha,* the elixir of life." He wiped his mouth with a napkin and leaned across the table toward Linn. "I've an invitation to speak in Kinsale tonight," he said suddenly. "Would you go with me?"

"Where is Kinsale?" Linn asked.

"On the water, several hours' drive from Bally," he said. "I have to give a talk on folklore to a student group there." He dropped his eyes. "To tell you the truth of it, I wasn't too keen on going and had thought about making my excuses, but now I feel like taking the trip." He looked up again. "That is, if you'll go with me."

Linn smiled at him. "Of course. I'd go anywhere in the world with you now."

"Would you, Aislinn?" he asked softly, watching her face. "Are you certain?"

"Certain sure," she answered, using a Bally expression.

He cleared his throat. "Let's be off, then," he said, rising. "I've a powerful load of rewriting to do on that manuscript today before we leave."

"Is it that bad?" Linn asked, walking with him to the register and waiting while he paid for their meal.

"If I could read it, I might be able to tell you," Con replied darkly.

"Oh," Linn said in a small voice. "I suppose that's my fault?"

"It is indeed," Con answered, pushing the door open for her. "I've been so distracted I could hardly put two coherent words together. Nothing like a woman to ruin a man's artistic integrity."

"I beg your pardon."

His eyes widened as he walked beside her down the street. "You mean you won't take the blame for my failure of inspiration?"

Linn stopped short. "Was it really my fault that you couldn't work?"

He folded his arms and faced her. "Well, Aislinn, let's put it this way. Every time I sat down at the typewriter, I wound up staring into space, mentally ravishing you, instead of putting the words onto the paper. I conjured up some rather creative fantasies, but no literary master-pieces."

Linn's lips twitched. "I'm sorry, Con."

He surveyed her critically. "I don't believe that you are. You take great satisfaction in the idea that you were driving me mad."

Linn grinned. "I do not."

Con continued to stare at her.

"Well, maybe a little," she admitted.

"I thought so." He ushered her into the car and edged his way out between the oncoming cars, joining the line of traffic.

"What will you speak about tonight?"

"Some of the legends that form the basis of our heritage here. I got most of my material from Seamus Martin. He knows the original version of almost all the stories."

"Like which ones?" Linn asked, interested.

"Oh, Tristan and Isolde, for example. Have you ever heard of them?"

"Hmm. The Irish Romeo and Juliet, right?"

"Not exactly. Isolde was an Irish princess who was betrothed to Mark, the king of Cornwall. Mark sent his nephew Tristan across the water to fetch Isolde, and to be cured of a festering wound that would not heal. During the time they spent together, and the voyage back to England, they fell in love. When Isolde arrived, she married Mark but still harbored a hopeless passion for Tristan. In despair, she ran away to the lepers, and Tristan rescued her from them. He tried to take her to safety, and during their flight he placed a sword between them to keep his vow of fealty to the king inviolate."

"It would take more than a sword to keep me away from you," Linn said.

"Thank you. Anyway, Mark caught up with them and banished Tristan from the kingdom, after which he was set upon by robbers and left to die. Isolde pined away without him, and Mark finally took pity on her and sailed away to bring Tristan back to her. But it was too late. Tristan was already failing, and through a misfortune Isolde thought that he was dead when his ship arrived, and she flung herself from a cliff in sight of the boat. They were reunited for a few seconds before they died together."

"Good Lord, that's terrible. Are all your stories so cheerful?"

"Most of the legends are pretty grim. Cuchulain and Niamh and Fergus and the Druid, all heavy-duty stuff full of tragic love affairs and heroes dying gloriously in battle. But the leprechaun tales are a little lighter, morality plays concerning wicked, scheming fairies who take perverse delight in outsmarting the foolish mortals who try to do battle with them."

"I thought leprechauns were sweet little men in green hats who show up in stationery stores on Saint Patrick's Day."

Con snorted, turning the wheel to bypass a bicyclist in the road. "That's the popular conception, the romanticized version. But in the old stories they're fallen angels, very bitter about it too, and constantly baiting mortals into traps, luring them into their downfall by appealing to their avarice."

"I never knew that."

Con nodded vigorously, warming to his subject. "You never heard of changelings?"

"No, what's a changeling?"

"A shriveled-up fairy brat left in a cradle in place of a human child who was snatched away to be a slave in the underworld. The wee folk rarely took girl children, and so my mother kept me in skirts until I was three in order to fool them.''

Linn stared at him, incredulous. ''Con, you're not telling me she believed that nonsense!''

He shrugged. ''She used to put a cup of milk out on the back step every night of her life for a passing fairy man to refresh himself. They love milk, you see, almost as much as drink. And she thought the bribe might keep the bad luck off the house.'' He shot her a sidelong glance. ''It was gone every morning.''

''Oh, I get it,'' Linn said derisively. ''Your house was the rest stop for the little people, sort of like the leprechauns' Howard Johnson's.''

Con laughed. ''No, I think it more likely that we were a soft touch for every cat in the parish.''

Linn shook her head. ''And how do you feel now, after being raised with all those fantastic imaginings?''

He turned his head. ''Well, as an educated man, I know that superstition is the enemy of enlightenment and progress. But I must admit that whenever the conversation turns to pookahs and banshees and things that go bump in the night, I'm Irish enough to listen with one ear.''

Linn sighed. ''I guess that never leaves you.'' She glanced at him and smiled tenderly. ''I hope it never does. I wouldn't change a thing about you.''

Con turned the car into the lane that led to Ildathach. ''Do you think Bridie is at the house yet?'' he asked.

Linn glanced at her watch. ''It's early still. Probably not. I think she'll go for the groceries first.''

Con looked over at Linn. ''Good.''

She smiled at him. ''I thought you were anxious to get to your manuscript.''

He coughed. ''Not that anxious.''

When they reached the house, he got out and followed Linn inside. Ned appeared from somewhere and demanded attention. Con picked him up and rubbed his ears, murmuring to him softly. Linn had time to put her purse on the table before Con dropped the cat and pulled her into his arms.

"Come inside to the bedroom," he said. "I want to conduct an experiment." He lifted her blouse from the waistband of her slacks and put his palm flat against her back.

"Would this be in the interest of science?" Linn murmured, closing her eyes as his hand traveled around her body to the front, seeking her breasts.

"You could say that," Con replied huskily, guiding her through the door to her room. "I want to see if you are as lovely under the sun as you are in the moonlight." He swung her up in his arms and deposited her on the bed, falling next to her immediately and gathering her close. He kissed her face and neck, leisurely at first, and then with mounting intensity as Linn responded, pressing eagerly against him. He rolled her over and undid her buttons, stripped the blouse off and threw it on the floor. Her bra followed, and with a muffled sound, half sigh, half groan, he began to make love to her as the morning sunlight streamed across the bed.

Con's exit beat Bridie's arrival by about ten minutes. Linn was looking for a skirt to wear that evening when she heard Bridie enter through the kitchen, accompanied by Terry, who was serving as beast of burden. They were unpacking the bags when Linn entered.

"Good morning," Bridie said, glancing at Linn. "I'll have some breakfast in a minute."

"Nothing for me, thanks," Linn replied, declining to explain that she had been to Ennis and back at the crack of dawn. "I'm not hungry."

Bridie peered at her narrowly. "What's up with you, miss?" she asked. "You're looking mighty smug."

Linn turned away, alarmed that the changes wrought by the night should be so apparent in her face. She wanted to avoid a discussion of the previous evening at all costs. She didn't need another lecture or an inquiry into the state of her relationship with Con.

"I have some letters to write," she said, glancing at Terry, who was watching her with a small smile on his face. She had the uncomfortable feeling that the kid could tell exactly what she was thinking.

"I'm off to school, Ma," he said, strutting past Linn and heading for the door. He glanced over his shoulder at Linn and then turned away abruptly, his boots clicking on the tile floor. Linn followed the progress of his slim, erect form as he departed, struck again by his aura of worldly wisdom, knowledge beyond his years. Then she looked back at his equally sharp mother.

"I think I'll be busy for quite a while," Linn said. "I'll be in my room if you need me."

Bridie examined her curiously, but Linn fled before she could say anything further. She shut the door of the bedroom behind her and locked it, feeling like a fugitive from an inquisition. She wanted to savor the wonder of the last twelve hours with Con, free from Bridie's well-meant but nagging probing. She flung herself on the bed and relived every moment from her meeting with Con in the glen, hugging the pillow in an excess of happiness.

And so, pretending to catch up with her correspondence, she dreamed the day away.

When Con arrived that night to pick her up, Bridie had left for the evening and Linn felt free to fling herself on him as he came through the door.

"Ah," he said, laughing, "missed me, did you?"

"I did."

"And where's herself?" he asked, glancing around for the housekeeper.

"Gone home."

"You said nothing to her about us?"

"Not yet. I want to keep it our secret for a while."

"That's fine with me," Con answered, "though I doubt you'll be able to conceal much for long. That woman operates from hidden signals, like radar."

Linn held him off at arm's length and glanced at his clothes. "Is that what you're wearing?" He was attired in a pair of jeans, slightly less disreputable that the ones he usually wore, and a soft woolen sweater the color of heather, which emphasized his eyes. He looked great, but hardly like lecturer material.

"Oh, aye," he said, "it's all very informal. We don't stand on ceremony here."

"Is this all right?" Linn asked him, spinning around to display her camel skirt and beige cotton top.

"It's more than all right. I love your clothes, and how you look in them," he replied, taking her hands. He transferred both of hers to one of his and traced her mouth with his other thumb. "I love these lips," he murmured, kissing them, "these beautiful eyes," he went on, touching them with a forefinger, "this glorious hair." He released her hands and bunched her hair into both of his fists, rubbing his cheek against the flaxen mass that spilled through his fingers. "I love every inch of you, Aislinn."

Linn swayed against him, her lashes fluttering downward. "Con," she whispered, "don't say things like that, or there will be no lecture in Kinsale tonight."

He let her go reluctantly, opening his hands and allowing her blond tresses to fall to her shoulders. "It's a good thing for my reputation that you're such a responsible little American," he said dryly. "As I recall, punctuality is highly prized in the States."

"That's right, and I'm going to get you to Kinsale on time. Let's go."

They left hand in hand. Linn noticed that Con was very pensive during the drive. He selected the southern route, along the water, and the salty sting of the ocean breeze invigorated Linn as they drove along with the windows open. The sky was inflamed with an orange sunset as they neared the seaport town of Kinsale.

"You've been so quiet," Linn commented. "What are you thinking?"

"I'm thinking about the chance that brought you to me," he answered, dropping his hand to the seat between them and clasping her fingers. "It might never have happened, you know. You might have spent your whole life in the States, separated from me by thousands of miles of land and sea."

Linn glanced at him in the failing light, a little frightened at his tone. At a time like this it was easy to believe his stories about his mother; he had a fey streak himself.

"Why worry about that now?" she asked softly. "It didn't happen, we're together, and that's all that matters."

He squeezed her fingers. "You're right. I don't know what's wrong with me." He smiled reassuringly. "It must be this sunset. There's a legend that a bloody one like this is a vision of the battle of Clontarf, where we lost Brian Boru."

"'Oh, how can I live, and Brian be dead?'" Linn recited.

Con shot her a look, impressed. "'Mac Caig's Lament,'" he said. "I'm surprised you know it."

"We have books in New Jersey, Con," Linn answered dryly. "Some of us even read them."

"I'll wager your father taught you that one," he said, unconvinced.

Linn sighed. "You'd win the bet."

Con nodded. "Seamus knows it in Gaelic. He cries every time he does it."

Linn looked around as Con turned off the main road and headed into Kinsale. It was a picture-postcard town right on the bay, with sailboats and other small craft tied up at the wharf, which jutted into the sea. Con drove through the cobbled streets down to the dock and parked at the water's edge.

"The meeting's in the library," he said, taking her hand. "It's just here, beyond the corner."

Con was welcomed like visiting royalty by the undergraduates who had assembled to listen to him speak. It was easy to see that this was no group of literary luminaries, but an eager bunch of students who seemed stunned that Con had even consented to talk to them. They hung on his every word, and Linn was touched that he had come so far to address this motley crew who had nothing to offer but their love of literature and their willingness to learn. But that was what had drawn him to them, she saw; they were kindred spirits, and he knew it.

By the time he finished talking and answering their questions, they were all old friends, and Linn found herself accepting an invitation to dinner at the local seafood restaurant. It was set up on pilings above the water on a sort of boardwalk that extended into the bay, and all the walls were glass. It was illuminated by floodlights from every side, so that while dining you felt as if you were in the middle of the inlet. Con drew Linn into the discussion, explaining that she was an English professor from America, and Linn was soon debating the merits of everyone from James Joyce to Oscar Wilde with the bright, informed college kids. Their lilting voices and the wine with which Con constantly replenished her glass combined to induce a state of euphoria that had her expounding at length on subjects she wouldn't have touched a few days before. Con smiled indulgently and encouraged her, and he laughed out loud when she protested that the dish she was served was not the scallops she had ordered. The things on her plate looked like fried eggs. These were fresh scallops, Con explained, not the cookie-cutter American version that were presented like little half-dollars. Linn tasted one gingerly and pronounced it delicious. She wound up eating all of hers, and half of Con's chowder. They lingered late, and by the time the group broke up she was full—and very tired.

Linn and Con wandered down to the quay, watching the boats bob at anchor in the moonlight. Linn put her head on Con's shoulder and gazed out across the shimmering water.

"Do you see how the moon makes a path across the waves?" she asked dreamily. "There's an American Indian legend that when a warrior dies, his soul takes that path to the next life, skimming over the sea to a place where animals are plentiful and everyone lives in harmony with nature. When I was little, we had a place at the Jersey shore, and during the summer I used to sit on the porch and stare out at the ocean, trying to catch a glimpse of a shadow that might have been a soul in transit."

"You must have been a fanciful child," Con said, hugging her close.

"I guess I was. Stories like that always seemed more real to me than the six o'clock news." She turned her head to look up at him. "It was very nice of you to come here and speak to those kids," she said quietly. "I could tell they really appreciated it."

He lifted his shoulders, dismissing it. "I enjoyed myself. That's the future, kids like that, and we'd best do what we can to shape it."

"I noticed that girl named Shelagh was an enthusiastic admirer," Linn added dryly. "She put her hand on your leg. Twice."

Con grinned. "She was touching me to make a point."

"Oh, I agree, but not the point you thought."

He kissed the top of her head. "Not jealous, were you?"

"Certainly not. But if she'd grabbed you one more time, I was planning to club her with my bottle of Liebfraumilch."

"I'm glad it didn't come to that," he replied, chuckling. Con raised his arm above Linn's head to look at the luminous dial of his watch. "We'd best be on our way, my lady," he added. "We'll get back in the middle of the night as it is."

Linn reluctantly let him lead her back to the car. She curled up next to Con on the seat and fell asleep with her head against his arm.

Linn woke as Con lifted her out of the door.

"Where are we?" she mumbled.

"Back home."

"At the house?"

"At the cottage."

Linn leaned heavily on his arm and sleepwalked inside, falling on the bed the instant she saw it. Con moved about the room in the dark, and Linn heard the clink of his keys against the desk.

"Do you want a fire?" he asked.

"It's not really cold, but that doesn't matter. They're so romantic, they always make me feel like Catherine Earnshaw staving off the chill of the Yorkshire moors."

"Does that mean you want one, or not?"

Linn took off her shoe and pitched it at him. It struck the wall and rolled harmlessly into a corner.

"You must be waking up if you're able to throw things at me," he commented, piling logs on the hearth.

"Con?"

"Hmm?"

"Did you ever bring Mary Costello here?"

There was a pause, and Linn was sorry she'd asked. Then he said shortly, "No."

"You don't have to talk about her if you don't want to," she added.

"There's nothing to say," Con stated flatly, setting a match to the kindling at the base of the stack. "I liked Mary well enough, but it was nothing like with you. She always knew that; I never misled her."

"She must hate me now," Linn said.

"I doubt it," Con said neutrally. "She is a practical woman; she'll move on and do well elsewhere."

"I don't think you're so easily forgotten," Linn replied.

Con pulled his sweater over his head and then joined her on the bed.

"Aislinn," he said quietly, "why do you do this to yourself? Forget Mary, forget Tracy, forget anyone else but you and me. The past is dead; it has nothing to do with us now. It was a hard lesson for me to learn. You know how I clung to that resentment of your father, but I can see that for what it was: blind stubbornness. If I can release that, can't you release these images you have of the time before I knew you?"

"Yes, I can," Linn said simply. "And I will."

Con stretched out next to her and drew Linn against him. She ran her hands over the smooth expanse of his chest and kissed his satiny shoulder. His skin was warm, fragrant, redolent of the life that pulsed beneath it.

"I'll never have to be alone again," she said.

"Neither one of us will ever be alone again," Con replied, stroking her hair. He kissed her brow lightly. "I love you," he whispered. "It's such a relief to be able to tell you that, to finally stop fighting it. When I said it last night, I felt as if a weight had been lifted from my shoulders."

"I thought I'd never hear you say it."

"Did you?" he asked.

"Yes, I did. I thought you'd let me go before you gave in to your feelings. I thought you were a pigheaded idiot."

"I was that," he agreed.

Linn sat up and kissed him, touching his lips lightly with hers. His hold tightened immediately, and he reached for the buckle of her belt, trying to undo it with one hand. Linn helped him and slid off the bed to undress. Con shed his jeans and pulled her back down to him. He just held her for a moment, running his hands over her body, and she shuddered with the exquisite sensation of his hard, capable fingers touching her everywhere, telling her without words that she was loved and cherished, desired and protected.

"Make love to me," Linn murmured.

Con didn't answer, but began to kiss her with an intensity that demonstrated he had heard. He moved over her, drawing her to him, caressing her with increasing ardor until Linn was writhing restlessly beneath him, demanding the ultimate embrace.

When he entered her, she clung to him, welcoming the sweet weight of his driving body on top of hers. And when it was over, she lay awake long after he fell asleep, staring over his dark head at the flames, which danced and blurred before her eyes.

Linn slept fitfully that night, perhaps because of the sleep she'd gotten during the car trips, and she finally gave up near dawn and rose, careful to steal away from Con without disturbing him. She drew a blanket over him to combat the early-morning chill and pulled on her clothes, then padded quietly to the kitchen to make a cup of coffee. When it was ready, she took it to the door and slipped outside.

It was barely light, and the birds were just beginning to sing. Linn hugged herself and sipped her drink, sitting on a tree stump at the edge of the clearing and watching the first faint streaks of pink and yellow brighten the eastern sky.

Do I deserve such happiness? she wondered. Does anyone? Could it last? She understood now why lovers savored every minute, having that which they feared to lose. She followed the progress of the sun as it climbed the sky until it was too bright to look at any longer. Then she went back inside.

Con was sleeping as she'd left him, on his stomach, his arm thrown out across her pillow. Crossing the room to put her cup in the sink, Linn paused at the stack of manuscript pages on top of the typewriter. A handwritten note was clipped to the first page. She picked it up.

"Dedication," she read. "For Aislinn, my woman made of moonlight, who saved me and enslaved me with her love. Everything I have to give is yours."

Linn blinked back tears and replaced the slip of paper, wiping her eyes with the back of her hand. At the same moment, a sound from Con made her glance in his direction.

He was sitting up in bed, foggy with sleep, calling for her.

"Aislinn?" he said, glancing around, his voice concerned.

She stepped into his range of vision.

"Good morning, darling," she said. "I'm right here."

He turned his head to look at her and smiled.

Chapter 9

THE NEXT TWO WEEKS FLEW BY IN A GOLDEN HAZE OF happiness. Linn resumed work on the house, while Con finished up his manuscript. He took frequent breaks to contribute to the renovations, putting up shelving, knocking down walls and generally making himself useful with hammer and saw. He made a daily supply run to transport necessary items and buy what he needed. He was in such high spirits, whistling, singing, and laughing at almost anything, that Bridie discerned the change immediately and began dropping broad hints about weddings and prenuptial consultations with Father Daly. Linn did her best to shut her up, but Bridie was not easily squelched.

Linn wrote a joyful letter to Karen Walker, telling her all about Con, and forced herself to ask Sean in when he arrived on his milk route. She apologized for her behavior the night of the festival, and Sean was gracious about it, making her task less burdensome with his understanding attitude. He said that he had known about Linn and Con

all along, and that he'd hoped to take advantage of their rift and ingratiate himself with Linn. He wasn't surprised that they had worked things out, and he wished them well. Linn was relieved, though she felt slightly guilty that she didn't receive the cold shoulder she thought she deserved.

One day in mid-August she and Bridie were hanging new drapes while Con nailed up freshly painted shutters outside the windows. He was roaring some old standard at the top of his lungs.

Bridie shook her head. "I've never seen that boy so happy, but I do wish he would give my poor ears a break."

Linn grinned sympathetically. Con couldn't sing worth a damn; all his efforts were droning and uninflected, like Gregorian chanting. This did not, however, prevent him from blistering the air with tuneless renditions of everything from "Kevin Barry" to "In Heaven There Is No Beer" (an obvious souvenir of Fordham).

"Aislinn?"

"Hmm?"

"What are you going to do about him?"

Linn glanced at the older woman, her mouth full of pins. "Do? I'm going to be with him and love him, that's what I'm going to do," she replied, mumbling around the pins.

"You know that's not what I mean."

Whatever Bridie was going to say was interrupted by Con's bustling entrance through the front door. He deposited an empty paint can on the floor.

"I'm off to buy more of that," he announced, seizing Linn around the waist and kissing her soundly. "How do you fancy a trip to Ashford Castle tonight?" he asked.

"Ashford Castle?"

"Aye. It's an eleventh-century castle converted to a fine hotel and restaurant, about an hour's drive from here in County Mayo. I wouldn't want you to think that the Kinnon Arms was all we had to offer."

"Isn't it late to get a reservation?"

He winked. "I have friends in high places. Get out your best, now, and I'll be back for you at six." He grabbed Bridie, danced her a few steps around the hall on his way out and then departed, humming loudly.

Flustered, Bridie patted her hair. "That man is impossible these days. I think I liked him better when he was miserable."

"What am I going to wear? I'm afraid my 'best' isn't very good. I only brought travel clothes with me."

Bridie shot her a look. "I never heard such nonsense; you have lovely things. What about that pink dress you arrived in? It's been cleaned and is hanging up there in the closet this minute, like new."

Bridie was referring to her rose linen chemise, which was the closest thing to a dinner dress she'd brought with her. "I guess that will have to do," Linn said, heading for her bedroom.

"We'll finish our discussion later," Bridie said warningly.

Linn was too preoccupied to reply. Bridie always wanted to discuss something.

She went to the closet to look for her dress.

Con arrived a few minutes early and was waiting for Linn when she appeared. She stopped short in the hall, staring at him.

He was wearing a dark suit with a light blue shirt and a figured tie. His hair was combed back off his forehead and gleamed wetly with his efforts to tame it. He smiled at her.

"You look wonderful," she said, awed.

He grinned. "You sound surprised, my lady."

Linn glanced down, embarrassed. "Of course I'm not surprised. I just never saw you dressed up before, that's all."

"Did you think I had nothing but caretaker's overalls?"

he teased. "I'm sorry if I shocked you, but I didn't think it fitting to show up at Ashford in my keeper's jeans." He leaned in toward her as if imparting a secret. "I don't think they'd let me in."

Linn crossed over to him and put her arms around his neck. "You just love to give me a hard time, don't you?"

He embraced her, pulling her hair aside to kiss her neck. "I just love you, and that's a fact. You're a gorgeous woman entirely in that dress. What do you call that color?"

"I call it pink, but the salesclerk called it desert rose. I think the truth lies somewhere in between."

Con's arms tightened, and his breathing quickened. "What do you say we skip the trip and stay here?" he murmured, reaching for the zipper at the back of her dress.

Linn slipped out of his grasp. "Nothing doing, buster. You promised me dinner, and I'm calling in your marker."

Con sighed. "I can see I'm not going to get out of it, so come along. But I will expect a suitable reward." He took her hand and swung her in a circle. "I booked us a suite overlooking the lake."

"We're staying the night?"

"That's the plan."

"Bridie will call out the garda if I'm not here in the morning."

"Leave her a note."

"She won't approve."

Con frowned. "Do you care what she thinks? She should better turn her attention to that motorcycle freak she's raising in her house."

"All right, all right." Linn scribbled a note and propped it on the kitchen table, where the housekeeper was sure to see it. Then she got a tote bag from her closet and put together some things for the night.

"I'm ready," she announced, stepping into the hall.

Con extended his hand and she took it, her small fingers lost in his big palm.

Ned watched them leave from his perch on the entry hall table.

Summer evenings are long in Ireland, and it was still full light as they drove. Linn stared out the window of Con's car, examining a road sign at the intersection they were approaching.

"That's funny," she commented.

"What is?"

"Well, I just saw a white sign that said, 'Dublin, 136.' Now here, a short distance later, there's that green sign saying, 'Ath Cliath, 219 km.' They both point down the same road. Which is right?"

"They both are. The white sign reflects the old system, using English and miles. The green sign reflects the new system, using Gaelic and kilometers."

"Oh," Linn said dryly. "That's clear."

Con grinned. "We do it to confuse the tourists."

"Take it from me, they're confused." She pointed to a marker at the side of the road. "Look at that. It says, 'When Red Light Shows, Wait at This Point.' Do you know what that would be at home?"

"I do. 'Stop Here on Red.' We like to take a little longer to say the same thing." He gestured to the right. "Off in that direction, toward the east coast, is the town where my father's ancestors came from, Cilleagh. It's on N25 between Cork and Waterford. When they emigrated to Liverpool it sounded like 'Clay' to the Brits, and Clay it became."

"It sounds like they shuttled back and forth between the two countries."

"They did, for many years. Some of them wound up in Belfast. The Titanic was built in the shipyard there, and I had a great uncle who was a cabin boy on that terrible

voyage. He survived and lived to be eighty-five. He talked
about it to his dying day. When I knew him, he was very
old and I was just a boy. I'll never forget that ancient man
describing the cries of the drowning and the sight of that
sinking ship. He would cry as he told the tale, staring into
the distance, and you could tell it was all as real to him as
if it had happened only minutes before.''

"That must have made quite an impression on you,"
Linn said softly.

Con looked over at her, slightly embarrassed. "Oh,
everything made an impression on me; I was like an ink
blotter.''

"You don't have to pretend with me," Linn said. "I
know you're a sentimental fool.''

He shot her a sidelong glance, and then dropped his
eyes, smiling.

Linn settled back against the seat and said, "Tell me
more about your childhood here.''

"What would you like to know?''

"Anything. I want to know about *you*.''

"Ah. Well, then, do you want to hear about the pansy
pint contest I won when I was seventeen?''

"Pansy pints?" Linn said faintly.

"Aye. Short pints, twelve ounces. Little snorts for
pansies, do you see?''

"I think so. Fire away.''

He proceeded to regale her with the details of a teenage
drinking contest that had her laughing so hard she wound
up crying. He was one of those people who could tell a
hilarious story without cracking a smile. Linn loved to
listen to him talk. His brogue had been moderated by his
education, and he sounded almost, but not quite, British,
like a Belfast news presenter for the BBC. In spite of this,
he retained many of the local expressions, including the
colloquial "aye," which a year in the States and four
years at Trinity had not managed to erase.

He was in the middle of another story when they pulled

up to the entrance of the castle. They drove through a stone arch and entered the grounds, rolling fields of green that stretched away from the road in all directions. The castle could be seen in the distance around a bend, and behind it the lake shimmered in the fading light.

"Con, it's beautiful," Linn breathed.

"I thought you would like it."

"It's an actual castle."

"Aye, it dates from the days of the Norman invasions. That's Lough Corrib in the rear and the Connemara mountains on the far shore."

"What's the name of the village here?"

"Cong, just off the Galway-Ballinrobe road. There's a wonderful history to this place. A great monastery was founded here, and the castle grounds saw many battles."

He drove up the winding road, past the battlements and the watchtowers, and parked the car in a lot before the main entrance. He got out and opened Linn's door, taking her hand.

"Come with me and see the courtyard," he said.

He led the way around through the greenery and banks of flowers to the open courtyard, which lay in the middle of the stone structure. A magnificent fountain splashed in its center, reflecting the sunset. A light breeze stirred Linn's hair as she tilted her head back and gazed at the top of the turret, which she thought must afford a view of the countryside for miles.

"There's our room," Con said, pointing to a window in the wing facing the lake.

"Oh, let's go inside. I want to see it."

Two suits of medieval armor flanked the entry hall, and the interior was furnished with heavy carved pieces and dark, patterned carpeting. Waterford chandeliers illuminated the staircases and the several dining rooms, and gilt-framed portraits hung on all the walls. There was a museum hush about the place, and even the modern reception desk with its uniformed clerk did not detract from the atmosphere of age and historical importance. The original stone walls of the castle could be seen beneath the hangings in the main corridor, adding to the aura.

Con got their key and confirmed their dinner reservations. They walked around the first floor hand in hand, and Linn gawked like the tourist she was as the dining room filled up with guests. Con had to practically drag her inside when the sitting was announced.

Blood red carpeting stretched from wall to wall, and the overhead lighting from the many glass fixtures bathed the vast room in a blaze of regal elegance. A hostess led them to a side table draped in beige damask, and immediately a wine steward appeared at Con's side.

It was soon apparent that this was no ordinary wine steward. This was, in fact, the friend in a high place who had arranged their seating on such short notice. A black-haired six-footer with vivid coloring, he examined Linn with interest when Con put his hand on her shoulder and introduced her as Aislinn aroon.

He asked Con something in Gaelic, and Con nodded. The man turned to Linn.

"I'm Christopher Dugan, miss, at your service. I'd be in a sorry spot if it weren't for your man here, as you may know." To her astonishment, he lifted her hand to his lips and kissed it.

Linn glanced at Con, who was watching this display with a hint of annoyance. "That'll do, Chris," he said sharply. "Go and get the list and leave off the Walter Raleigh act."

Christy grinned and pulled out Linn's chair, bowing. Con shot him a black look and he left.

"Well," Linn said as she sat down, "so that was the friend you rescued from a camp. I never expected to find him working here."

"And why not?" Con asked as he pushed in her chair and sat opposite her. "We all have to work somewhere."

''He's quite a charmer.''

''So he thinks,'' Con said sarcastically.

''What happened to his brother? Where is he?''

''In an Antrim jail, where he belongs,'' Con answered grimly. ''He won't be fixing any Molotov cocktails to incinerate babies from his cell.''

Linn stared at the tablecloth, sorry she'd asked.

Con's hand covered hers. ''I'm sorry, Aislinn. Matt Dugan is a sore subject. It's animals like that who give all of us in this country a bad name.''

Christy returned with the wine list, and Con ordered. He assisted Linn with the menu, and she selected smoked salmon, prawn cocktail and rack of lamb, which Con related to the waiter when he arrived.

Everything was delicious. Christy hovered nearby, along with the waiter and the maitre d', who paid frequent visits to their table. Con was either very popular, or all the employees shared Christy's moonlighting activities.

By the time they were ready for dessert Linn had worked up an appetite of another kind. The waiter brought coffee for Linn and tea for Con, and then wheeled a heavily laden pastry cart up to their table. Linn took one look at the Black Forest gateau and the kiwi flan, the chocolate mousse and the rum torte, and then her gaze sought Con's across the eggshell linen tablecloth. She saw the blue flame ignite in his eyes as she said, ''I think I'd rather see my room now, Con.''

He signaled for the check without taking his eyes from hers. Linn reached for his fingers and raked her nails across the back of his hand. He sucked in his breath and shoved back his chair.

Con settled the bill so fast Linn was sure he overpaid outrageously just to get finished with it. Christy stood watching their hasty exit with a smile of vast amusement illuminating his dark face.

Con tapped his foot impatiently while they waited for the elevator in conspiratorial silence. He was looking yearningly toward the stairs when it finally arrived. It carried them in plush, carpeted splendor to the third floor. They were the only guests in the hall, with dinner still underway, and their feet made no noise on the Oriental runner as Con unlocked the door to the suite and led Linn inside.

He embraced her the instant the door shut behind them. Linn closed her eyes and laid her cheek against the lapel of his jacket, inhaling his clean, masculine fragrance, the scent of his soap, the starch of his shirt. Music began in the distance, drifting in through the open windows, and Con started to sway in time to it, carrying Linn along.

"They're dancing downstairs," Linn said dreamily.

"We're dancing upstairs," Con replied, stepping back from her and whirling her in a circle the length of the sitting room.

The tune being played below them was "Begin the Beguine," and as the music swelled, Con led her through the steps of an intricate ballroom waltz, dipping and holding her tightly for dramatic pauses. He was remarkably easy to follow, skilled and graceful, and as the song ended he bent Linn back over his arm and kissed the soft skin at the base of her throat. She put one hand up to the back of his head, holding him against her as his hand found the hem of her dress and inched it upward, his fingers gliding smoothly up her thigh.

"Con, the door," Linn murmured. "Lock the door."

"Bother the door," he answered, pulling her upright and seeking her lips. She put her hand across his mouth to forestall him, and he bit gently into the soft roundness of her palm. His tongue flickered across her wrist, leaving a hot trail of wetness which cooled abruptly, making her wish for the caress again. Linn swallowed hard; she couldn't believe she was so aroused by the mere contact of his mouth with her hand.

"The light, then," she persisted. "The curtains are open and it's getting dark."

His leg jerked backward, and he pulled the plug from the socket with his foot without interrupting the movement of his lips against her bare arm. His kisses traveled upward, pausing in the hollow of her elbow to linger over the tender, unweathered flesh, and Linn fancied that his mouth might burn through to touch the delicate tracery of veins just below the surface. This is ridiculous, she thought; all the erotic awareness of her being was centered on the most prosaic and unglamorous part of her body. She sank her fingers into his hair, trying to raise his head.

"What do you want, Aislinn?" he murmured as her tugging became more insistent. "Tell me what you want."

"Kiss me," she moaned. "I want you to kiss me."

"I am kissing you," he muttered, his lips traveling lightly over her inner arm.

"On the mouth," she gasped, frustrated, "kiss me on the mouth."

He straightened immediately and crushed her lips with his, taking her breath away with the quickness and force of his response. Linn ran her hands up his arms, feeling the hard muscles tense beneath the coarse fabric of his jacket. Her fingers worked the coat back from his shoulders, and he slipped it off, moving his mouth to her ear, rimming it with his tongue. Linn shivered as he cupped her chin in his hand and turned her face up to receive another searing kiss, forcing her hips against his with his other hand splayed open on her lower back. She shifted her stance to fit more closely between his legs, and he groaned, lifting her and setting her on the edge of the bed. He crouched on the floor and slipped off her shoes, then pushed up her skirt to remove her panty hose. Pulling the stockings off her legs, he ran his hands over her bare skin. She leaned back on her elbows as he knelt and clasped his arms around her waist, pressing his face into the folds of cloth in her lap.

Linn arched against him. "Hurry," she whispered.

He stood and undressed rapidly, flinging his clothes on the rug. Linn watched him with heavy-lidded eyes, studying his hard body hungrily, unable to move. When he bent to remove her dress, she surged forward as if released from a trance and kissed his naked chest greedily, smoothing the mat of dark hair with her cheek, clinging to him as he ran her zipper down its track and bunched the sheath in his hands.

"You must let me take this off," he ground out, but Linn ignored him, reaching for him with frantic fingers and caressing him wildly. He growled an oath under his breath and pushed her down, falling on top of her in a tangle of limbs.

Linn received him eagerly, lifting her hips off the bed as he fumbled with her underclothes. The thin silk of her briefs was very strong; when more delicate measures failed, he drew back to rip them off, but Linn stayed his hand.

"I'll do it," she said, and he rolled to the side to let her get up. She pulled the dress over her head and let it fall from one hand, shaking out her hair and standing barefoot in her slip.

Con watched her from the bed, prone and fully aroused, his hot blue gaze following every move she made. With deliberate slowness Linn lifted the hem of her slip and worked it up over her hips to her waist, pausing to tilt her head back and stretch. Con inhaled sharply.

Linn raised the silken material further, drawing it sensuously over her breasts, but then she let it slide from her fingers to settle again around her knees. Con groaned aloud. "Come on," he muttered thickly. "Come on."

Linn began again, raising the slip over her head slowly and then tossing it aside. Con reared up from the bed and pulled her over him, yanking the scrap of flimsy material that remained from her body in one swift movement. Linn sat on his thighs as he fell back, feeling the delicious friction of his hair-roughened legs on her sensitive skin.

He was ready, full and pulsing against her, as he buried his face in the damp valley between her breasts and encircled her waist with his hands.

"Aroon," he whispered. "Aislinn aroon."

Linn bent her back like a bow, curving inward to meet his lips as they sought her nipples, pebble hard and flushed dark with passion. "What does it mean?" she asked tenderly, stroking his hair. "You always call me that."

"Beloved," he replied, sinking his teeth into one ripe bud. Linn sighed and pulled him closer. "My beloved," he added, "and so you are." He moved to slide her under him, but Linn resisted.

"Let me," she said. "Let me love you."

His eyes went smoky, becoming clouded sapphires, seducing her with a glance. His hands slipped to her buttocks, guiding her onto him. When she enclosed him, an involuntary sound of gratification escaped his lips. He grimaced, baring white teeth, and Linn's own cry was stifled as she reveled in his pleasure.

"You were made for me," he rasped. "I was made to join myself to you." Linn put her hands against his chest and felt the tensile power coiled in his body, building in the exquisite agony of anticipation, preparing for the headlong rush of release. She clung to him with all her strength; he reacted to her every movement, gripping her hips to impel her into a steady rhythm. His eyes were shut tight, as if he were lost in a fevered dream.

Linn leaned back from the circle of his arms and felt him touch her deeply. She gasped aloud, trembling, and fell forward, her hair surrounding Con's face. Con pulled her down to him and kissed her fiercely, the salt of their mingled perspiration lingering on his lips. When Linn drew back to kiss his brow, his cheek, she saw that his thick dark lashes were wet. She touched the tip of her tongue to his lids and heard his long, shuddering sigh.

He lay back and allowed her to set the pace, confident in his masculinity, encouraging her to explore the delights they could share. But Linn did not have his control. Carried away by the new, heady experience, directed by his forceful hands on her hips, she was soon caught up in the elemental quest for fulfillment, driving frantically to a conclusion that left them both spent and drained. Exhausted, she slipped slowly downward into the haven of his arms.

There was silence in the room for some time. Then Con said, "Marry me. Quit your job in the States and stay on Ildathach with me."

Linn didn't answer.

She felt him stiffen. "Aislinn? Do you not wish to marry me?" he inquired evenly. His regular tone was a facade for his true feelings; she could actually feel him holding his breath.

She kissed his damp shoulder. "Of course I want to marry you, more than anything in the world," she answered. "But I can't quit my teaching position just like that. It's not a job, it's a career. I have students, people are depending on me . . ."

The tension left him in a wave of relief. "Career, is it? God save me from American women," he growled.

"He's too late to save you from this one. You've proposed, and I've accepted. Now all we have to do is work out the details."

"Aye, like what continent we're going to live on."

"Oh, I see. Now that you've turned me into a shameless hussy, you're going to give me trouble about every little thing."

"I consider turning you into a shameless hussy my finest accomplishment," he replied, shifting onto his side to pull her closer.

"Con, be serious." Linn propped herself up on one arm to face him. "Why don't you come with me to the States? You can write anywhere, and you'd be a minor celebrity there now."

"Heaven forbid," he said with real feeling.

"Come on, why not? We could keep Ildathach for when I'm not working, and have two homes."

He shook his head. "This is where I belong. What would I be in America?"

"You'd be an Irish immigrant, of which there are millions, most of them flourishing like green bay trees. One of them even grew up to be president."

"Aye, and look what happened to him," Con said darkly.

"You're being ridiculous. You know you are."

"Where is your flat, your apartment?" he asked suspiciously.

"In suburban Jersey, about thirty minutes from New York."

Con groaned. "New York. I knew it. I hate New York; I hate that city."

Linn eyed him mischievously. "You sound like my godmother's husband, except he talks that way about the country. He's lived on Christopher Street in Greenwich Village all his life. Anytime he hears a suggestion about a picnic or a hike or anything rural, he uses a line he heard in a movie once: 'I don't like the country, the crickets make me nervous.'"

"The *subways* make me nervous. I was always lost."

Linn chuckled wickedly. "I promise I won't handcuff you and force you to ride the subway."

"You may well laugh," he said grimly. "I remember spending half a day riding back and forth endlessly until I finally found myself on the right street, but twenty-five blocks in the wrong direction. I walked twenty-five blocks uptown in the rain rather than get on a train again."

"Poor Conchubor," Linn mourned, grinning.

"Poor indeed. That was my second grandest New York adventure. The first was my arrival. There was I, all of twenty, sounding like a potato eater right off the boat, asking directions to the Solarium."

"The Solarium?" Linn asked, puzzled.

"I got the name wrong; I was looking for the Planetarium. It's no mystery I never found it."

They both dissolved in laughter. Linn sobered, still smiling, and indented his lower lip with a forefinger. "Con?"

He bit her finger gently. "What?"

"How did you learn to dance like that, the way you were dancing with me before? That was ballroom dancing; you wouldn't learn that growing up in Bally."

"Tracy taught me. I was groomed to have all the skills that would make me a suitable escort."

Linn absorbed that in silence. Then she said, "She really hurt you, didn't she?"

He kissed her forehead. "You've healed me entirely."

"Did you ever hear from her again after you left the States?"

He didn't answer for a moment, and then said, "She followed me back home the summer after I finished school. She called me from the airport and I met her there."

"And?"

"She wanted to resume our former relationship. I told her that I was one toy that was not for sale."

"Oh, Con, she must have cared to come so far after you."

"She didn't care enough." He left her abruptly and walked, naked, to the window. Linn followed, pulling the sheet around her as she went.

The view was breathtaking. In the glow of the floodlights Linn could see beyond the battlements to the islands in the center of the lake. The mountains loomed out of the evening mist like sentinels. The only touch of modernity was the splashing fountain; in all other respects it was a scene from a previous age.

"It looks like Camelot," Linn murmured. She pulled

the drapes closed and replugged the lamp, looking around at the suite. "And this is lovely, Con." It was. The sitting room contained a love seat and two Queen Anne chairs upholstered in the same flowered yellow silk that covered the walls. Their bed was a pine four-poster flanked by matching nightstands. The taupe antique satin drapes blended with the neutral Kirman rug on the floor. The transformation from medieval castle to luxurious hotel was so complete that it was a shock to look from the window and realize where she really was.

Con put his arm around her shoulder. "Only the best for you, my lady."

The band below them, which had taken a break, started playing again.

"Do you want to get dressed and go back downstairs? It's still early," Linn said.

"I want to stay undressed and go back to bed with you," Con answered.

"Okay," Linn agreed, and dove onto the mattress.

Con joined her and was wrestling her playfully into submission when there was a knock at the door.

They froze and looked at one another.

Con shrugged and got up to pull on his pants.

"Open up in there," a deep Irish voice said in a bad imitation of American gangster movies. "This is a raid."

Con turned back to Linn and rolled his eyes. "It's Chris," he said. He went to get the door.

Linn couldn't see anything from the bed, but there was a muffled conversation followed by subdued male laughter. Con returned shortly with a bottle and two long-stemmed glasses, a towel over his bare arm. He saluted Linn with the wine.

"Dom Perignon '67," he announced. "A gift from Mrs. Dugan's boy Christy."

Linn's eyes widened at the name of the expensive champagne. "You don't suppose he paid for it himself?"

Con wrestled with the cork, holding the bottle between his knees. "I doubt it," he grunted. "Nicked it, more likely."

"He stole it! He'll get into trouble."

"He will not. The chief steward is his brother-in-law. How do you think a lout like him got such a fancy job?" He popped the cork and poured the foaming, sparkling liquid into the glasses. He handed Linn one of them. She tucked the sheet under her arms and took it.

"*Slainte*," he toasted her, touching her glass with his.

"*Slainte go soaghal agat*," she replied.

Con took a sip, grinning, and rattled off a sentence in unfathomable Erse.

"Oh, shut up," Linn said, disgusted. "You're perfectly aware that the toast is the only phrase I know." She drank deeply, enjoying it.

Con set his glass on one of the night tables. "Then I must teach you," he said, taking her glass from her hand and putting it next to his.

Linn looked longingly after it but was distracted as Con picked up one end of her sheet and started peeling it away from her.

"Don't you want the wine?" she asked.

"I'd rather have you," he replied, tossing the sheet aside. He dropped next to her and began to caress her lightly.

"We'll lose the bubbles," Linn protested faintly, unable to muster up any real concern about it.

"That is a shame," he murmured, nibbling her earlobe.

"I like it better flat," Linn said, and pulled him down to her.

Linn awoke to a delicious sensation. She was face down on the bed, pale dawn light filtering into the room, and Con was leaving a trail of kisses along her spine. She stirred, sighing contentedly.

"Good morning, my lady," he murmured. "Lie still, now. Don't move."

Linn did as he said, remaining motionless as he crouched next to her and slowly kissed every inch of her body, from the soles of her feet to the tips of her fingers, until her whole frame of reference was limited to the velvety sensation of his lips against her skin. He continued with deliberate precision until she was squirming restlessly, trying to turn over, but he held her fast, tightly enough to stay her but not tightly enough to hurt.

"No," he said urgently. "I want you this way." He moved onto her, easing his weight down slowly on his arms. He slipped his hands under her and found her breasts. Linn raised her arms above her head and arched against his fingers eagerly, luxuriating in the hard fullness of his manhood pressing into the backs of her thighs.

Con slipped his hands down her body, molding her to him, impelling her upward and backward into his encompassing warmth and strength. He gently moved her legs apart, pushing her knees up to allow him access. When he entered her, Linn cried out softly with the sweetness of it, the sudden union with him and the tactile pleasure of his body against her back. She felt enveloped by his love for her, as if he were a shield to protect her from all harm. I could get pregnant, Linn thought for a brief moment; it would be so beautiful. Then all thought fled.

"Always so ready for me," he said in her ear, sweeping aside her hair to kiss the back of her neck. "I love you so much."

Linn met and matched his ardor, surging with him to a quick and satisfying completion. Con rolled to the side, pulling her with him and gathering her into his arms. With her eyes still closed, Linn pressed her face against his chest, not trusting herself to speak. His heartbeat slowed and steadied beneath her ear.

"I'll think about going to America, Aislinn, if you want it," he said quietly. "I'm not promising anything, mind, but if it means that much to you, I have to consider it."

Linn moved to look up at him, settling the back of her head into the curve of his arm. "Are you sure, Con? Could you be away from Ireland so much of the time? It's your home."

He lifted her to kiss her lips tenderly. "My home is where you are, Aislinn," he said. "You're my home."

Con settled back into the pillows with Linn folded against him, and they both fell asleep again as the sun rose.

Several hours later they had a leisurely breakfast in the Ashford dining room before Con drove back to Ballykinnon. He had several appointments in town that day, including what promised to be a long one with Larry Fitzgibbon concerning the foreign rights to one of Con's books. Linn had also been nagging him about getting Neil McCarthy to take a final look at his leg, and he promised to stop by the doctor's office and get it checked before he returned. Linn dropped him off at the lawyer's office, and Con said that he would get a ride back to Ildathach with Neil. It looked like Con would be occupied most of the day, so Linn took his car back home.

Driving Con's Bentley was an adventure in itself. Not only was the steering wheel on what Linn thought of as the wrong side of the car, but everyone drove on the wrong side of the road. The first time she was behind the wheel in Ireland she had the unsettling feeling that all the other drivers were aiming at her. She was getting better at dealing with the reversed situation on the road, but nothing could improve the quality of the local drivers. Irishmen drove cars the way they rode horses: like maniacs. Irish roads are for the most part narrow and winding, but that didn't slow the drivers down. Passing on two wheels on a curve was a favorite maneuver, along with riding the shoulder and using the horn for an armrest.

Linn arrived back at the main house to find a note from Bridie telling her that Father Daly had called on her and requested that she get back to him. This was not as surprising as it seemed; Bridie had doubtless put a flea in his ear about a potential wedding. Well, it wouldn't hurt to see him, and perhaps get some of the preparations under way. Linn put the note down, smiling at the penmanship. Bridie still wrote like the parochial school fourth-grader she had once been, with uniformly spaced letters and carefully drawn loops. A postscript indicated that she had gone grocery shopping and would be back later with Terry.

Linn looked up the telephone number of Saint Michael's rectory and went through the usual song and dance to get through to the priest's home. The only thing worse than Irish "telefon" service was Irish plumbing; all the showers dribbled cold water and the toilets gurgled menacingly with every flush. Despite such inconveniences, Linn was madly in love with the place. So much for Yankee materialism.

She drummed her fingers impatiently while waiting for an answer and finally was greeted by the voice of the housekeeper. Father Daly came on the line at once when he heard who was calling.

"Miss Pierce, I wonder if you could give me some time today," the priest began without ceremony. "There is something I must discuss with you."

Linn frowned at his tone. He didn't sound as though he was getting ready to talk about a wedding.

"Is something wrong, father?" she asked.

There was a pause. Then, "I would rather discuss this subject in person, Miss Pierce. Do you think you could come over to the rectory?"

"Now?"

"If it's convenient."

"Why, yes, I can, if you want me to."

"I do. I'll expect you directly, then. Good-bye." The line went dead.

Linn stood staring at the receiver in her hand, wondering what was going on. Had something happened to Karen, or Anne, one of her friends at home? But no, she would have been notified at the house. Feeling vaguely alarmed, Linn picked up Con's keys and went back outside to the car.

Linn drove back to the town she had just left, passing Larry's office on the way. She could see the top of Con's dark head through the window, above the lower frosted portion. He was sitting in the client's chair, facing Fitz's desk. He didn't see Linn go by in his car.

Linn parked outside the rectory and rang the bell. She was received by a gray-haired lady in a lace apron who led the way inside after Linn had announced herself. She was left in a spare, very clean sitting room by the housekeeper, who went to get the priest.

Father Daly was prompt. He arrived seconds later, walking over to shake Linn's hand as she stood to greet him.

"Miss Pierce, sit down. Alice, would you get us some tea, please?" he asked the other woman, who had returned with him.

The housekeeper nodded and departed in silence.

"I came as quickly as I could, father," Linn began.

The priest sat across from her and folded his hands in his lap. He looked like a man about to perform an unpleasant but necessary duty.

"Miss Pierce, this will be a difficult interview," he said slowly. "I have something to tell you that I think will upset you greatly."

"What is it?" Linn replied, her uneasiness growing.

Father Daly sighed heavily. "I have been observing

your relationship with Connor Clay and have heard the talk in the town. I generally disregard such gossip, but I saw for myself your attraction for the man at the Fleadh.''

Linn stared at him, baffled. Was this going to be a morals lecture?

Father Daly was stalled. ''Go on,'' Linn said sharply.

The priest closed his eyes. ''There is no easy way to say this, Miss Pierce.''

Linn waited.

Father Daly opened his eyes and looked at her.

''Connor Clay is your brother.''

Chapter 10

Father Daly's voice seemed to be coming from a distance.

"Are you going to faint, Miss Pierce?"

Linn shook her head, unable to speak.

The housekeeper came through the door with the tea tray, and the priest said quickly, "Bring Miss Pierce a glass of water."

The woman set down the tray and left, then returned from the back of the house with a tumbler of water. Father Daly turned to offer it to Linn and then thought better of it. He went to a mahogany rolltop desk which stood in a corner of the room and removed a bottle of Napoleon brandy from a drawer. He added a healthy slug of the liquor to the water and then held the glass out to Linn, signaling for Alice to leave.

Linn turned her head away.

"Take it, girl," he urged. "You need it. You're as white as boiled rice."

Linn accepted the drink mechanically, swallowing some of the burning liquid. She licked her lips and whispered, "It isn't true."

Father Daly examined her sadly, looking suddenly very old, the lines in his kindly middle-aged face seeming more pronounced. "It is true, more's the pity. Kevin Pierce, your father, was Con's father as well. I did not interfere before this because of promises I made long ago, when I was a young man, but when I saw the serious turn events were taking, I knew I had to speak up to prevent a tragedy."

Linn had a hysterical urge to laugh. *Prevent* a tragedy? This man, with one sentence, had just ruined her life.

"How?" she asked dully. "How did it happen?"

"Kevin made Con's mother pregnant before he left for the States," the priest answered simply. "Her marriage to Trevor Clay was made in order to cover her condition and give the child a father."

Linn looked up sharply, feeling a wild surge of hope. "Con told me he was born ten months after his mother and Clay were married," she said rapidly. "He knew that his mother had been in love with Kevin; he said she had never gotten over it. But Trevor Clay was his father."

Father Daly shook his head slowly, clearly unhappy to be dashing her argument. "No, lass. He thinks he was born ten months after the marriage because that's what he was told. Everyone here believes it too. He was born in England, you know, where Trevor supervised the mines, and when he and Mary came back to Ildathach they said the baby was three months younger than he actually was. A discrepancy of three months is easy to hide in a babe that age, an infant." He dropped his eyes from Linn's and turned away. "I'm the only one left who knows the truth," he added quietly.

"Tell me," Linn said evenly. "Tell me about it." She was amazed at her own control; while one part of her wanted to run screaming into the street, another part wanted to hear the chain of events that had conspired to separate her from Con before they had ever met. Even the pain of listening to the story would be preferable to the numbness that seemed to be engulfing her. The Ice Princess, freed from her cold prison by Con's love, was being enclosed again in a wall of ice.

Father Daly sat again and folded his hands in his lap. "If there is a villain in this piece," he began, "it was your grandfather, Dermot. A hard man, very hard. Con can be like him in that way, stubborn and unyielding. Dermot kept those two from having the life together that they should have had. He's paying for it now, I'll warrant, getting justice from a higher judge."

Linn listened, her eyes fastened on the priest's face.

"Mary Drennan worked at the house, a lovely girl, you have no idea how beautiful she was. Con doesn't resemble her much, except in the eyes. Hers were green, not blue, but had that same light, and the beautiful, full lashes. She was a sight to behold at twenty-one, slim, with a quick, graceful step and soft hair the color of honey."

Father Daly smiled at the memory, and Linn thought he sounded as if he'd been half in love with Mary himself.

"Kevin fell in love with her, and she with him. They were able to keep the affair secret for a while, but your grandfather had ways of finding out everything that went on about him. He was furious that his son was consorting with a servant—not up to standard, you see. Dermot was an awful snob. He packed Kevin off to the States on business, and while he was gone Dermot discovered that Mary was pregnant. He scared that poor girl half to death, let me tell you. You can't imagine what a terrible thing it was for a woman to be with child and unmarried thirty years ago, especially in this country. Dermot told Mary that Kevin would not be back, that he'd left the country expressly to be rid of her. Dermot persuaded Mary to marry Trevor Clay, an employee of his who had met Mary during a visit to Ildathach and admired her. Clay was a mining supervisor from England who looked after some interests Dermot had there. As I said, he liked Mary, and a few words from Dermot about the future of his position convinced him that he should marry her. So Mary was sent to Derbyshire, and the child was born there. After a while, when Dermot considered it safe, he brought the couple and the little boy back to the estate so he could keep an eye on his unacknowledged grandchild. Dermot gave the Clays the gatehouse, rent free, to live in all their lives, and when Con reached college age he paid for his education anonymously under the guise of a parish scholarship.''

"How could he play God like that?" Linn cried. "Those poor people, being manipulated by him as if he were a puppeteer and they were his marionettes."

The priest was silent, watching her closely to see if she was about to crack under the strain. Linn noticed his scrutiny and deliberately modulated her voice.

"And my father?" she asked quietly.

"Oh, when he heard that Mary had married in his absence, it broke his heart. I was his childhood friend, lass; we were at school together. When he received the news, he wrote to me and said that he could never come back to Ballykinnon and see Mary married to another. And as you know, he never did. He stayed in the States."

"And a few years later he married my mother," Linn whispered.

"Aye, so he did," the priest agreed. "But the whole situation caused a permanent break with Dermot. Kevin knew his father had had something to do with Mary's marriage, though he never knew about the child."

"How is it that you're the only one who knows this story?"

"The principals kept silent for obvious reasons, and they're dead now. I was brought into it after the fact when Mary and Trevor returned to Ildathach. Mary came to me and begged me to help her, telling me what had happened and asking me to keep her child's true paternity a secret. I could see no reason to hurt her and the innocent baby any more, so I altered the records, which had been sent from Britain, changing the date of Con's birth and listing Trevor as his father. I thought I was acting for the best, but look what has come of it." He bent his head. "God forgive me."

"He should forgive you for telling me about it!" Linn burst out, overcome with anger and despair.

The priest raised his head, his eyes wide. "Girl, the man is your half brother! Could I keep silent and abide an abomination?"

Linn closed her eyes, his final word lancing through her like the stroke of a knife. An abomination? Her love for Con, and his for her? It was the most precious, sacred, beautiful thing in her life, and he was trying to turn it into something foul and dirty.

"Don't you say that," she said in a low, dangerous voice, rising from her chair. "Don't you use that term again."

The priest stood also, alarmed. What was he going to do with a hysterical woman on his hands? He grabbed Linn's forearms and steered her back into her chair.

"Calm yourself," he soothed. "It will avail us nothing for you to become so upset."

Linn subsided, shaking, forcing herself to see reason. This man was not her enemy; none of this was his fault. He thought he was doing the right thing, and taking her feelings out on him wasn't fair.

"Where is your proof?" she asked coldly. "How do I know you're telling me the truth?"

Father Daly regarded her sadly. "Would I lie about such a thing? Think, girl, what reason would I have to inflict such cruelty?"

"I want to see the proof," Linn said flatly.

Father Daly sighed. "And so you shall, if you go to the office of patient records for Holy Rosary Hospital in Limerick. Con was brought there for a childhood illness, and the officials there consulted his birth records in Derbyshire for information. The hospital has a copy of Con's real papers." The priest bit his lower lip. "Don't fight it, child. That will not help you to accept it, as you must. You know in your heart that I have told you the truth."

Linn was silent, unable to disagree.

"You love Con very much, don't you?" the priest asked softly.

Linn nodded, her lower lip trembling as she fought off tears.

"Then don't tell him," Father Daly said. "Just go, and let him remember Trevor Clay as his father. Clay was a good man who cherished Mary and her child, and Con was devoted to him."

"I know that," Linn said, remembering Con's anguish over Trevor's unhappiness.

"Then just leave, without destroying his illusions. Your loss alone will be enough to bear without adding the hurt the truth would cause him."

Linn nodded again, dumbly.

"You must go now," the priest added sternly. "You cannot remain; you cannot stay together, surely you see that?"

Linn broke down. "I don't know how I can leave him," she sobbed. "I'll be leaving my soul behind on Ildat-hach."

The priest's resolve faltered for the first time. For just a second he forgot proprieties and biblical injunctions and the laws of the church he'd served for thirty-two years. His heart went out to the slight, pretty girl in the chair before him, crying as if she would never hope again.

He went to Linn and put his hand on her shoulder. "There, there. You must be strong, my child. God never sends us a burden heavier than we can bear." He took a wad of tissues from the pocket of his cassock and handed them to Linn.

She wiped her streaming eyes ineffectually. "I think he has this time. I don't want to live without Con. I can't."

"You can, and you will." Father Daly's expression became thoughtful. "Where is Con today?"

"He's in town, with Larry Fitzgibbon. They had some business to discuss."

Father Daly nodded. "That's good. You can pack while he's occupied and be gone before he gets back."

Linn stared at him, stunned. "Now? You mean I can't see him ever again?"

The priest eyed her levelly. "What would happen if you saw him?" he asked sternly.

Linn put her hand over her eyes. She knew what would happen. He would want to make love, and when she refused, he would demand to know why. She would wind up telling him about his father. She recoiled silently, afraid to think of the other possibility, the one uppermost in Father Daly's mind. If Con pressed her, would she give in? She loved and wanted him so much; would she sleep with him rather than tell him? And if so, what would that make her? She swallowed a shuddering sob and looked up to meet the priest's concerned gaze.

"I'll leave this afternoon," she said.

Father Daly sighed in relief. "How can I help you?"

Linn stood on legs that threatened to give way under her. She grasped the back of the chair for support.

"No one can help me," she said quietly.

The priest watched her struggle with admiration. This

was a brave lass. He knew he had dealt her a mortal blow, and she was staggering but still on her feet. Kevin would have been proud of her.

"Did you drive here?" he asked. "Can you drive back?"

"Yes. I have to return the car and get my things." She glanced around the room. "May I use your phone?"

"Certainly," Father Daly answered, indicating that she should go to his desk. As she picked up the receiver, he tiptoed past her and quietly left the room, shutting the door after him.

Linn called Bridie at Ildathach, hoping that she would be back. She was. She answered on the third ring.

"Bridie, it's Linn. I want you to do me a favor," Linn said, trying to keep her voice normal.

"Aye, what is it?"

"I'd like you to pack a bag for me, enough for overnight, and get my passport and travel things together. I'll be back in a few minutes, and I want to be able to just pick up and go."

"Where are you going?" Bridie asked, her voice unsure.

Linn put her hand over her mouth for a second, and then gained control. "I have to go back to the States right away. I can't explain now; it's too much to go into over the phone, but please just do as I ask. I'll be bringing the car back, and I'd appreciate it if you could look for that car rental information I got once before. I think I left it in the library on my grandfather's desk. I'll be needing transportation to the airport."

"What about Con?"

"Con can't know I'm leaving," Linn answered.

"Wait a bit! What is happening, Aislinn? Something's amiss. Tell me what it is."

Linn cleared her throat. "Please, Bridie, just do as I ask. If Con should call or come back early, just stall him or get rid of him for me, just long enough for me to get away. I know you don't understand, but do this on faith. I'm begging you. Please.''

There was a heavy sigh from the other end of the line. ''I'll pack for you. But I want an explanation when you get here.'' The line went dead.

Linn sagged against the wall and then steeled herself to make a second call. This one would be more difficult.

Larry Fitzgibbon's secretary answered.

''Hello, this Aislinn Pierce from out at Ildathach. Can you tell me if Mr. Clay is still with Mr. Fitzgibbon?''

''He's just after leaving, Miss Pierce. He was going on to Dr. McCarthy's, I think he said.''

Linn exhaled on a long breath. ''Then may I speak with Mr. Fitzgibbon, please? It will only take a moment.''

''Just as you say.'' There was a pause, and then Larry's vaudeville brogue came over the wire.

''Well, Aislinn. Connor was just here; you've missed him. If you wanted to give him a message, you're too late.''

''No, I wanted to ask you to do something for me.''

''Oh, aye? Whatever you say.''

''Larry, you're a lawyer and I'm your client. If I ask you to do something and keep it strictly confidential, would you?''

''Of course.'' The lawyer's tone had become guarded.

''All right. I want to deed Ildathach over to Connor Clay.''

The response was stunned silence for a moment, and then, ''You mean you want to convey it to him alone? But when you get married you can hold it jointly—''

The mention of marriage made Linn interrupt almost rudely. ''Larry, can you do it? I know you need time . . . and the proper papers . . . and witnesses, but can you set the process in motion? I don't want anyone to know about it, not even Con until it's done, but I want him to receive full title.''

There was another long pause, and then, ''I can do it.''

"Good. I'll be in touch with you about it again." Linn
didn't say that she would be calling him from New Jersey.
"And thanks, Larry. You were my first friend here, and
you've helped me. Good-bye."

It was only after she hung up that she realized her last
words to the lawyer had a definite ring of finality.

There was one more call to make, and Linn dreaded
making it. She wiped her eyes, then dialed the overseas
operator for international long distance and called Karen
in New York, asking the operator to make it collect.

To Linn's enormous relief, Karen answered. She ran
her own business from her brownstone and was often out
making deliveries. The operator identified the caller, and
Karen accepted the charges, her tone changing to de-
lighted expectation when she heard that it was Linn.

The sound of her godmother's voice almost caused Linn
to falter. She waited a few seconds before saying tentatively, "Karen?"

"Linn? Is that you?"

"Yes."

"Oh, it's wonderful to hear from you! How is that
gorgeous man you wrote me about?"

"Karen, I'm calling because I need you to pick me up at
Kennedy tomorrow. I don't know the time or the airline or
the flight number, nothing is arranged yet, but I will be
arriving sometime during the next day or so. When the
flight's booked, I'll send you a telex and you'll get it on
the machine in your office."

"Fine, honey," Karen answered, sounding puzzled,
"but why are you returning so soon? Are you bringing
Con with you? Do you want us to meet him?"

Linn's knuckles on the hand that held the phone were
turning white. "No, he isn't coming. I just need a ride
back from the airport. I left my car at home on the way
over; I took a taxi from my apartment."

"I understand that, but there's something you're not
telling me. Did something happen with your beau?"

"Yes," Linn whispered.

"What is it, Linn?"

The line crackled with interference, and Linn was grateful because it gave her an excuse to cut the conversation short.

"Karen, I can hardly hear you. Just look for the telex, and come for me when I get in, okay? Thanks a lot. I'll see you soon." Linn hung up the receiver, realizing that she had broken into a cold sweat. She took the last of Father Daly's tissues and wiped her forehead with them. Then she picked up her purse and left the room.

The priest was waiting in the hall. He walked her out to Con's car and offered again to drive her back to Ildathach.

"I'm all right, father. I'll get there in one piece."

"Take care of yourself, Aislinn Pierce. It's sorry I am that things turned out this way."

Linn got into the car and looked through the window at the man who had brought her the most unwelcome news imaginable. She didn't know what to say to him.

Father Daly understood. "Just go now. God go with you."

Linn drove away from the rectory, not looking back.

She went out of her way to avoid the main street for fear of seeing Con, and drove halfway up the mountain and down again to reach Ildathach by the other route. She couldn't see too well; her eyes kept misting over, and once she was forced to stop. The trip took twice as long as it should have, but she finally got back and left the Bentley parked in front of the main house.

Bridie was waiting for her in the front hall. Ned emerged from the kitchen to greet her, winding himself sinuously about her legs.

"Your bags are there, ready to go," Bridie said, pointing to the hand luggage on the floor. "Do you mind telling me what this is all about?"

Linn picked up the tote and checked for her passport and other essentials. Everything was there.

"Did you find the number of the auto rental place?" she asked.

"I did not. You're not renting anything. If you're going anywhere, Terence will take you; he's out back working on his bike. But first you'll be explaining yourself, Miss America, or my name isn't Bridget Conlan Cleary." She folded her arms on her chest and stood between Linn and the door.

Linn almost wailed with frustration. She'd guessed Bridie would do this, but facing her, knowing Con's secret, was worse than she had imagined. "I have to go," she said wildly. "I just have to go, that's all."

"Without a word of explanation for that boy who loves you like part of himself? You won't get past me, my girl."

"I'll leave him a note," Linn said desperately.

"A note! That's a fine thing," Bridie said disgustedly. "He'll be very happy with that, I'm sure."

Linn decided to take a different tack and play her departure down. "I'm just going back to teach a pre-session course at my school," she lied. "I'm not vanishing from the face of the earth."

"Tell it to the Scots," Bridie said, shaking her head, not buying it for a minute. "This looks like headlong flight to me, and it will to Connor as well. What am I supposed to say to him?"

Linn twisted the strap of the tote in her fingers, trying to think of a reply. The events of the day were proving too much; her mind was a blank.

"He'll follow," Bridie said softly. "You know how he is; he'll follow wherever you go."

"You mustn't tell him where I am!" Linn cried, alarmed.

"I certainly will. I never saw such tinker's manners in my life. He thinks that he's going to *marry* you, lass. Doesn't that mean anything to you?"

"I'll call for a car and you won't know where I've

gone. There are hundreds of hotels in this country. I'll be on a plane before he finds me.''

Bridie planted her feet more firmly on the tile floor, indicating her unwillingness to budge. ''I don't think you're as heartless as that.''

Linn was almost in tears. Time was passing, as Bridie knew, and Linn suspected she was trying to delay her long enough for Con to return. She simply could not face him. She would have to tell Bridie so that the housekeeper would help her get away.

''What is it, girl?'' Bridie asked, sensing her weakening resistance. ''It's no good lying to me. I can see you're on the verge of collapse.''

Linn blinked rapidly, pushing back the wayward strands of hair falling across her face. ''Bridie, will you swear never to tell another soul? Will you swear before God to keep what I tell you a secret?''

Bridie's eyes went wide; she was very religious and took such things seriously.

''I will. What has happened, Aislinn?''

''Say it. Say that you swear before God you won't ever repeat what I'm going to tell you.''

Bridie pronounced the oath, blessing herself at its conclusion, and Linn was satisfied. The housekeeper would take whatever Linn told her to her grave.

''I went to see Father Daly today. He told me that . . . that . . .'' She squeezed her eyes shut. ''He told me that Kevin Pierce was Con's father. He told me that Con is my half brother.''

When Linn opened her eyes, Bridie was leaning against the entry hall table, her face ashen. ''It's never true,'' she whispered.

''It is. Father Daly wouldn't lie, and besides, Con told me all about our parents when I met him. I knew that Kevin and Con's mother had been in love, but Con thinks he was born ten months after his mother married Trevor

Clay." She dropped her eyes. "It was seven months. Father Daly changed the records."

"Merciful Jesus," Bridie murmured. "You poor lambs."

"You never guessed?" Linn asked. "I don't understand why no one even suspected, if everybody in town knew about my father and Mary Drennan."

Bridie shrugged, recovering slightly. "Why should anyone suspect anything? Kevin left, and Mary got married on the rebound to a man who'd always admired her. Rejected, abandoned women do that all the time. And when she showed up back at Ildathach almost two years later with an infant, why would anyone think it wasn't her husband's? A baby is a baby at that age. What's three months?"

So Father Daly had thought thirty years ago, and his small act of kindness to a distraught young mother had led to Linn's present heartbreak.

Bridie straightened up. "I'll get Terence to drive you; you can't wait for a car. Don't tell me where you're going. Con will try to get it out of me and it's best I don't know. Hustle up, now, here's your jacket."

Linn's revelation had immediately altered Bridie's thinking. She was now as anxious for Linn to go as Linn was. She ran to get Terry.

The boy appeared, wiping his hands on a greasy rag, puzzled by the air of urgency about the two women. He nodded at his mother's directions and picked up Linn's bags, taking them outside to stow them on his bike.

Linn grabbed a sheet of paper and dashed off a note to Con, repeating the story about a presession course that she had tried out on Bridie. It was feeble at best, and if it had failed to convince the housekeeper, Con would see through it in a second. She was too distraught to think of anything else, and yet she couldn't accept the cruelty of departing without a word to him.

Bridie flung her arms around Linn as she picked Ned up from the floor and kissed him a quick farewell. He leaped down to avoid being crushed.

"I know you must go, but write to me. I'll miss you so," Bridie said, her mouth working. "Oh, my poor Aislinn. My poor Conchubor."

"I'll write as soon as I can," Linn replied, embracing her tearfully. "I'll miss you almost as much as . . ." She let the sentence trail off, and they both understood. "Try to take care of him," she sobbed, and left.

Terry was waiting for her, the bike idling under him. She climbed on behind him and glanced around at her beloved Ildathach.

Good-bye, my home, she thought. Good-bye, my love.

Linn put her face against the back of Terry's leather jacket and let the hot tears stream down her face as the boy pulled away.

"Take me to Holy Rosary Hospital in Limerick," she said in his ear, and Terry nodded, taking Linn down the lane to the road for the last time.

Terry's bike had just vanished around the bend toward Limerick when Neil McCarthy's Ford Cortina appeared at the gates of Ildathach.

Con was inside it, sitting next to the driver, gesturing broadly, punctuating some story.

He was laughing.

Linn took her leave of Terry on the sidewalk outside the hospital. She didn't want him to be able to tell Con where she went.

"I'll be fine here, Terry, you can go. I have some business inside, and then I'll get a cab. Please tell your mother I'll send for the rest of my things, and thank her for everything."

Terry's face changed. "You're leaving for good, miss?" he asked.

Linn nodded. Of course he didn't know; Bridie had been careful to tell him very little.

"Safe journey, then," he said quietly. "Good luck to you."

Linn looked at him, feeling a rush of affection for this canny, comely teenager who had chauffered her around for six weeks without complaint when he doubtless had better things to do. Despite his Casanova tendencies, he was as generous in his own way as his darling, fussbudget mother. She took a step toward him and hugged him impulsively.

To her surprise, he pulled away, taking a deep breath, shaking his head.

"Your man told me to keep off from you, and I'll not tangle with the likes of him," Terry said.

Linn sighed. "It's all right, Terry. Con was just trying to protect me, but it doesn't matter now. Don't worry about it."

"You really aren't coming back?" Terry asked.

Linn shook her head.

"But he loves you, miss, he really does."

Linn closed her eyes to clear her vision. She opened them and said, "I know that, Terry. I have to go in now. Be good to your mother, and stay out of trouble." She turned and ran up the broad steps of the hospital, head down, intent on her mission.

At Holy Rosary, the files weren't computerized and microfilmed as in American hospitals, but they also didn't have American confidentiality-of-records laws. A very helpful clerk looked up the patient lists for the years during which Linn guessed Con might have been admitted. Everything was alphabetized, and Clay was only the third letter in the alphabet. It didn't take long to discover that Connor Liam Clay, age seven, had been there in March of 1959 for a problem that had necessitated his physician's sending for his birth records. A faded copy of his handwritten birth certificate was attached. It stated that Connor Clay was the child of Mary Drennan Clay, age twenty-two, of Horsham, Derbyshire, England, an Irish citizen, and Kevin Michael Pierce, age twenty-six, of Elmwood Park, New Jersey, U.S.A., also an Irish citizen. The birth date listed was February 18, 1952.

Con had told her that his birthday was in May.

Linn gave up her last shred of hope. Her father had still been living in Elmwood Park when he met her mother; Linn had gone to school there until she was ten. There was no mistake.

She and Con had the same father.

Linn thanked the clerk politely for her help and walked outside into the mild, slightly cloudy Irish day. She hailed a cab in the street and told the driver to take her to a hotel with easy access to the airport. And when she got there, she booked a 9:30 A.M. flight for New York from her room phone.

Then, even though it was only late afternoon, she fell on the bed in exhaustion, grateful for the oblivion of sleep.

Linn was awakened in the middle of the night by the sound of Con pounding on her hotel room door. Confused with sleep, terrified of what she might do if she saw him, touched him again, she stumbled out of bed and backed a chair against the door.

"Go away," she screamed, trying to make herself heard over his shouts for admittance. "I don't want to see you."

The response was a splintering crash as Con broke down the door, overturning the chair and kicking it out of his way. He confronted her wildly, his face dark with stubble, brandishing the note she had left for him. He was drunk, or very close to it, swaying slightly on his feet, his eyes narrowed and mean. For the first time since she'd known Con, Linn was physically afraid of him. She had never thought before of the damage he could do with his tremendous strength, his powerful body, because he had always been so gentle with her. But now she remembered Bridie's comment about his temper: You don't want to be around when it erupts. He had demolished the hotel's door as if it were made of cardboard. She backed away from him, and he advanced menacingly.

"Don't be frightened, Aislinn," he said softly, the drink—or his emotions—enhancing his brogue. "Another man might break you in half for this loving farewell," he sneered, waving the piece of paper, "but I will not. I haven't come to kill you; I've come for an explanation."

Linn swallowed, squaring her shoulders. She would have to calm him down or he might destroy the place, using the hotel's furniture as a substitute for her.

"Your explanation is in your hand," she said, striving for a normal tone. "That says I'm going back to New Jersey to teach a presession course."

"Don't give me that!" he shouted, lunging forward. "Do you think for a moment I don't know what this is? This is the kiss-off, the—what do you call it—the Dear John letter. You're running out on me!"

The scene was interrupted by the hotel manager and a security man, summoned by the noise. They came through the ragged doorway, looked at Con and glanced at each other. The security man reached for his gun.

Linn raced across the room, putting herself between Con and the men. "I'll pay for the damage," she said rapidly. "I'll pay for everything. Please just let me handle this. He'll be all right."

"I will not," Con said belligerently, moving toward the newcomers, his progress made slower and clumsier by his condition. He lurched to a stop, his jaw thrust forward pugnaciously. He collared the manager and said, "You got something to say to me, boyo?"

Linn could see that any discussion would be concluded

with the use of Con's fists. He was itching for a fight in order to give vent to the pain she had caused him.

"Please go. He won't break anything else. He wanted to talk to me and I wouldn't let him in; this is my fault," she said, clinging to the security man's arm.

He looked down at her.

"You didn't mash in the door, miss."

Linn closed her eyes. "If you try to take him out or call the police, he will trash you and your hotel before you get him to the street. Please just trust me and go."

This argument clearly carried weight. The manager and the other man sized up Con, who was still gripping the former's lapel. Linn could see that they believed her.

"Well, all right, miss, just as you say," the manager agreed. "But if I hear another sound from this hall, I'll be calling the garda, and no mistake." He shrugged loose from Con's hand and turned away.

"Thank you, thank you," Linn babbled, ushering them from the room. "Just add the cost of the door to my bill."

"I will that, and mind what I said," the manager flung back at her, having the last word. "No more noise, now."

Linn nodded and turned back into the room, where Con awaited her.

"Don't you think you should have kept them for protection?" he demanded. "You might be in mortal danger from the likes of me."

Linn met his eyes. "I think you'd cut off your arm before you'd hurt me."

She saw the impact of her statement in his face. He closed his eyes and bowed his head.

"That's the truth of it," he said quietly.

Linn dug her nails into her palms to prevent herself from running to him. Being forced to witness his pain was the cruelest torment she had ever experienced.

"How did you find me?" she whispered.

"Terry. Terry told me where you were."

"Con, you didn't hurt that boy!"

He gave a snort of mirthless laughter. "Oh, I didn't have to, not at all."

"But he didn't see where I went."

"Oh, aye, he did. He waited outside while you were in the hospital, and then trailed you here when you took the cab."

"But why?"

"Because he felt sorry for me!" Con barked, flinging his hands wide to indicate his amazement. "My lady was taking off, ditching me like a bundle of trash for the dustbin, and he thought I should have another chance to talk to you. That's what you've done to me, Aislinn. I'm reduced to being pitied by romantic teenagers." He shook his head as if he still couldn't believe it.

"I'm sorry, Con," Linn murmured. She could well imagine how that had injured his pride.

"Oh, sorry doesn't cover it," he responded, eyeing her. "There was I, in every hotel and hotel *bar* in Shannon, looking for you, and as I'm leaving one place Terry comes roaring up on his bike to tell me the news. What were you doing in the hospital, Aislinn? Why did you go there?"

She didn't answer.

"Not talking, are you? You and Bridie have suddenly turned into the silent sisters." He reached out and grabbed her arm. "Tell me why you're leaving me. Tell me."

Linn hung her head until he thrust his hand under her chin and forced her to look up at him.

"What is it? Did you decide you couldn't leave your grand job in America, that you couldn't take the chance I wouldn't go with you to the States? I realize I hardly stack up against such a wonderful *career*."

Linn's heart was breaking. He was stabbing at improbabilities in his desperate struggle to understand what could not be understood.

"Or is it that you can't commit yourself to a real man

after that pansy you were married to?'' he spat. ''Well, you might not be able to push me around, but I'll promise you would never have a cold bed.''

She willed herself not to cry. She would endure this, and then he would go, and it would be over.

He released her so suddenly that she stumbled. ''You're no different from Tracy,'' he said disgustedly. ''You've had your fun and now the vacation's over and it's time to go home.''

''Please don't say that,'' she whispered. ''It isn't true.''

''Then tell me what is true,'' he demanded.

''I have to go back to teach a course,'' she repeated pathetically.

Con seized her and backed her against a wall. ''Oh, you are a liar,'' he gritted between his teeth. ''I would shake you senseless if I thought it would make you tell me, but it will not.'' He spun her around and flung her away from him. ''Go, then. Go back to America, go back to teaching, go straight to hell.''

I'm there, Linn thought. I'm there already.

Con took a deep breath and steadied himself with his hand on the bedpost. The liquor seemed to be having less effect on him now; his anger was clearing his head.

''But you remember this, Aislinn,'' he said softly. ''You are *mine* and will be mine always, no matter where you go or what you do. You bear my mark, invisible though it may be, and it can never be removed.'' He took a step forward and slid his hands beneath her hair, encircling her neck with his fingers. ''You will never want another man the way you want me, and you will never experience with another man what you have with me.'' He rubbed his thumbs along her throat, and she responded, as he'd known she would. ''In your American bed, with whatever American lover you choose, you will wish that I were kissing you, holding you, loving you. And when you feel him move inside you, it's my name you will call.''

A hot tear slipped from her lashes and fell on his hand. He lifted the salty droplet to his lips.

"Tears, Aislinn? Why? Are you sad to go, or do you just wish that *I* would go? Well, how's this. You tell me that you don't love me, and I will leave you alone."

"I never said I didn't love you," Linn moaned, hardly realizing that she'd spoken the words.

His fingers dug into her shoulders. "Then why would you leave me and create a torment for us both?" He pulled her violently into his arms. "You are the love of my life," he whispered, his hands moving over her body. "I will have no other." He drew back and looked into her eyes, his own vulnerable and filled with feeling. "I will have no other," he repeated, moving his head slowly from side to side.

Linn sagged against him, unable to keep up the facade. This was Con, and she loved him so. He sensed the change in her and pressed his advantage, reasserting his claim on her in the most fundamental way possible. He lifted her gently and lowered her to the bed.

"You promised me you would never leave me," he said feverishly, "and I'm not going to let you go." He covered her face and neck with wild kisses, murmuring incoherently under his breath, and Linn writhed beneath him, famished for his touch. The smell of the liquor and his heated body only intensified her reaction; she had thought never to feel his mouth, his hands again. He pulled at her clothes, slipping his hand inside her panties.

"Ah, you want me," he moaned, his fingers stroking her. "You love me still."

"Yes, yes," Linn whispered, "I love you, Con. I want to stay with you." She sought his mouth again, kissing him deeply, and a sound like a sob tore from Con's throat. He fumbled for the buckle of his belt.

Linn stirred restlessly, impatient for him, and her half-closed eyes rested on the scrap of paper lying on the floor. It was the note she'd left for Con, and in an instant she recalled the reason she'd written it. Dear God, what was she doing? This was her brother!

She wrenched away from him violently, pushing him off her.

"Let me go!" she cried hysterically. "Get away from me!"

Con crouched next to her on the bed, staring, sobered instantly by her irrational vehemence. His own emotions slipped into the background in his concern for Linn. She was afraid, but not of him. She was afraid of herself. Something was terribly, frightfully wrong. He reached for her again, to comfort her, and she recoiled in horror.

"Don't touch me!" she gasped, holding out her hands to fend him off. "Please don't touch me. Con, oh Con, you're my brother."

He froze in shock, his eyes widening, fastened on her face. He couldn't speak.

Linn nodded, her lips bitten raw with her efforts at self-control. "Kevin Pierce was your father."

Con swallowed hard, then rasped, "I don't believe it." He was trembling, his accent intensified.

"Oh, it's true, it's true. My God, do you think I would leave you for anything else?" Linn pushed herself off the bed, putting some distance between them. If he tried again, her will was not equal to the test, and she knew it.

"Who told you this?" Con asked hoarsely.

"Father Daly. He changed your records in Bally to make it look like you were born three months later than you were. Your birthday isn't in May, Con; it's in February. My father got your mother pregnant before he left Ireland, and Dermot arranged her marriage to Trevor Clay."

Con dropped his eyes, trying to comprehend it. He had the expression occasioned by sudden death, sudden tragic loss: the blank, inward stare of a person who is simply trying to absorb what has happened.

"I went to Holy Rosary Hospital to check on your

records. They have a copy of your birth certificate there, and it confirms what Father Daly said. That's why I was leaving Con, not because I want to, but because I must.''

"There could be a mistake," he muttered. Linn closed her eyes. It was agonizing to watch him take the same path that she had taken, clinging to straws, refusing to accept that this awful thing was true. Sweet Jesus, could she spare him nothing? She was hurting the one person she loved best in the world, and she was powerless to stop it.

"There's no mistake. But my father loved your mother, Con; he didn't know about you, ever. Dermot tricked him, making it look like Mary had decided to marry Trevor while he was gone. He told Mary that Kevin wasn't coming back. My father—and yours—was no monster, but the good and decent man that I remember.''

"That's cold comfort when I can't have you!" Con ground out. "I would rather fate had given me a monster for a father than sentenced me to a life without you!"

"I didn't want to tell you," Linn said sadly. "I tried not to tell you.''

"Maybe . . ." Con mumbled, looking around him urgently. "Maybe the birth certificate is wrong. . . .''

"Darling, darling, listen to me. Don't do this to yourself; I've been through it all already. Now that I know it's true, I can see the signs. Why do you think I felt that instant bond with you? How could I have trusted you when I had gone for years alone after my disastrous marriage? I think now it was because, in some unconscious way, you . . .''

"I reminded you of your father," he finished dully.

"Yes," she whispered, destroyed by the knowledge. "You don't look like him, except for the color of your hair, but you have some of his mannerisms. The way you incline your head . . .''

"What?" he said. He was unaware of it.

"And," she went on, as if talking to herself, "that half

smile, like you have a secret on the world. He used to smile that way too. Oh, Con, I didn't want to admit it either, but it is true."

His eyes drifted away from hers and looked into the distance.

"What will become of us?" he said. "Aislinn, what will become of us?"

Linn wiped her cheek with the back of her hand, shaking her head.

"I don't know," she said on a trembling sigh. "I've done nothing else but wonder the same thing."

Con stood abruptly and took out his wallet, dropping a wad of brightly colored Irish money on the dresser. "This will pay for the door," he said dazedly. He adjusted his clothes and tucked his shirt back into his jeans.

"Where are you going?" Linn asked, suddenly frightened. Armed with this awful knowledge, what might he do?

"I have to get away," he said, moving toward the door. "Don't worry, I'm not going to hurt anybody, but I must go."

Linn put her hand on his arm. He shrugged it off.

"Leave me be, Aislinn," he said in a strangled voice. "Leave me be!"

He dashed out through the doorless entrance and Linn heard his footsteps pounding down the hall.

She sank into the hotel armchair and put her head in her hands.

Con ran out through the lobby and into the adjacent alley. He stopped, panting, and leaned against the brick wall of the building he had just left. After a moment the night silence was broken by the sound of choking, wracking sobs, the crying of a man who has forgotten how to cry, a man who hasn't cried since childhood. His broad shoulders shook with the force of his emotion, and he wiped his streaming eyes with the back of his arm. He hadn't cried since his father had died. No, not his father. The man who had raised him, but not his father.

Aislinn, he thought, moaning softly. His Aislinn was lost to him forever.

Con took a deep, shuddering breath and looked up at the night sky. The stars shone; the clouds drifted across the moon, just as they had before and would again. Why wasn't there some sign that two lives had just been thrown away by the mistakes of a previous generation? It wasn't fair. No, it wasn't fair!

He thought about how she loved his book of poetry, envisioned her rapt face as she'd listened to him tell the story of its title. *The Eden Tree*.

They had created their own garden, with a new tree, and the forbidden fruit was each other.

Chapter 11

LINN FLEW BACK TO NEW YORK THE NEXT MORNING. SHE had little recollection of the flight, except for one interruption from a stewardess who asked her if something was wrong. Linn had been listening to music through the headphones, a sad song about a lost happy past. When the vocalist got to the line that said, "I remember a time I knew what happiness was. Let the memory live again," Linn started to cry. The attendant had seen the silent tears flowing down her cheeks.

Linn lectured herself sternly as she walked through the airport reception building. "I have to stop crying all the time; I have to start eating; I have to call a halt to this walking nervous breakdown." She repeated this line as she moved along, but it didn't help. The double loss of Con and of Ireland was too much. She couldn't think of going back there; the country was tied up with the man. Never again to see the green fields, the cloudy, opalescent sky, feel the cool, salty breeze, or hear a soft voice saying, "I will," or "I am." The Irish disliked the use of "yes" and "no"; there were no words for them in Gaelic, and they carried their custom over into English. The vaguely Celtic "aye" was the only concession they would make.

And the people themselves—generous, witty. Gone, all of it, never to be recaptured. Linn mourned the passing of her emerald summer with Con.

Karen was waiting for Linn at the gate. She took one of Linn's bags from her hand silently, and then said, "I don't have to tell you that you look awful."

"Please, Karen, I appreciate your coming for me, but no lectures, all right?"

"Aren't you even going to tell me what happened?"

"I can't talk about it now; it's too painful. I'm exerting all my energy to deal with it. Don't press me for details, okay?"

"You're not pregnant, are you?"

Linn shook her head. Before her visit to Father Daly, she hadn't been concerned about getting pregnant; in fact, she had been half hoping. . . . But after she knew about Con's true parentage, it had become a possibility too horrible to contemplate. She'd found out on the plane that she was safe, one small spark of relief in a dark cloud of misery.

"I don't like the way you look," Karen insisted. "I think you should see a doctor. I can make an appointment with Dr. Cross if you like."

"All I need is rest. I'd like to go home and get to bed, if you don't mind."

Karen eyed her warily all through the drive back to Jersey but maintained a tactful reserve. She dropped Linn off in front of her apartment complex and said, "Are you sure you don't want me to come up for a little while? I could fix you something to eat; you can't tell me you couldn't use a decent meal."

"No thanks. I'll call you tomorrow. Don't worry, I'll be fine."

"Where is the rest of your luggage?"

"I'm having it sent."

"You left in a hurry, I see."

"Karen, I'll call you tomorrow. Good-bye." Linn slammed the door of Karen's station wagon and wearily walked up the path to her apartment.

She unlocked the door to find everything as she'd left it. It was odd; she felt so different, and yet the furniture, the pictures on the walls, the potted plants all stared back at her with customary indifference. It was the same old place, but she wasn't the same old Aislinn. She tossed her bags on a chair and collapsed on the sofa.

Well, Linn thought, what happens now? I go back to my job, back to loneliness, back to my empty former life. And as for the future, who could know? Would she wind up batty like Amanda Wingfield, patient in chiffon, waiting for a gentleman caller who never came? Would she become one of those crazy old ladies who bore people endlessly with stories of a lost youthful lover? She sure as hell wasn't going to fall headlong into happiness. There was only one Connor Clay.

Linn got up slowly and went to the bedroom, putting her copy of *A Terrible Beauty* on the shelf above the bed. It was the hardcover edition, which she'd purchased at the airport on her return trip. She already owned a paperback edition, but this one had Con's picture on the back. Above the caption "Trevor Drennan" and the brief biography, his beloved eyes looked into hers. He was standing on a Dublin street corner, a corduroy jacket hooked over his shoulder, his hair stirred by the wind. The photographer had captured that faintly quizzical look she loved: Con's head tilted to one side, his chin lifted, his mouth firm and serious. She stared at the dust jacket for a moment, and then flung the book across the room.

She crawled onto the bed and stared at the ceiling until she finally fell asleep.

Several days passed, and Linn was determined to keep busy. She went in to her office and began organizing things for the fall term, drawing up book lists, compiling course outlines. Work helped during the day, but the nights were endless. She took long walks; she went to the movies alone; she went shopping with Karen—anything to occupy her time. Unoccupied hours left her free to think, and that was a mistake.

She was having a cup of coffee in the faculty lounge one afternoon when the secretary opened the door and said, "Linn, there's somebody here looking for you—tall guy with curly dark hair, sounds sort of British or something . . . ''

Linn dashed past her and went running down the hall.

Con was waiting in front of her office, his hand on the nameplate that read Dr. Aislinn Pierce. He looked around at her approach and dropped his hand.

Linn stopped a few feet away from him. "Hello, Con."

He smiled his slight, all-eyes-and-very-little-mouth smile. "Hello, Aislinn."

Just the sound of her name on his lips was enough to make her knees weak. She unlocked the office door and they entered her small, paneled cubbyhole. Linn locked the door behind them.

Con stood until she indicated that he should sit. They were both very formal and restrained, as if one wrong word would send the earth spinning out of orbit.

Linn perched on the edge of her desk and looked at him. He was wearing a beige turtleneck and tan chino pants, which was dressed up for him. He looked thinner, preoccupied, but as attractive as ever. Linn wanted to feel his arms around her so badly that it was a moment before she could trust herself to speak.

"How did you find out where I worked?" she asked him.

"By the same method I discovered that I'll shortly be coming into a piece of real estate," he answered, watching her face.

Linn sighed in defeat. "I asked Larry not to tell you. He promised me he wouldn't."

"He didn't. His secretary is Mary Costello's aunt."

Linn nodded slowly. She should have known better than to think that such a thing could be kept quiet in Bally.

"I'll not take it, Aislinn," he said quietly. "That's no prize to substitute for you."

"It should be yours, Con, by right. By primogeniture, the property passes to the eldest son. That's still the custom, if not the law, in Ireland."

He stood abruptly, thrusting his hands through his hair. "Christ, Aislinn, don't quote me common law. You know what I mean. Too much has happened; I'd rather see the place go to charity."

"You can give it away if you want once you get it. Dispose of it any way you please once it's yours."

"You wouldn't care?"

Linn met his eyes. "I feel the same way you do, Con. Too much has happened." She forced a smile. "How have you been?"

He stared at her as if she were deranged. "Oh, smashing, what do you think? I've been grand, just grand."

Linn looked away.

He grabbed her arm and forced her to face him. "I'll tell you how I've been. I can't sleep again. Couldn't sleep before I met you, can't sleep now. I can, however, drink. I've been just a little drunk every day since you left." He put his palms on either side of her face, looking into her eyes. "I love you. I wake up loving you. I drink myself to sleep loving you. All day long, I love you. What am I going to do with all this love?"

Linn tried to twist free of his hands. "Don't, Con. Please don't."

He held her fast. "Aislinn, listen to me. The only one who knows our story is Father Daly. We could go anywhere else in the world but Bally and live as man and wife. Who would know?"

Linn looked back at him despairingly. "We would know, Con. We would. Can you live with that?"

"I can't live without you!" he ground out, letting her go. "I'm trying, but it's like being condemned to a punishment when there's been no crime."

"We could never have children," she whispered.

"I don't care, if I can have you," he answered, his eyes pleading.

Linn wrenched herself away from his tortured gaze, emotionally ravaged by the depth of a need which would prompt such a desperate suggestion. "No, Con, no. Our lives would be haunted by the knowledge of our true relationship, and in the end it would destroy us both."

Con seized her again, pulling her into his arms. "You're destroying me right now. Come with me, Aislinn. Don't let me go back alone."

Linn stood like wood in his arms, forcing herself to remain unresponsive.

"Please don't touch me, Con," she said quietly.

He released her immediately, stepping back and looking at her with huge, defeated eyes. "I can remember a time when you begged me to touch you," he said in a low tone heavy with surrender.

She met his gaze, acknowledging the memory of words that could never be spoken again.

He cleared his throat. "All right, Aislinn. I can't force you, and God knows I don't want to." He put his hand into his pocket and came out with a small jeweler's box. "I thought you should have this. It was my mother's and I had the inscription put on before . . ." He stopped, and then continued. "I don't know what the bloody hell to do with it; I can't bear to look at it anymore." He picked up her hand and put the box into her palm.

Linn opened the hinged cover. It was a Celtic cross, wrought in silver and studded with marcasites. She turned it over and looked at the back.

"Ildathach," she read aloud, "August 2."

It was the date of the Fleadh, the first time they'd made love.

"Thank you, Con," she whispered. "I'll wear it always."

"Think of me," he said, his voice breaking. He turned away, and she knew that he was choking back tears. It was terrible to see him so wretched; even his strength and force of will could be sapped by the hopeless need of something, someone, he could never have.

When he turned back to her he was composed, even attempting a smile.

"I'll go now; I don't want to upset you more than I already have." He took her chin in his hand and said, "Good-bye, my lady. You *are* my lady, Aislinn, and you always will be, though we may never see each other again. A hundred secrets from the past could not change that." He ran his thumb over her lips, and Linn finally, despite every effort, started to cry.

"Don't, Aislinn," he said gently. "I want to remember a smiling face."

"I'm sorry, Con; I was trying to be so brave. But I'm no good at it. I'm just too weak."

"You are not; never say that. You are the bravest, strongest woman I've ever met. There aren't many who could go through what you have these past few weeks with only a few tears to mark the experience. I will always think of you as that plucky little lady who took on the whole town and sang for me, showing them all how you felt."

Linn closed her eyes. She was dangerously close to begging him to stay with her. "Please go, Con," she said softly. "Don't say anything else; this is too hard."

His hand fell away from her face. She felt the touch of his lips on her brow, and then he said, "Farewell, Aislinn. I love you now; I'll love you forever."

She heard him cross the room, and then the sound of the lock being released. In the next instant the door had closed behind him and his steps were fading down the hall.

Linn clutched Mary Drennan's cross in her hand and said good-bye to Mary's son.

In the next few weeks Linn learned what despondency was. She acquired dark circles under her eyes, which no amount of makeup could cover, and she lost weight to the point where her bones were beginning to show. She started wearing bulky sweaters when it was still too warm for them in order to camouflage her appearance. She had to get in shape to face her classes; students weren't easily fooled, and already some of the early arrivals, coming in for conferences, were watching her curiously, as people study someone with a debilitating illness.

She tried to go on and be cheerful; there is nothing romantic or even interesting about despair, she told herself. But she bored herself with her own dullness and couldn't understand how Karen or Anne could bear to be in the same room with her. Linn grew to understand Hamlet's description of her current state of mind: "How weary, stale, flat and unprofitable seem to me all the uses of this world." No one ever expressed a thought quite as accurately as Shakespeare.

The semester was about to begin when Karen stopped off at Linn's apartment one morning on her way back from a delivery. She sat across from Linn at the kitchen table and said, stirring her coffee, "Don't you think this has gone on long enough? Don't you think it's time we talked about it?"

Linn sighed wearily. "How much time do you have?"

Karen patted her frosted hair and adjusted her sweater. "For you, Linndy, I've got all day."

Linn got up. "You might as well come into the living room and get comfortable. This is going to take a while."

Karen picked up her cup and followed Linn, settling on the couch. Linn slumped into a wing chair and began her tale.

Karen never interrupted once. She refreshed her coffee twice, signaling for a pause by lifting a finger and going into the kitchen to tap the pot on the stove. Otherwise she was still, listening wide-eyed with that particular attention that had always made her a confidante of many. She knew how to concentrate and knew when to keep her mouth shut.

"And so," Linn concluded, "we have the same father. Kevin Pierce and Mary Drennan were Con's parents."

Karen nodded thoughtfully. "And that's why you broke with him, because you think he's your half brother?"

"I don't think, I know. I saw the birth certificate myself. Believe me, I checked. I wouldn't be here with you if there were any doubt about it. I would be with Con on Ildathach."

Karen rose, putting her cup and saucer on the coffee table. "I see." She wore an odd expression—not the sadness Linn would have expected, but consternation, as if she were troubled.

"Don't look like that, Karen; there's nothing you can do about it. There's nothing anyone can do."

Karen smiled mechanically and picked up her sweater and purse. "I have to go, Linn. Thanks for telling me. I can understand better now what you've been going through. I'll give you a ring tonight." She offered Linn another wan smile and left.

Linn picked up the dishes and brought them into the kitchen, wondering what had caused Karen's abrupt departure. Her behavior had been odd. Linn shrugged mentally and dismissed it.

She had enough on her mind as it was.

Linn was awakened by the sound of the doorbell ringing in the middle of the night. She sat up in darkness and glanced at the fluorescent dial of her bedside clock. Not night, early morning. Who on earth would be ringing her doorbell at 5:45 in the morning?

It was Karen, who obviously hadn't slept at all. She looked exhausted and emotionally spent. She brushed past Linn and collapsed on the sofa.

"Karen, what are you doing here at this hour?" Linn asked. "You look as though you've been up all night."

"I have. I've been sitting in the Catholic church in Fair Lawn, the one that's open twenty-four hours a day."

"Saint Leo's?"

"That's right, Saint Leo's."

"You drove out from the Village to sit in Saint Leo's all night? Karen," Linn said, laughing, "you aren't even Catholic."

Karen shrugged. "Same God. It was the only church I knew would be open."

"Why did you have to go to church?"

"I had a big decision to make and I needed advice from a higher authority."

Linn belted the sash of her robe and curled up next to her godmother on the couch. "All right, what's going on?"

To her surprise, Karen took her hand and held it in her lap. Her face was very serious.

"Linn, I was your mother's dearest friend. I have loved you all your life, looked after you as best I could when your mother died."

Linn smiled. "No one could have done a better job."

Karen squeezed Linn's hand. "I did my best, anyway.

But I hope I've come to the correct decision here. I am about to break a promise I made to your mother before you were born.''

''What do you mean?''

Karen took a breath. ''Regardless of the allegiance I feel to your mother's memory, I can't stand by and see you ruin your life for nothing. I know she would want you to be happy.''

''For nothing?'' Linn echoed. What was this?

''Linn, you can have your Connor for a husband. There is no blood relationship between you. Con may be Kevin's child, but *you* are not.''

Linn didn't move, didn't dare to breathe.

''Kevin married your mother when she was already pregnant by another man, a married man who deserted her when he learned of her condition. You were born early, weren't you?''

''I was told I was premature,'' Linn said softly. ''Everyone said they'd been a good match, happy together. It never occurred to me that they might have married for anything but love.''

''Your mother never wanted you to know. She was afraid you would think badly of her for her mistake. Your father knew all about it when they got married. He had lost someone he loved very much, and he sympathized with your mother's plight. I think it started out as a gesture of kindness, his marrying her, but it seemed that they grew close in the short time they had together. I know for a fact that he never regretted doing what he did, and that you were the joy of his life.''

''And when my mother died, you and he kept silent for her sake.''

''That's right. Kevin knew how much she wanted your good opinion, and he saw no purpose to be served by telling you the truth. He also wanted you to inherit from Dermot, as you did.''

"Dermot never knew," Linn murmured softly. "He *did* leave me his property; he *did* think I was his grandchild."

"I suspect that was your father's last laugh," Karen said, smiling slightly.

Linn's eyes roamed the room, seeing nothing. It was too much to take in at once. A wild surge of joy was building inside her, but she was afraid to unleash it, afraid that if she did she would be thwarted again. Could this possibly, wonderfully, be true?

She sought Karen's gaze. "No one knows?" she asked.

"No one knew except Kevin and me. That leaves me. There are no records to check, Linn. Kevin listed himself as your father on everything. You have only my word, but it's the truth, darling. Go back to Ireland and find Con. Have the happiness your mother would have wished for you."

Linn put her hands on Karen's shoulders and searched the other woman's face.

"Karen," she whispered, "you wouldn't lie to me about this? I know you want to help me. You wouldn't make this up out of some misguided good intention to end my current unhappiness? Because if I went back after Con, and found out later that Kevin really was my father, I don't know how I could bear it."

Karen closed her eyes and moved her head slowly from side to side. "No, Linn. I do want to help, but I would never take it upon myself to twist fate like that. My decision concerned breaking your mother's trust, betraying her confidence, and that's all. I believe in my heart that she would agree I made the right choice."

Linn threw her arms around Karen and hugged her until the older woman was squealing. "God bless you for telling me. Of course you made the right choice. You were never a better friend to my mother than you are today."

Karen embraced her tightly and then sat back. "All

right, enough of this mush. I think you have a plane to catch."

Linn didn't know what to do first. She stood, sat down and then stood again. "Oh, I'm so happy," she breathed. "You'll never know what you've done for me."

"I think I have a rough idea," Karen said, standing up herself. "I'm dying for a cup of coffee."

"Help yourself," Linn said, pulling off her robe and heading for the shower. "On the way to the airport, will you drop me off at the college so I can explain that I need some time off?"

"Why don't I just open a limousine service?" Karen asked from the kitchen, reaching for the canister of coffee.

"Would you call Aer Lingus and book me on the next flight to Shannon?" Linn yelled from the bathroom. "I'll take anything they have."

"Is the number in your directory?" Karen called.

She was talking to empty air. She heard the hiss of running water through the door to the hall. Linn was already in the shower, doubtless trying to wash and dress at the same time.

Karen sighed, replacing the metal tin on the counter. She went back into the living room and dialed New York information.

By the time Linn emerged, dripping, pulling on clothes over her wet body, she was booked on a flight to Shannon.

Linn peered down through the gauzy curtain of clouds at the green landscape visible beneath the wing of the plane. She was back—back where she most longed to be. The pilot circled lower, coming in for a landing, and she could pick out the runways and the clapboard outbuildings of the airport. *"Cead mille failte,"* the sign in the lobby read. A hundred thousand welcomes. Linn felt every one of them. She was coming home.

As the air hostess made her final announcements to the

passengers, Linn unfolded Bridie's latest letter and read it again. It was light and chatty, skirting the most salient issue, and said that Con was doing "tolerably well, considering."

Linn had no idea what that meant. He could be drinking himself to death or trying to get himself killed in Ulster, and she doubted if Bridie would tell her about it. She wouldn't want to deliver any more bad news to Linn, who'd had enough.

When she landed, she called both the gatehouse and the main hall and got no answer at either. She tried Bridie's house and got Terry.

"Terry, this is Aislinn Pierce. May I speak to your mother?"

"She's at my sister's in Donegal, miss. She'll be back later this day. You sound awful close; where are you?"

"I'm at the airport."

"In Eire?"

"Yes, Terry, I'm back."

"Does that mean you've worked it out?"

"As soon as I find Con, everything will be fine. Do you know where he is? His number doesn't answer."

There was a pause. "I don't know where he's gone, miss. He's been away some days now. I know Ma's been worried about him." Terry hesitated. "He's been in a bad way since you left him—drinking, picking fights, you know the sort of thing."

Yes, indeed. She knew the sort of thing. She voiced her greatest fear. "Terry, do you think he's gone north? It might be like him to make himself a target."

"Don't think so, miss. His car's still at the cottage, and Mr. Fitz said something to Ma about him going off someplace to write." Terry sighed. "Sounded like an excuse for a roaring drunk to me."

Linn hoped it was a roaring drunk. She would much prefer that to a dangerous excursion above the border.

"Terry, do you think you could come and get me?"

"Sure thing, miss. Sit tight and I'll be there."

"You're an angel."

Terry chuckled wickedly; it was the first time Linn had ever heard him laugh. She stared in amazement at the phone.

"You didn't think so the night of the Fleadh," he said.

"You're right about that. Would you bring your mother's key to the house? I gave mine back to her when I left."

"Right. Sit in the outside lounge and look for me. I should be there in half an hour."

"Okay, kid. Good-bye."

Linn was perched on a chair in the lounge, her feet on her single bag, when Terry pushed his way through a crowd of departing passengers who were heading for the duty-free shop to spend their last pounds. When he saw her, he grinned and unzipped his black leather jacket to reveal a blue sweatshirt underneath. He had a way of doing that which promised untold delights beneath the clothes. Linn spotted a teenage girl watching him covertly and smiled to herself. Bridie was in for a few more gray hairs from that one, for sure.

"*Failte a bonnla,* miss," Terry said. "Welcome home."

"Thanks, Terry. You can't know how wonderful it is to be here, and that's a big change from the way I felt the last time I was in this place."

He picked up her bag as if it were weightless and took her arm. "Ma came back as I was leaving. She wants to see you."

"Do you have the key to the house?"

Terry shook his head. "She wants me to bring you to our place first." He shot her a sidelong glance. "She was a bit bothered that you were back. I think you'd best talk to her."

Linn could understand why Bridie was upset. She

didn't know what Linn now did, and she probably thought that Linn's return was going to be the cause of more misery for all concerned.

"All right, Terry. Let's go to your house."

Linn followed Terry down the escalator and through the long corridor to the main reception room on the first floor. She waited while he retrieved his cycle, and then she climbed up behind him. There was a work stoppage in progress, and Terry threaded his way through the circling protestors, one heel on the ground, and then gunned the motor once they reached the open road.

Linn closed her eyes and let the fresh, wet breeze bathe her face and whip through her hair. The roads around the airport were wide and well traveled, but it wasn't long before they were immersed in the countryside, skimming along a narrow ribbon of road that skirted huts with their original thatched roofs, and others where the straw had been replaced with corrugated metal, now rusting from the damp. Every once in a while Linn would peek to reassure herself that she was actually back in County Clare. As they rounded a bend, she glanced up and saw a medieval stone tower looming up from the side of the road, an enchanting anachronism in the middle of the modern landscape. She was in Ireland, all right. She blew it a mental kiss and closed her eyes again.

By the time Terry roared down Bally's main street and ground to a stop in front of his house, Linn was so anxious to see Con that she felt like wrenching the bike from Terry's grasp and taking off on it alone. She had no idea where to go, though, so she trudged dutifully behind him through the yard and followed him into the kitchen.

Bridie stood up as Linn and Terry came through the door. She ran to Linn and grabbed her hands.

"I've been thinking," she said rapidly, "and I know that something has changed or you wouldn't be back here. What is it?"

Linn glanced uncertainly at Terry.

"Terence," Bridie said crisply, "put Miss Pierce's bag in the hall and then take yourself outside. We have some talking to do."

"Will it blister my ears to listen?" Terry asked, offended.

His mother raised her hand. "I'll blister them for you if you don't do as I say. Look sharp, boy. Out you go."

Terry shrugged, grabbed an apple from the bowl on the table and sauntered out, slamming the door behind him.

Bridie turned back to Linn immediately. "Tell me, girl, before I burst."

Linn took a deep breath and recounted Karen's story quickly, watching the news transform Bridie's face.

"And so I took the first flight back here to see Con," Linn concluded.

"It's a miracle," Bridie said reverently. "A miracle, to be sure."

"I feel as if I had been facing execution and then suddenly got a full pardon," Linn said. "But I don't know where Con is, Bridie. His phone doesn't answer, and Terry says he's disappeared. He also says that Larry Fitz might know where Con is. Is that so?"

Bridie's mouth pursed at the mention of the lawyer's name. "He may," she said disdainfully, "but I'm not sure. Connor's tight-lipped when he's unhappy, as well you know."

Bridie clearly didn't relish the thought that Fitzgibbon might have information unavailable to her, but Linn was in no mood to cater to Bridie's ancient grudges. "I'll go to see Larry, then," she said. "Terry told me that Con's car is still at the cottage, so he didn't go far." Linn's eyes sought Bridie's anxiously. "Bridie, tell me the truth. How has he been?"

Bridie bit her lip, silent.

Linn sighed, her heart sinking. "That bad?"

"Not good, lass. Not good."

Linn watched Bridie steadily, waiting.

Bridie extended her hands, palms upward. "He's been tearing up the town, if you want the truth; turned the Arms out twice with terrible rows. Mick the barkeep won't let him through the door anymore."

Linn dropped her eyes, her expression defeated.

"He fights at the drop of a hat," Bridie went on, "starts swinging if anybody looks at him cross-eyed. Everyone thinks he's behaving like a madman. All in town know you left him and think he's been jilted, but of course they don't know the half of it."

"I have to find him as soon as possible," Linn said urgently.

Bridie shook her head. "You'd hardly recognize him, girl. The last I saw of him his hair was all grown over his collar, shaggy like, and he had a full beard. The best you can say of him is that he's clean, but as for the rest, he goes around looking like a crazed apostle and acting worse."

"Why didn't you tell me this in your letters?" Linn asked quietly.

"Why add to your misery?" Bridie answered. "There was nothing you could have done. I'm only telling you now because I see you've come to end it, and I want you to know what to expect."

Linn picked up her purse. "Bridie, I'm going to see Larry now. Do you think Terry could give me a lift back to the house when I'm finished?"

Bridie nodded. "I'll keep him close and wait for your call."

Linn turned to go, and then looked back over her shoulder. "Do *you* think Con's gone north?" she asked in a low tone.

Bridie's face reflected her shared concern. "I don't know, Aislinn," she answered softly. "I just don't know."

Linn pushed open the door. "I'll call you as soon as I'm

through," she said in farewell, and strode out across the rear yard.

Linn covered the distance from Bridie's house to Fitzgibbon's office in record time. His secretary turned red when she looked up and saw Linn standing before her.

"I'd like to see Mr. Fitzgibbon," Linn said coolly to Mary Costello's chatty aunt.

"He's busy with a client," the woman said, becoming quite busy herself shuffling papers.

"I'll wait."

"He may be some time," the secretary added.

"Then perhaps you'd better tell him I'm here," Linn said firmly, staring her down.

The woman eyed her back huffily.

"Madam," Linn stated with dangerous sweetness, "I have come all the way from New Jersey to talk to that man, and I'm very sure he would want to know that I am here. Now are you going to get him, or am I going to march in there and announce myself?"

The woman left hurriedly and returned in about ten seconds. "He'll see you directly," she said shortly, and sat at her typewriter. She began to bang out a letter as Linn stared at the door from which Fitz would emerge.

He came out finally, calling over his shoulder, "Be back in a minute, Margaret." He studied Linn and then said, "Come into the other office." He walked off down the hall and Linn followed him into a book-lined room.

Larry indicated that she should sit but remained standing himself. His attitude was not friendly.

"What do you want?" he asked curtly.

"I'm looking for Con," Linn replied, somewhat startled by his hostile tone.

"Are you indeed? And what makes you think I'd tell you where he is?"

"What?" Linn said, bewildered.

"I said, what makes you think I'd tell you where he is,

assuming that I know? You almost killed him when you left him. Have you come back to finish the job?"

"Larry—", Linn began, finally getting his drift.

"Don't Larry me, my girl," the lawyer said, folding his arms. "I believe I asked you a question."

"Larry, you don't know the whole story. I can understand why you're not happy with me at the moment, but it's not the way it looks, believe me."

"Perhaps, then, you'll be kind enough to tell me what way it actually is." Without waiting for a reply, Fitz leaned forward and peered into Linn's face. "I picked him out of a ditch last week after he got into some dustup. Drunk as a lord, he was, and beaten almost senseless. Took on four Cork men at once, I heard, and came out much the worse for his trouble. Neil had to patch him up at three A.M.; he was bleeding like a stuck pig from a cut beside his eye."

Linn winced. Poor Neil. Con was becoming his full-time career.

Larry's eyes narrowed. "How could you do it? You *know* what it took for him to open himself to you. You know how hard it was for him to haul down that guard and let you inside. But no, you spend the whole summer chipping away at that reserve of his until he's as defenseless and vulnerable as a child, so in love with you a fool could see it at twenty paces, and then you hop on a plane back to America and leave that boy to rot." He shook his head. "It was a terrible cruel thing to do, lass, and no mistake."

Linn opened her mouth, but Larry raged on.

"And then," he said, spreading his hands, "what do you do? You leave him that wretched piece of land, as if that would make up for the loss of you. You can't buy that man with Ildathach, my girl, have no doubt of that."

Linn held up her hand to stem the flow of his invective. While she wasn't enjoying his tirade of abuse, Linn felt a certain grudging warmth for the lawyer, whom she had previously viewed as somewhat pompous and certainly self-centered. She hadn't realized before how very fond of Con he was. They all were, she thought; Bridie, Terry, Neil—all of them. In his own quiet way, Con had made each of them his. Even now, when his behavior to an impartial observer might appear questionable, or even childish, it was Linn whom Fitzgibbon blamed, not Con.

Larry stopped talking, and Linn said into the silence, "I'm sorry, Larry. I never meant to hurt him; you must believe that. I'm here now to straighten things out once and for all, but you have to tell me where he is in order for me to do that. If it's any consolation, I haven't been having much fun either."

"Have you not?" He examined her closely, taking in her thinness and pale complexion. "Hmm, perhaps not. You *are* looking a trifle peaked. What is going on, Aislinn?" he asked in a milder tone.

"It's a long story, Larry, and I'm wasting time as I sit here. I want to get to Con as soon as I can. I promise that I'll fill you in later. Now, if you know where he is, will you please, please tell me?"

Fitzgibbon deliberated a moment longer and then reached for a pad on the desk at his side. He leaned over Linn and began to sketch a map on the paper.

"Did Con ever speak about the shepherd's hut in the foothills where he used to go when he was boy?"

Linn thought that over. "I think he mentioned it once or twice. He said you could only reach it on foot, that the roads don't go up there. It's beyond Cool Na Grena, isn't it?"

"It is. It would be a trek of several hours to get there, and the way isn't well marked. But it's my guess that's where he's gone. He used to run away up there like a kicked coinin whenever he got into trouble, which was often enough when he was a lad. I think you'll find him there now if you've a mind to look." Fitz had been drawing all the time he talked, and he presented Linn with a rendering of the route to the hut. It showed the paths that led up the side of the mountain, and the one she was to take was done in bolder lines.

"You go up to the ruins," he explained, "and then take the well-traveled road that leads up to the right. After about fifteen minutes' walk you'll come to a dry well made of gray stones." He pointed to the place on the map with his pencil. "Take the turning there that leads west, toward the sea. After that it's just climbing almost to the summit, where you'll see the grazing land for the flocks. The hut is off in the brush; you'll have to search for it, but it's there." Fitz drew back and studied her doubtfully. "Do you think you can find it?"

Linn stood. "I don't know, but I have to try."

"Shall I go along?"

"No, no, you have your work here, and this is something I have to do alone. But thanks for the thought."

"Take the boy Terence with you, then. He knows those hills almost as well as Con."

"I said alone," Linn repeated firmly. "I appreciate your giving me the directions, and I promise you won't be sorry that you told me where to find him."

The lawyer nodded. "I'm almost certain he's there. Tell me if he's not, because then we'll have a problem on our hands."

Linn agreed, then asked to use the phone to call Bridie. Minutes later Terry arrived on his bike to take her back to Ildathach.

Linn unlocked the front door to the house, and Terry followed anxiously behind her.

"I don't know that you should go alone, miss," he said for the third time. "The way is easy to lose, and there's nothing up there for a long stretch if you go wrong."

"Terry, I'll be fine."

"Have a care, then," he said. "Watch how you go."

"I will." Linn glanced up at him, stepping aside to disentangle herself from the fervent embrace of an enthusiastic Ned, who was wrapping himself around her legs. "You're a good kid, Terry, do you know that? And if you dropped that skirt-chasing leather-boy act more often, people would be able to see it."

Terry smiled slightly. "Can't fool you, eh?"

Linn smiled back. "Not anymore."

Terry turned to go. "Shall we keep it between us?" he said, teasing. "You wouldn't want to ruin my reputation."

Linn laughed. "It will be our secret."

Terry raised his hand in farewell. "Ma will call tonight, and if there's no answer here, I'm coming up after you, so return here if you find him, will you?"

"I will. Good-bye."

Terry left, and Linn went to the bedroom, changing quickly into the jeans and shirt she'd left behind. She got down an old backpack she'd uncovered during her cleaning frenzy, and put blankets, a sweater and a bottle of water in it, along with some apples and cheese. Then she pocketed Fitz's map and set out on foot to find her beloved.

The search took three hours. By the time Linn saw the hut in the distance she was filthy, sweaty, sore, and hopelessly lost. If Con wasn't inside it, she was in trouble.

He was. She pushed aside the sheepskin covering on the door to see him asleep at an old-fashioned deal table, his head on his arms, a partially filled tumbler of whiskey before him. His hair was wild, and his face was obscured by a luxuriant beard. A thick dark scab bordered his left eye.

Linn unstrapped her pack and tiptoed over to him, putting her hand on his shoulder.

"Con, wake up. Con, it's Aislinn."

He stirred and his eyes opened. Joy flooded his face when he saw her, to be replaced immediately by tortured comprehension.

"Why have you come?" he demanded. "To show me

again what I cannot have?'' He shrugged her hand off and turned his head.

"No, Con. To stay with you forever.''

He stared at her for a moment and then sighed. "You're mad. You've gone mad, and I don't blame you. I'm half there myself.''

"Listen to me, Connor. Here I am and here I'll stay, and you're not going to get rid of me.''

He shook his head. "There's no mistake in the records, Aislinn. I went to Holy Rosary. I flew back to Derbyshire and saw my original birth certificate. Kevin was my father.''

"I know. But he wasn't mine.''

She watched the import of her statement register in his eyes. He stood up so fast his chair crashed to the floor. He seized her and searched her face.

"What are you saying?'' he demanded breathlessly.

"I'm saying that you're the only rightful heir to Ildathach; you're Kevin's only child. I'm about as Irish as lasagna. Does it matter?''

Con picked her up and spun her around the tiny shack, laughing and crying and yelling at the top of his lungs. "Are you sure, Aislinn? Are you sure?'' He set her down and they both sat on the floor.

Linn calmed him enough to listen, and she happily recounted Karen's story. He watched her every movement, absorbed her every word. When she was finished, he gathered her tenderly into his arms and kissed her hair.

"I hope I'm sober enough to make sense,'' he said. "I love you and want you to marry me. Immediately.''

"That makes perfect sense to me.'' Linn tugged at his shirt, pulling it free of his pants. "Are you sober enough for something else?'' she asked, kissing his exposed chest.

He pulled her on top of him and began removing her clothes. "We may shock the sheep,'' he said huskily.

"As long as we don't shock the shepherds. Are there any around?''

"I hope not, but I don't care. Do you?"

"Certainly not. I'm the lady who likes to make love in the grass." She caressed him eagerly. "Remember?"

Bells tinkled in the distance. "I think they're on their way," Linn said.

"So are we," Con replied, and silenced her with a kiss.

EYE OF THE STORM

MAURA SEGER

A powerful portrayal of the events of World War II in the Pacific, *Eye of the Storm* is a riveting story of how love triumphs over hatred. In this, the first of a three-book chronicle, Army nurse Maggie Lawrence meets Marine Sgt. Anthony Gargano. Despite military regulations against fraternization, they resolve to face together whatever lies ahead.... Author Maura Seger, also know to her fans as Laurel Winslow, Sara Jennings, Anne MacNeil and Jenny Bates, was named 1984's Most Versatile Romance Author by *The Romantic Tim*

READERS' COMMENTS ON SILHOUETTE INTIMATE MOMENTS:

"About a month ago a friend loaned me my first Silhouette. I was thoroughly surprised as well as totally addicted. Last week I read a Silhouette Intimate Moments and I was even more pleased. They are the best romance series novels I have ever read. They give much more depth to the plot, characters, and the story is fundamentally realistic. They incorporate tasteful sex scenes, which is a must, especially in the 1980's. I only hope you can publish them fast enough."

S.B.*, Lees Summit, MO

"After noticing the attractive covers on the new line of Silhouette Intimate Moments, I decided to read the inside and discovered that this new line was more in the line of books that I like to read. I do want to say I enjoyed the books because they are so realistic and a lot more truthful than so many romance books today."

J.C., Onekama, MI

"I would like to compliment you on your books. I will continue to purchase all of the Silhouette Intimate Moments. They are your best line of books that I have had the pleasure of reading."

S.M., Billings, MT

*names available on request